The Migration of Willie Mackerels

by

Mike Clarke

Robert D. Reed Publishers
San Francisco

Copyright © 1999 by William M. Clarke

All rights reserved

No part of this book may be reproduced without prior written permission from the publisher or copyright holder, except for reviewers who may quote brief passages in a review; nor may any part of this book be transmitted in any form or by any means electronic, mechanical, photocopying, recording or other, without prior written permission from the publisher or copyright holder. Permission inquiries should be addressed to Robert D. Reed Publishers, 750 La Playa, Suite 647, San Francisco, CA 94121.

ISBN 1-1-885003-30-7

Library of Congress Catalog Card Number: 99-066899

Robert D. Reed Publishers
San Francisco

To my wife, Helene, still my best friend
after all these years.
And to three wonderful children,
Terri, Patti, and Michael.

Mike Clarke

Thanks to my sister, Patricia Thomas, for all her support and help with past writing projects.

Thanks in memory to Tom and Esther for having installed in their son a love for both reading and athletics.

A hearty thank you to Joe Schriener for faithfully reading my material and for his encouragement.

And a special thanks to Bill O'Meara for reading, listening, and crucial editorial assistance.

Prologue

The pitcher stares in menacingly from the mound. But it's all a facade. He's jittery—I can tell. But what pitcher wouldn't be? The unmoving killer eyes of the American League's leading homerun hitter have him somewhat mesmerized.

Finally, the pitcher takes a brief economical windup, and at last the pitch is on its way. I've guessed right—it's a fastball. And as luck would have it, it's thigh-high and out over the plate. Now comes the short stride of the right foot, the coordinated swivel of the powerful hips, and the graceful, controlled swing of the bat.

I'm standing here at the mall, watching the Mariners on a giant screen in Sears' TV department. I've got a few minutes to kill, while the wife finishes shopping for a wedding present. Ken Griffey Jr. is the batter. I love Jr. as a ballplayer but hate the way he wears his baseball pants. You know—all the way down to his shoe tops. There are no baseball socks showing at all, not even the stirrups or the sanitary hose.

It looks really bush league if you were to ask me. Back in my day, the players had lots of colorful sock showing beneath the fluff of their baggy flannel pants. Griffey and the others look too much like softball players. In spite of that fact, though, Griffey hits the first pitch over the right field fence, and the Mariners take the lead. Now if Randy Johnson was pitching, that's probably the only run they'd need. But of course, the brilliant Mariner front office had to go and trade the Big Unit away—right when he was in his prime.

As the Kid goes into his homerun trot, an older white-haired gentleman over closer to the fifty-four-inch TV gets all excited and starts jumping up and down and clapping his hands. I say old, but the guy's probably only in his sixties, just like me. And then, as Edgar Martinez pops up (a rarity for him), I get to looking more closely at the older fellow. He's dressed nicely, in sports coat, tie, and well-creased slacks, and there's something very familiar about him. He's actually a pretty good-looking guy for his age and all, although his hair is pretty thin, and he's got a pretty good gut on him. I notice too, that his face is on the reddish side, and he's got a few veins showing in the ol' schnozzola. I wonder if he hasn't been hitting the sauce a little too hard. He flashes a real nice smile with big strong-looking white teeth when Jay Buhner rips a double into the gap in right center. It's a sneering kind of smile, though, to tell you the truth. And it's that odd smile and those big white teeth that keep me staring at the guy. I'm almost sure I know him. Then it hits me.

"Excuse me," I say, "but...uh...you wouldn't be Teddy Snodgrass by any chance?"

The guy eyeballs me for a second with a puzzled look on his face and then says, "Yeah, I'm Ted Snodgrass...*Do* I know you?"

"Well," I say, "we used to play ball together a long time ago...and against each other too." I wait then to see if he shows any sign of recognition. When people from the past don't recognize me, it bums me out. It really does. Then I begin to wonder if I'm beginning to show my age as well.

"Hmm...well...uh...I probably ought to remember...but...uh..."

I can tell right then that the guy doesn't have a clue. Of course, that doesn't necessarily mean that it's because I've taken on an old timer's appearance. It might be just because *his* memory is not so hot. Maybe I'm right about the sauce and all.

I'm about to try giving him another hint, when crowd noise draws our attention once again to the giant screen there in the Sears TV department. When we try to see, though, a high school kid, wearing baggy short pants, walks rudely across our line of vision. Seeing him makes me feel all the older. In my day, you showed more respect, and besides, if you were caught wearing short pants from about the fifth grade on, the other kids were apt to throw rocks at you. Of course, they might have thrown rocks at Griffey Jr., too, what with him wearing an earring and having his cap on backwards and all.

It seems the rookie up from Tacoma has just blown away the Oriole leadoff hitter with a blazing fastball. He looks to be every bit as tall as Randy Johnson and with that fastball, he does sort of remind you of the Big Unit. Back in high school, the girls all used to call Roderick Remblinger, "The Big Unit," even though he wasn't all that big of a guy. But in those days, I was too naive to understand why they'd tagged him with an unlikely nickname such as that.

Teddy Snodgrass jumps straight in the air with hands clasped high overhead like a prize fighter. "Yes!" he hollers. "Give'm the old fastball, kid. He turns to me and says, "That's like I used to do."

"I remember," says I.

Then ol' Teddy gets the quizzical look on his face once more and says, "You say *we* played ball together?"

"Yeah, we both played for good ol' Scandia High back there in '51...before I moved away. Then I pitched *against* you."

"Huh...I'll be damned," he says. He doesn't have a clue. His eyes are big, round, and empty—just like Little Orphan Annie's from the funny papers.

"Bill Michaels," I say, as I stick out my hand. I'm real disappointed in his hand shaking technique, if you want to know the truth. For a strong-looking guy like him, he offers a handshake my Dad would've called a "dead fish"—no strength or enthusiasm to it whatsoever. But I can tell by the slight glaze that's come over his eyes that he's still mystified as to who I am.

"Well...I used to go by *Willie* Michaels." Still no sign of recognition. "In fact...people usually called me Willie *Mackerels*."

Teddy's eyes light up at last, just as he withdraws the sweaty, dead fish from my grasp. "God yes!" he exclaims. "I remember now...hah, hah, hah...the guy with the wienie arm...Willie Mackerels. I'll be damned. How in the hell do you remember back that far, anyway? I got trouble just remembering what I had for breakfast this morning. Well hey...it's been good seeing ya, but I'm kinda late for an appointment. I been standin' here watchin' this stupid game when I ought to be out sellin' cars. Hey...you take care now." With that, he strode off with a show of great purpose, as though he had to sell a Lincoln Town Car to the governor or something.

Talk about rude. But I never liked Teddy anyway, if you want to know the truth. He always was stuck up. And though he doesn't seem to remember the time we faced each other in the big game, I'll never forget, especially since Trudy Trammell was in the stands watching us both.

When I glance back to the TV, Alex Rodriguez, makes a sparkling play on a ground ball behind second base. The Mariners should feel real fortunate to have a humble player like an A-Rod on their team. Back in our day, we had to put up with an A-Hole—Teddy Snodgrass.

Mar. 7—51

Dear Auntie,

    I guess it's about time I was writing you folks. You're probably wondering what's ever happened to your favorite nephew (I've got to be your favorite—since I'm the only one you have—ha, ha). The last time I wrote, we were sort of safe about 50 miles south of Seoul, but now we're on the move again. We've liberated Seoul and are now starting to drive the reds back across the 38th parallel. All things being equal, I think I had more fun throwing baseballs for good ol' Lincoln High than I'm having throwing hand grenades at the North Koreans—ha, ha. I hope that this letter finds the Michaels family all in good health. How is cousin Willie doing with his baseball career? I'll bet he's blowing that fastball of his right by all those hitters. Well, that's about all the time I have for now. Write soon.

Your loving nephew,
Harvey

Chapter 1

Oh, by the way, I'll have to explain where the name Mackerels originated. Former neighbors of ours, the Jensens, had a son who wasn't quite developed mentally and all. He had a heck of a time pronouncing my last name, Michaels, so that's why I'm called Mackerels to this day. That's okay, I guess, although I don't particularly like being named after a fish and all, especially one as ugly as a mackerel. But I don't much care for the name Willie, either, if you want to know the absolute truth. It's definitely not a movie star-type name. I've told my folks over and over that I'd rather be called Bill, but do you think they'd pay any attention? At one time, I'd sort of entertained the notion of maybe being a movie star, like Errol Flynn for example. But in the sixth grade, it was pointed out to me by several of my classmates that perhaps my nose was a little too big for a career as a matinee idol. I guess the ol' snout might be a little too large to be considered Errol Flynnish at that, although I've often thought that they were all just a trifle jealous of my movie star-looks in the first place. Besides, thanks to my baseball career, my nose has a pretty good bend in it now, but there'll be more about my nose later.

Speaking of that baseball career, it's sure bum luck I've been stuck with a coach who can't recognize talent when he sees it. You'd think that maybe good ol' Willie Mackerels would finally see a little action in this last game of the year. After all, we're ahead seventeen to nothing in the bottom of the seventh and last inning, and the opposition, the Happy Valley Milkmaids, is hardly likely to make any kind of a comeback. Heck, they're the last place team in the league and have yet to win a single game this whole season. I mean, if the coach won't even put me in the Hapless Valley game, I must be way down at the bottom of the ol' totem pole.

And if I'm ever going to be a major league ballplayer, I'd better start seeing some action right here and now. Being the final game of the year and all, this is my last chance to show the coach what I can do. Since I'm a junior, I've got to plant some seeds in his mind for next season. If I don't win some games my senior year, it'll be almost impossible to attract the attention of the baseball scouts.

Our senior starter, Danny Johnson, is showing signs of weakening. The temperature has reached the mid-eighties, and that's awful hot for the middle of May here in the Puget Sound area. Yep, ol' Danny is sure enough struggling out there. He's just hit a batter after walking another on four straight pitches.

"Mackerels!" Coach Rattebaugh yells once again. "Better warm up."

"Come on, Twink," I say to Elmer Finley, the freshman reserve catcher, and we hurry out to what passes for a bullpen behind the visitors' bench. This is the fourth time Coach Rattebaugh has called on me to warm up, and I feel like I've already pitched about a game-and-a-half.

I'm walking behind Elmer, as we make our way, and I can't help but chuckle to myself at the appearance he presents. Elmer is only about five feet tall, perhaps the shortest catcher in all of high school baseball. And as he trudges along toward the bullpen, little puffs of dust rise up from his big ol' catcher's mitt, as it drags along the ground.

I glance across the diamond to the Happy Valley bench and can't help but feel a little pity for those poor sodbusters. What a crude-looking bunch they are. They don't even have real baseball uniforms for Pete's sake. Instead, they wear blue jeans and what looks like some beat-up hand-me-down football jerseys. What kind of a name for a high school is that, anyway? If you were to ask me, Happy Valley sounds more like it'd be a rest home for old folks—or maybe even some kind of asylum. And Milk Maids—that sounds more like the name of a girls' team or something.

But what I see when I steal a peek into the crudely-built stands, makes me forget all about pitying the poor Milkmaids. I start feeling a little sorry for myself instead. There she is, the prettiest girl at Scandia High. It's Trudy Trammell—the would-be love of my life.

If you could see Trudy, you'd know what I mean. She's got a dazzling smile, beautiful honey-colored hair, and just enough freckles to give her this wholesome farm girl look. And her figure is pretty danged wholesome too. In fact, it's so wholesome, it makes heads turn wherever she goes.

The funny thing is, though, she doesn't seem to realize what a knock-out she is. She treats everyone the same and never acts stuck-up like most good-looking girls. She's only got one fault as near as I can see—she's going steady with Teddy Snodgrass. The fact that she's going steady with anyone at all is hard enough to handle, but to have it be Teddy Snodgrass is enough to set a guy's stomach on fire.

Teddy and I go way back, and we're not on the best of terms. But I'll tell you more about that later. Right now, I've got to concentrate about how I'm going to get the Milkmaids out, just in case Mr. Dumbhead Rattleballs finally sends me in. And if I *do* get in and have a good outing, maybe Trudy will sit up and take notice.

I wonder if I might be facing that white-haired left fielder of theirs. Last inning when I was warming up, I noticed him giving me the eye. He just kept gawking at me. It seemed like he was more interested in me than the actual game. It made me sort of nervous, to tell you the honest truth. He was kind of a funny-looking kid, anyway. Once, when he took off his cap to scratch his head, I could see that his hair was completely white. I don't mean the sort of blonde you see on albino circus freaks. Instead, it was more like the bluish-white you might see on your grandparents. If you had to judge this kid's age by just his hair, you'd swear that he was at least eighty, for Pete's sake.

I was getting pretty danged sick of his staring, though, I can tell you that much for sure. I didn't care how old he was. I was about to ask him if he was getting ready to propose or what, when he finally hollered over to me.

"Hey, Speedy, when they gonna put *you* in? I wanna fatten up my battin' average...hah, hah, hah." He obviously wasn't any too impressed with my warmup pitches and all. I suppose it was because they weren't exactly popping good ol' Elmer's mitt. You wouldn't expect a sodbuster from Hapless Valley to be able to recognize a finesse pitcher, anyway.

"You better hope they never do, Whitey," I shot back. Sometimes I can be real quick on the comeback. I really can.

"Kiss my butt," he says.

"Looks too much like your face," I say.

"That's the beauty of it," he says. He's obviously played this game before.

"There's no beauty in a horse's ass," I should have said. But he throws me off the track when he makes a crude obscene gesture with his middle finger, and I forget to say it.

The more I think about it, our opponents' ragtag looks remind me an awful lot of the first team I ever played for, Willie's Wonders. As I continue to throw to Elmer, whose tiny body is back there somewhere behind the big ol' catcher's mitt, my mind sort of drifts back to the beginnings of my baseball career, back in Seattle. The more I think about it, the game was a lot more fun in those days. I got to play, rather than spending all my time just warming up or sitting at the end of the bench for the Scandia Vikings.

Chapter 2

I didn't really get into baseball until the sixth grade. Until then, my spare time had been pretty-well taken up with the fighting of World War II. The war broke out when I was six years old and for the next few years was probably the greatest concern in the lives of most Americans. It was an especially big deal to the kids in our neighborhood, and we spent a lot of our free time playing war. We kept up on all the war news by watching Movietone News—the Eyes and Ears of the World. That was during our weekly Saturday afternoon trips to watch the matinee at the Green Lake Theater in Seattle's north end.

If you want to know the truth, the Green Lake Theater played a pretty big role in my early education. I learned a heck of a lot more about our wartime enemies, the Germans and Japanese, at the theater than I ever did at school. The war was not part of the curriculum at good ol' Fairview Elementary. The teachers there were more into talking about pilgrims and Indians and stuff like that. A guy could learn all he ever wanted to know about John Alden and Miles Standish but very little about Hitler or Hirohito.

At the theater, though, I learned all about the axis powers as they did battle with John Wayne, William Bendix, and some young blonde actor who always managed to get killed about three-fourths of the way through the movie. They fought over and over again in such places as the Sahara Desert, Wake Island, Bataan, and Corregidor.

By the time I reached the sixth grade, though, the war was pretty much all over. The allies had things pretty well in hand, the young, blonde actor could no longer make a living being bayoneted over and over again, and the city of Seattle no longer worried about Japanese air attacks. Sports and an awakening interest in girls had replaced playing war as the main recreational activities for sixth graders.

No longer did we wear goofy ol' aviator hats, complete with goggles, as we flew to school each day. And no longer did we wear surplus army jackets completely covered with a variety of military insignia patches sewed on by our sometimes reluctant mothers.

"Willy—you think I have nothing to do around here but to sew these crazy patches on your jacket?" To my way of thinking, Mom didn't always show the proper enthusiasm for the war effort.

But now, we were nattilly attired in green rain slickers with our names spelled out on the back with white adhesive tape. And on the slicker's draw strings was the mandatory collection of metal tax tokens with holes in the center. A guy with lots of tax tokens was never broke; three of the tokens made a penny. And for five pennies, you could buy enough candy to make you sick for the rest of the day.

It was the spring of that sixth grade year that the boys of Fairview Elementary made the amazing discovery that girls were different. We'd always known they were different, of course, but not in the many ways that were becoming increasingly more apparent. Until the sixth grade, girls were different because they preferred dolls and jumping rope to playing marbles or war. They were different because they actually studied and completed their homework assignments. And they were different because they never seemed to get sent to the danged principal's office. Until the sixth grade, the goofy ol' girls were good only as targets upon which to sharpen your rock throwing skills.

Suddenly, the girls were beginning to look a whole lot better to us. Their hair, once greasy and ratty like ours, was now apt to be freshly-shampooed, well-brushed, and all gussied up with brightly-colored ribbons. And instead of dingy socks and badly-scuffed shoes spattered with mud, they now wore sparkling white bobby sox that contrasted nicely with their shiny, black patent leather shoes. Many of the girls had also shot up in height, dropped their baby fat, and were now beginning to show the first traces of a feminine figure.

Unfortunately, most of them towered over the average sixth grade boy as amazons would over a pygmy. Yet, the goal of every red-blooded sixth grade boy was to acquire one of these suddenly-delectable creatures for a girlfriend.

But to tell the honest truth, having just any girlfriend didn't necessarily increase the ol' social standing. If the girl you'd attracted wasn't Jessica Bell, it didn't count. She was the reigning femme fatality of good ol' Fairview Elementary. Jessica, slim and tall, had an olive-skinned beauty, highlighted by two enormous brown eyes and a long mane of lustrous chestnut-colored hair. A smile from Jessica could make your danged knees go all wobbly. And that's the honest truth.

As the spring progressed, Jessica went through boyfriends faster than Grant took Richmond, but she appeared not to be interested in tall, dark, Errol Flynnish types like me. Instead, she seemed to go for shrimps like George McCorkle and David Lewis. Maybe it was a latent motherly instinct that drew Jessica to little twerps that came only to her waist.

Day after day, I waited for Jessica to notice my obvious Flynn-like qualities and announce to the world that I'd been selected as her current boyfriend. But I was having absolutely no luck, if you want the whole sad truth of it all. But one day late in the spring found me with hopes up higher than usual. Having jilted Kenny Brantley the day before, Jessica dumped David Lewis by morning recess, and since just about every other kid had been rejected at least three times by now, I figured it just about *had* to be my turn at long last.

Well, later in the day I got a real shock to the ol' self esteem, when Jessica let it be known that instead of *me*, she'd selected Rollo Bean to be her current squire. Come *on*! Rollo *Bean*? I was completely stunned, if you want to know the whole sad truth. Rollo was the fattest kid in the whole danged school. Later in the day, I expressed my dismay to my friend, Jerry Robbins. Surely he'd understand. Jerry was a three-time loser himself. "I just don't understand what Jessica Bell sees in a guy like Rollo," I said.

"Heck, me neither," Jerry said.

"Shoot, I think I'm better lookin' than *that* fatso," I said.

"Yeah—I guess—uh—probably."

The ol' confidence was not overly bolstered by the way Jerry said, "probably," if you want to know the truth of it all. "Of course," Jerry went on to say, "there is that problem with your nose."

"What problem with my nose?" I asked.

"Well—umm—it is sort of on the big side."

Could that be? I wondered. I stole a glance at Jerry's nose; it was quite small—almost button-like in appearance. Maybe he just meant that my nose was large in comparison with *his*—or did he?

I spent the rest of the school day alternately staring at the noses of my classmates and comparing my own in the mirror in the boys' lavatory. But the more I checked the ol' snout, the bigger it appeared to be. By the end of the day, I was sure that I ranked right up there with Pinocchio and Cyrano de Bergerac.

When I got home from school, I entered the living room with head down and shoulders bowed. It was becoming increasingly more difficult to support the weight of my out-sized nose. I was forced to affect the rolling gait of a sailor, as the pendulum-like swing of the giant appendage no longer allowed me to walk like a normal human being. I more nearly resembled an African elephant, as I slowly lumbered to the davenport. I wearily took a seat, being careful not to sit on my big ol' nose in the process.

"Jesus H. Christ, Mackerels, what's wrong with you, anyway? Got a sore neck or something?" Dad was working swing shift and hadn't yet left for work.

"Nuthin'," I said, as the sound of my reply trumpeted out into the room.

"Well, you don't look so good to me. Looks like you lost your last friend."

"It's my nose," I said.

"What's wrong with your nose—forget to keep your guard up again?"

"Naw, Jerry Robbins said I got a big nose."

"Hmmm," Dad said, as he eyed me for a moment or two. It was as though he was taking a mental measurement. "Well—yeah," he said, "you got a slightly-bigger nose, all right—but it's not as big as Jimmie Durante's."

Much relieved upon hearing that, I slowly shuffled off toward the sanctity of my bedroom (Inka dinka DOO a dinka—). It was in that cozy haven that I finally decided to give up my pursuit of Jessica Bell for the remainder of the school year and turn my attention to baseball, where it belonged. I wouldn't be having time for any goofy ol' girls while I pursued a career as a major league ballplayer.

GREEN LAKE REPORTER LOOKING FOR CARRIERS
Green Lake Reporter Staff Writer

The Green Lake Reporter needs reliable carriers to deliver their weekly newspaper door to door. Many people depend upon the Reporter for local news and shopping bargains in the Green Lake area. Lately, however, there has been a rash of unreliability among some of the carriers. In some instances, papers have been delivered late or not at all. The Reporter apologizes for this and promises to make some personnel changes among existing carriers. The job pays $6.75 per week. If interested, come to the desk of the Reporter Circulation Department for a personal interview.

Chapter 3

It was right after the ol' Jessica Bell fiasco when I had my first taste of organized baseball and also my first run-in with the great Teddy Snodgrass. Until then, the kids on our block amused themselves by playing in pick up games against kids from other neighborhoods. We had no coaches, no umpires, and hardly any equipment, but the games were hotly contested, and we always had lots of fun.

In these games, the kid that brought the bat and ball usually had a good chance of being coach, pitcher, and first up to bat. So it was in these games that I got my start on the mound. My dad had been an outstanding pitcher in Seattle's fastest semipro league, until he hurt his arm, so we always had lots of leftover bats and balls lying around the house.

Umpires were almost impossible to find for the neighborhood games, so usually the catcher of the team in the field called balls and strikes. As you could probably guess, the catchers often had a little problem staying objective. Quite often, the games would come to a halt, and arguing, name-calling, and shoving matches would take over.

"Hey, that was no strike!"
"Heck if it wasn't!"
"Heck it was!"
"Was!"
"Wasn't!"
"Was!"
"Oh yeah...well just wait 'til you guys get *your* ups!"

Although Dad didn't play ball anymore, he still liked to play catch with me after dinner and show me lots of stuff about pitching and all.

One evening, I was pitching, and Dad was alternating the target of his old catcher's mitt from high and inside to low and outside. I think Dad was beginning to worry a little about my velocity as he kept on encouraging me to try for a little more zip on my fastball. Once, when he signaled for the hummer high and inside, I tried a little too hard for some extra smoke on the ball, and it sort of got away from me.

"Jesus H. Christ, Willy, watch where you're throwing!" Dad shouted. I couldn't figure out why he was so upset. I put the ball right where he wanted it—high and inside. It was high—high over the back fence. And it was inside—inside the Jensens' garage, having broken one of that building's windows during the flight. But heck, it only cost Dad one Saturday morning of his time. He'd decided to replace the window himself, rather than to pay a professional glazier to do the job.

As much as I admired my dad, I'll have to admit that pitching in the neighborhood games was a lot more fun than throwing to him in the backyard. In the games, I didn't have to worry about hitting the high-inside or low-outside targets all the time. I only had to get the ball somewhere close enough to the plate for our catcher to have sort of a realistic shot at calling it a strike. A lot of that depended upon just how tough of a guy your catcher was.

Then suddenly, the neighborhood games were replaced with organized ball, mostly as a result of my mom's browsings through our local shopping guide, the Green Lake Reporter. She'd been a little nervous about the 265 unfolded copies lying there on our living room floor. It was getting sort of late in the day, and I hadn't quite got around to delivering them as of yet. But anyway, she spotted an article she thought I might want to know about.

"Willie," she said, "it says here that the Green Lake Recreational Department is starting a summer baseball league for boys your age. Are you interested in something like that?"

Hah! Would a fox be interested in a free pass to the hen house? According to the newspaper, all I had to do to enter a team was to get some kids together and then contact the recreation director. There was no entry fee, but each player had to provide proof of his correct birthdate. The recreation department would furnish the necessary bats, balls, and catcher's equipment.

Oh boy! I thought, a chance to play in a real league, with a real umpire, and with real baseballs. That meant that we would no longer have to play with baseballs that had the covers half off or with those whose hides had been replaced with black friction tape.

There wasn't much standardization to the size or weight of the tape balls, if you want to know the truth. A skillful ball repairer wouldn't use all that much tape—only what was absolutely necessary to do the job.

Then we'd have a product that was only slightly larger and heavier than a regulation ball. But with a less-accomplished artisan at work, we were apt to wind up with a ball more the size and weight of a shot-put.

What would really be great, though, would be the use of the catcher's equipment. Our catchers had never known the luxury of catching while wearing masks, chest protectors, or shin guards. Because of this lack of protective gear, our catchers always got about fifteen to twenty feet behind the batter. They didn't actually catch the ball; they just tried to stop it on about the fourth bounce. Because of that fact, we always waived the rule that said a batter could advance to first base on a third strike not caught in the air by the catcher. If you missed a third strike in the neighborhood games, you were automatically out—no matter what the goofy catcher did.

With all this in mind, I immediately set about the job of organizing a team. I rounded up all the good players I could and delivered our formal entry into the hands of the recreation director. Several on the list would probably never show, but at least they wouldn't be playing for some other team if they were locked into our roster.

Because I had gone to all that work, I thought that it was no more than right that I should lay claim to the team's captaincy. And what the heck, as founder of the team I might just as well be the starting pitcher. I'm sure Teddy Snodgrass would have claimed that position, but he left to stay with his grandparents shortly before the season began. Teddy had flunked a grade and was a year older than the rest of us but still satisfied the league's age requirement by five days. He'd been on our original roster.

Since Teddy's fastball had a certain amount of Chinese mustard on it, I might have had a little trouble justifying to the rest of the team just why it was that I should pitch rather than Teddy. Not only that, since he was older, he was bigger and stronger than the rest of us kids and had a tendency to get his way by bullying. So when Teddy left for his grandparents, I wasn't all that unhappy he'd gone away.

A little shorter than I, Teddy was blonde and blue-eyed and possessed a terrific physique. The girls at Fairview Elementary were all madly in love with him. In fact, rumor had it that he'd talked Jessica Bell into going into the woods and doing a bad thing with him on the day of the school picnic. That piece of information just about knocked Jessica right off the ol' pedestal as far as I was concerned.

No one else could think of a suitable name for the team, so I made an administrative decision. We proudly made our entrance into the Green Lake Recreational League under the name of Willie's Wonders.

There were still a few weeks left before the league schedule was to begin, so we increased the number of practice games with the other neighborhoods. We needed the work in order to sharpen up for league competition. Meanwhile, as captain and founder of the team, I took on the added chore of researching the league regulations.

But rats! Would you believe it? According to the league rules, a catcher had to catch the third strike, or the batter could try for first base. This posed a real serious problem for us, if you want to know the truth. There was no one on our roster capable of getting right up in the catcher's box and catching a third strike in the air.

Rollo Bean had always been our catcher. Why? Partly it was because he was too fat and slow to play any other position. Also, he was the only kid on the team who had a catcher's mitt. It seems the parents of fat kids have always bought catchers' mitts for their chubby offsprings. I guess they must possess some sort of special instinct that tells them that the purchase of a fielder's glove would be a heck of a waste of money.

I suppose Rollo was as good as most of the other neighborhood catchers, but under league rules, he would undoubtedly be worthless at that position. In our practice games, it became pretty darn obvious that he wasn't going to stay in a crouch right behind the batter like a real catcher was supposed to do.

He'd start each game with the best of intentions. But with each succeeding pitch, he'd work himself farther and farther from the plate, until he reached his comfort zone some fifteen feet behind the catcher's box. There, he'd cower against the backstop as he tried to hide behind his new catcher's mitt.

Then I was struck by a brilliant idea. "Rollo," I said, "you pay attention to me, and I'll make you into the best catcher in the league." I knew that was stretching it quite a lot, but there was no need to tell him that. Rollo was going to need all the confidence he could get.

First, I talked him into getting back into the catcher's box where he belonged. Then, I put a batter up to the plate and sent our second-string pitcher out to the mound. "Now, Rollo," I said, "Jerry's gonna pitch the ball to you, and Dave's gonna swing at it." Rollo, I noticed, flinched quite a bit at the word, "swing." I continued. "Only thing is...Dave's gonna miss the ball on purpose. In fact...he's gonna miss it by a mile. So don't pay any attention to him at all. It'll be just as though he isn't even there. Pretend you're just playing a game of catch with good ol' Jerry."

We got ready for the great experiment. Jerry took his windup and came in with a medium-soft lob. Dave did as instructed. He took a vicious cut at the ball but missed it by quite a lot.

To tell you the truth, I was sort of surprised when Rollo caught the ball so easily. We repeated the experiment several times, and in each instance Rollo came through like a champ.

"Way to go, Rollo," I said. "Now we'll do it again, only this time Dave won't miss by quite as much." Once more Rollo passed the test, and I began having visions of myself joining the ranks of John McGraw, Connie Mack, and some of the other great baseball managers of the past.

"That's great, Rollo. Now that you're used to the batter, we'll have Dave actually try to hit the ball. You won't have any trouble at all."

"You betcher boots I won't," Rollo said…"cuz I ain't gonna do it. I ain't gettin' behind no plate when there's a batter really swingin' at the ball."

I was pretty danged frustrated by this sudden turn of events, if you want to know the truth of it all. "Why *not?*" I said. "You've been catching really great back there."

"Yeah, but we ain't got no catcher's gear," Rollo shouted. He looked to be as upset as I'd ever seen him. "What if Dave hits a foul tip back at me. I got no protection at all. I ain't as dumb as I look." At that point, his big ol' round face was as red as a spanked baby's butt.

When I told Dad about the failed experiment, he said, "Remember, Mackerels, you can't make chicken soup…out of chicken poop."

Rollo had a point there about the catcher's gear and all—I had to admit it. But to be perfectly honest, I guess I hadn't really thought too much about the possibility of a foul tip. Actually, it wouldn't be much of a problem once the league started. Then we'd have the catcher's gear furnished to us. But that would be too late to begin breaking in a new catcher. So in the meantime, who *did* we have that might be as dumb as he looked?

Well, the next practice game found yours truly crouching behind the plate—without a mask, of course. I was doing pretty well, too, probably catching at least three-fourths of the pitches. That was right up until I experienced one of those darn foul tips Rollo'd been talking about. The opposition's cleanup hitter fouled one back that caught me right on the tip of my left ear. As I hopped up and down and rubbed my throbbing ear, I could see Rollo's smirk all the way from his new position way out in right field.

Though my confidence was pretty well shot after that, I managed to hang in there and finish the contest from the catcher's box. Once the game was over, though, a brilliant bit of coaching strategy suddenly came upon me. I decided that our team had now reached a fine cutting edge and wouldn't be needing any more practice until the league started. After all, I had to guard against the team becoming stale didn't I?

Besides that, no more practice games meant that I would no longer have to catch without the benefit of the recreation department's catching equipment.

When league play finally started, Willie's Wonders enjoyed great success. Even though we had to suffer along without my pitching, we were undefeated going into our last game. Our opponents, the Green Lake Lions, were also without a loss, and so the game would decide the league championship. The Lions were sponsored by a service club of the same name. The club not only sponsored the Lions but provided them with real fancy uniforms to boot.

If you were to ask me, the Lions were sure a cocky-looking bunch. All togged out in their flashy white suits trimmed in green, they strutted onto the field like they thought they were real hot stuff. While they began to zip the ball around the infield, we sort of slouched around our dugout like we were ashamed or something.

But compared to the Lions, we were a pretty raunchy-looking outfit. I'll have to admit it. Most of us just wore jeans and sweatshirts. And lots of the jeans had holes in the knees, and hardly any of the sweatshirts matched. Several of the guys didn't even have ball caps, and it didn't help matters any, either, when Rollo showed up wearing a multi-colored beanie with a propeller on top.

Our appearance didn't bother me nearly as much as did our sagging morale; our spirits were at a low ebb. Jerry Robbins, our number one pitcher since I'd taken over the catching duties, had to go and pick this time to come down with the chicken pox. We had absolutely no other pitcher on the team, except for me, and I hadn't pitched a single ball since the league started.

But if I pitched—who would catch? The idea of Rollo Bean behind the plate was a scary thought to say the least. What was best? I had only a few minutes left to make up my mind. Should I stay at catcher—leaving us with no pitcher at all? Or should I pitch and take a chance on Rollo behind the plate? I think that's what they call one of those Hobsen's Choices. But then I had a sudden inspiration.

"Hey, Rollo," I said, "you got a nickel I can borrow for the phone?"

"Yeah," he said as he fumbled in his pocket, "but you gotta promise to pay it back—and I don't mean next year."

"Thanks, old buddy. Don't worry. I'll pay ya back tomorrow. Don't let 'em start the game until I get back—I'll just be a few minutes." With that said, I took off on the dead run for the pay phone up the street. On the surface, it seemed like a probable waste of money, but I'd never know if I didn't give it a try.

I'd decided to give ol' Teddy Snodgrass a call. He was probably still at his grandparents, but there was a slim chance he might be back in town. And if he was he wouldn't know a thing about our championship game unless someone told him.

Fifteen minutes later, a snazzy black Lincoln Continental pulled up alongside the playing field. Suddenly, the rear door opened, and good ol' Teddy Snodgrass stepped out. When the team spotted him, you could almost see the gloom rising from our dugout in waves. But that was all behind me now. I clapped good ol' Teddy on the back and said, "Boy, am I glad you were home. You're gonna pitch, and I'm gonna catch."

Teddy was terrific. I'll have to admit it. He hit three homeruns and a triple and mowed down one Lion hitter after another with his blazer. I was having a little bit of tough luck, though. Teddy's pitching was a lot faster than I was used to, so I stuck a piece of sponge rubber in my glove to try to absorb some of the sting. After that, my mitt was a little too springy, and I had a little trouble holding on to the ball. I dropped a few more third strikes than I should have. I'll have to admit it. I guess it was my fault that so many Lions were reaching first base. It was the darn sponge. But what else could I do? My hand was burning up as it was.

Still, we were ahead seventeen to sixteen in the bottom of the seventh and final inning. My continual dropping of the strikes was beginning to get to me. It must have been getting to Teddy too, because every time I turned to chase a pitch back to the backstop, I could feel his eyes burning holes in the back of my neck. The danged pressure was making me tense up all the more.

As the last inning began, Teddy had a brief spell of wildness. The first batter walked on four straight pitches and then, quick as a wink, stole second. My somewhat tardy throw arrived there on the third hop. I still wasn't used to the regulation ball, I guess.

"Come on, Mackerels, get an arm," Teddy snarled. Then he struck out the next batter, but again I dropped the third strike. Now the Lions had runners at first and third. Teddy glared in at me, and I could almost feel the daggers. Next, a slow roller to the mound handcuffed Teddy momentarily, and he couldn't make a play. The runner on third had to hold, but now the Lions had the bases loaded with still no outs.

At that point, I could see our championship slowly riding off into the sunset. But good ol' Teddy gave us a new life, when he daringly picked the runner off first base for out number one. At that point, I was hoping he'd pick the other runners off too. Then I wouldn't be in the horrible position of having to hang on to any more of Teddy's rockets for third strikes.

The next batter lofted a high pop fly right out in front of the plate. This was a new experience for me, but at least I remembered to remove my catcher's mask. A pop fly would be hard to locate looking through a mask. On wobbly legs, I staggered out onto the diamond to do battle. I lurched to the left, stumbled to the right, almost fell over, but then righted myself and prepared to make the catch.

But why was I standing there holding my catcher's mask? I wondered suddenly. Dang! In the excitement, I'd become confused, kept the mask, and thrown my mitt out of the way. Nevertheless, I continued to track the ball, and to the amazement of my astonished teammates, I managed to use the mask to make the catch.

"Two outs...get the easy one," I bellowed, as I bounced jauntily back to my position.

Now, all the chips were on the table as big Frank Marsden, the Lions' powerful cleanup hitter, strode up to the plate. Although Marsden seemed to be oozing confidence from every pore in his body, I had no fear of him whatsoever. What I *did* fear was the Teddy Snodgrass fastball. At that moment, Teddy was really pumped, and I could well imagine the massive gobs of adrenaline zipping through his veins.

I'd been having enough trouble handling the normal Teddy projectile without having him reach back for something extra. I could just visualize the count reaching three and two and the game's outcome depending upon my ability to hang on to a third-strike Snodgrass fireball.

There we were—the count full, Frank Marsden switching the ol' Louisville Slugger, and Teddy Snodgrass glaring in menacingly from the mound. Meanwhile, Lion runners were dancing off every base, while there I was, crouched behind home plate with my knees shaking like a dog trying to crap a bowl full of peach seeds.

"Time," I called suddenly. To this day, I don't know what possessed me or where I got the nerve, but at that moment I decided to be a tough guy and take the sponge out of my mitt. I didn't want to risk dropping the ball because of the extra bounce the sponge seemed to provide. "Time in," I said.

Snodgrass, pitching from the stretch, finally rocked back, kicked his left leg high in the air, and came right straight over the top with the ball. Not only was it covered with Chinese mustard but had liberal coatings of horseradish, Tabasco, and chili powder as well.

Marsden took a hefty swing but was clearly overmatched right from the start. A Teddy hummer rocketed right on by the Lion hero, to where it should have buried itself deep into the pocket of my catcher's mitt. But without the sponge, my hand stung so much, I dropped the ball anyway. It popped right out there on the ground in front of me, and it looked as though I'd lost us the game.

Big Frank Marsden was a little slow getting out of the batter's box, however, and I still had a chance to throw him out. I bounced out from behind the plate, scooped up the ball, and fired it to first.

But then I was a victim of some incredibly bad luck. I hit big Frank right in the back of the head with the ball, and it ricocheted out into right field while the tying and winning runs crossed the plate for the Green Lake Lions.

*****

Now, between warm up pitches, I steal another furtive glance toward the happenings on the rocky Happy Valley baseball diamond. I look just in time to see a line shot to right field for an apparent single. But the ball hits a big ol' rock right in front of Nathan Risberg and bounces clear over his head for a triple, driving in two more runs. It's now seventeen to four. Maybe Mr. Willy Mackerels will be seeing some action at long last.

Now, if only I had a fastball like my cousin Harvey Bodenheimer. Then I'd be sure to be out there on the ol' mound. You can bet on that bit of information. Harvey was good enough to play in the St. Louis Cardinal farm system.

> The Scandia Vikings lost to the Central Kitsap Cougars last Thursday by a score of 9 to 8. The Vikings were leading 8 to 5 until the last inning, when the Cougars, featuring Sam Lund's grand slam, erupted for 4 runs to win the game.
>
> Coach Rattebaugh, of the Vikings, was visibly upset at the conclusion of the contest. "That's the last time I put an inexperienced pitcher in an important game like that," he said.
>
> By Leonard Beacraft
The North Kitsap Herald

Chapter 4

I've switched to my money pitch by now, a big, slow, wide-breaking curve. It can make a batter look really silly. Little Elmer has the ol' catcher's mitt anchored on the low, outside corner. I throw at his glove and let the curve break down and away from the target. My control is practically pinpoint, and I feel more than ready for the Hapless Valley Milk Maids. They'll be like putty in my hands—the poor sodbusters.

As I throw another near-perfect curve to Elmer's mitt, I hear a mild burst of excitement coming from the sparse Milk Maid crowd in back of the Happy Valley dugout. I glance back to the playing field and see a routine ground ball carom off a rock and go trickling out into left field for a base hit that scores yet another Milk Maid run. Won't be long now, I think, and I bear down even harder, preparing myself for the inevitable call to the bullpen.

I feel more than ready, and I desperately want a last chance to salvage what has so far been a disastrous and embarrassing season for me personally. Though I'd been mentioned in the North Kitsap Herald's pre-season review as a returning veteran, goofy ol' Rattleballs seemed unimpressed with my scientific assortment of junk pitches. He was more inclined to go with stronger arms on the mound.

And to tell you the truth, I hadn't done myself a whole lot of good in my only other outing to date. In a relief appearance earlier in the year, I'd had a terrible piece of luck. The stupid umpire couldn't seem to see that my big, jug curve was consistently nipping the outside corner. Trying to protect a three-run lead, I walked three batters in a row.

Finally, I had to throw a fastball in order to get a strike, and the batter tagged it out of sight for a grand slam in the bottom of the seventh and final inning.

I'm afraid that fiasco pretty much sealed my fate as a pitcher for the Scandia Vikings. For the rest of that season, I've stayed nailed to the far end of the bench.

*****

But that was then, and this is now. Two walks and one double later, Johnson is definitely finished, and the game is getting a tiny bit scary. Rattleballs gets up and looks nervously towards the bullpen. He watches as I break another of my big, sweeping curves into Elmer's mitt. My control is awesome.

"Snodgrass, warm up," Rattleballs yells. Yep, you guessed it. This is the same Snodgrass that was my teammate back in the days of Willy's Wonders. Teddy moved to Scandia the same year I moved to Kingston. His dad had purchased the Ford dealership there. Teddy quickly gets off the bench and trots out in our direction. When he reaches the crude pitching mound in the makeshift bullpen, he extends his hand to me for the ball.

"Coach says you can go back and sit down." Of course, he's got the usual sneer on his face when he says it. He's never really forgiven me for losing the championship of the Green Lake Recreational League.

Greatly embarrassed, I surrender the ball and head dejectedly back to the bench. I glance up to the stands to see if Trudy Trammell is watching, but fortunately for me, she's busily engaged in a conversation with a couple of girl friends.

Two walks later, Johnson comes out, and Teddy is in the game. While he takes his preliminary warm ups, I sit at the far end of the dugout with my head in my hands. How did I ever end up here on a team that doesn't even appreciate my talents? I wonder. What kind of a baseball career will I ever have mired here at the end of the Viking bench? Then I think back to the chain of events that brought me to Scandia High in the first place.

POPE & TALBOT WATERFRONT LOTS
FOR SALE

Pope & Talbot Realty announces that they are selling some of their properties in the Apple Tree Cove area in Kingston. These wooded waterfront lots, roughly three-quarters of an acre in size, begin at $7,500. Within walking distance to town, these sites would be an excellent choice for those wishing to commute to jobs in Seattle, while escaping the hubbub of living in the big city.

By Leonard Beacraft
The North Kitsap Herald

Chapter 5

It was at the dinner table during the winter of my eighth grade year at John Marshall Junior High that Dad made an important announcement. "Mackerels," he said, "we're selling this house and are going to move to the country."

Dad had been becoming steadily more disenchanted with the hustle and bustle of city life. He'd been wanting to move from Seattle for some time. He'd grown up in primitive surroundings on the shores of Hood Canal, where he'd had access to lots of hunting and fishing and an a wide assortment of other outdoor activities. I think he wanted me to have the same opportunity to enjoy that more rugged and manly style of life. Still, the suddenness of his decision to move sort of rocked me back on my heels, if you want to know the truth. Actually, I was quite comfortable with my sheltered life in the city. And besides, what would I do without the Green Lake Theater?

"Uh...the *country?*" I said.

"Yeah, your mother and I bought some property over in a place called Kingston."

"Uh...where's Kingston?"

"It's over across the sound. We have to take a ferry boat from Edmonds to get there."

Until then, the only view I'd ever had of the Puget Sound was from downtown Seattle. Having never been particularly strong in geography, I had not a clue of what might exist on the other side of that body of water. It could have been the end of the world over there for all I knew. I could now understand some of Columbus's fears back there in 1492.

"What school will I go to there, Dad?" I'd never heard of a Kingston High. I'd been all primed to go to Seattle's Roosevelt High and star for the Roughriders.

"You have to take a school bus to the high school at Scandia. It's about twelve miles away."

"Oh," I said. But I'd never heard of Scandia either. I was a little worried about making new friends and all, but to tell the honest truth, I guess I didn't have all that many friends here in Seattle, except maybe Jerry Robbins. And what kind of friend tells a guy he's got a big nose, anyway?

So, the spring of '48 found us commuting to Kingston every weekend to work on the site of our future home. Kingston turned out to be a rather quaint little town. Mainly a ferry terminal, it's sole purpose, it seemed, was to serve as a link from the mainland to the Kitsap and Olympic Peninsulas. Much like the animals on Noah's Ark, everything in Kingston seemed to come in twos. There were two grocery stores, two cafes, two taverns, two churches, and two roads out of town. Too bad there wasn't at least a couple of decent-looking girls in beautiful downtown Kingston.

"This place must have been founded by a Gemini," Mom said. Mom was somewhat interested in astrology and horoscopes and weird kinds of things that dealt with the occult and such as that.

Unfortunately, there was lots of land clearing to do before we'd ever be able to build on the Kingston property. We'd have to keep our noses to the ol' grindstone if we expected to get a house constructed before the beginning of the next school year. That meant that I soon was to become a little too familiar with the brush-hook, the crosscut saw, and the double-bitted ax.

We spent our weekend nights in little, dinky summer cabin that belonged to a friend from Seattle. The days were filled with slashing, hauling, piling, and burning, and as a rule, we worked right up to the last light of day.

After the dinner dishes were done, the folks often went downtown to the tavern, so they could become acquainted with some of the native Kingstonites. Dad was a pretty good pool player, so he was often able to pay for our cross-sound ferry trips by hustling some of the locals in what *they* thought was a friendly game of pea pool.

The owner of the summer cabin had a pretty good collection of girlie magazines, so that's how I often spent *my* evenings. The only naked ladies I'd ever seen before were on page 334 of the only art book in the Green Lake Library. And those were all extremely plump red heads with tiny boobs and great big bottoms. They were painted by some guy named Titian, way back in the 1500s.

The figures of the girlie magazine ladies were a lot more exotic. You couldn't deny that. The only problem, though, was that the magazines always inserted these little white stars to cover the most interesting parts of the female anatomy. I'm a little ashamed to admit that I often tried to imagine Jessica Bell in one of those skimpy, little, girlie magazine outfits. But I had a heck of a time eliminating the little white stars from the ol' imagination.

During the few breaks we took from the land clearing, Dad liked to tell about the idyllic, pastoral life we'd lead once we were finally settled into our country estate. Good ol' Dad—he painted quite a rosy picture.

"We'll have ducks, and chickens, and rabbits, and maybe even a pig or two. And we'll have a nice big vegetable garden...and lots of fruit trees. How's that sound to you, Mackerels?" I tried to get Dad talking about the forthcoming Utopia whenever I could. After all—talking about paradise was a lot more restful than working on it. That's one thing for sure.

To tell you the truth, I must have sounded a whole lot like the half-wit, Lennie, from Steinbeck's classic, Of Mice and Men. "Tell how it's gonna be, Geee...orge...tell about the rabbits again...huh, George, huh."

When the Seattle schools were finally out for the summer, the long-awaited move to the country came about at last. Our new house had been erected during that last week of school, although we hadn't even seen it yet. It was some sort of new-fangled pre-fabricated construction that had taken the carpenters only a couple of days to put together.

On the first visit to the new domicile, I gave it a thorough inspection. I wasn't all that impressed either, to tell you the honest truth. It was definitely a much smaller and simpler house than the nice one we'd left behind in Seattle.

What first caught my eye in the combination living room-kitchen, was a strange-looking iron contraption called a wood range. "It's a Lang," Dad said, "and it's brand spanking new. It'll heat the house, and your mother will cook our meals on it."

Right off the bat, I didn't like the looks of the darn thing. It was throwing off some really bad vibes. I liked it even less, when I found out that I was going to be the official supplier of wood for the stupid thing.

As I continued on my tour, I found two small bedrooms in the rear of the place, and they didn't even have doors. Instead, in keeping with the general austerity of the place, there's just curtains hanging over the entrances. Great! Not only will I have to listen to my dad's, horrible snoring all night, but also, I'll probably not be able to listen to the radio after I'm supposed to be asleep. I Love a Mystery comes on at 10:30. I'll miss Jack, Doc, and Reggy. They have some danged scary adventures.

As I continue to inspect the new house, I'm vaguely aware that something else is missing. "Er...Dad...uh, where's the bathroom?"

"Out back, Mackerels," Dad said. "We don't have any water yet. We'll have to kind of tough it out for the first year. It'll be one of your jobs to haul water from the neighbors' well next door. We'll dig our own well and build a bathroom next summer. "Some Utopia," I should've said.

*****

I'm rudely jerked back to the present, when our bench lets out with a big cheer. Teddy Snodgrass has struck out the first Milk Maid batter he's faced with one of his patented blazing fastballs. No art to the way he pitches at all, I think to myself. I glance into the stands to get Trudy Trammell's reaction. She and some other girls are bouncing up and down and clapping wildly for ol' Teddy. It's enough to make a guy sick to his stomach. It really is. Although, it is sort of fun to watch ol' Trudy bounce up and down. I've got to admit that.

The hardness of the danged wooden bench starts to raise heck with my rear end, but I adjust the ol' cheeks a tad and then seek escape back into the recesses of my mind. To relieve the boredom of it all, I try to recall my introduction to baseball here on this side of the Puget Sound.

> The North Kitsap Recreation Department will once again be running a summer baseball program for teenaged youths of the local area. Department director, Richard (Dick) Urquhart, hopes to once again attract teams from Scandia, Kingston, Pearson, Suquamish, and Port Gamble. Adults wishing to coach or umpire should contact Urquart as soon as possible. League play starts June 15.
>
> By Leonard Beacraft
> The North Kitsap Herald

Chapter 6

I hadn't been in Kingston long before I discovered that the town had a baseball team for kids my age. They played in a summer league against such neighboring towns as Scandia, Port Gamble, Pearson, and Suquamish. I was really looking forward to trying my assortment of junk pitches on these country bumpkins.

At that time, I'd just begun my Eddie Lopat phase. I'd read where the famed Yankee junkballer had command of three different pitches, thrown from three different levels of arm release, and at three different speeds. I didn't have all twenty-seven combinations mastered just yet, but I was working on them faithfully, whenever I could find a catcher.

There was lots of batting practice to do, too—not to mention the endless hours of shagging fly balls. Pitchers had to do these things to keep their legs in condition. I had to explain this to my mom from time to time, whenever she grew anxious over the ever-shrinking woodpile.

Every so often, Dad would put a temporary restraining order on my ball playing, in order to get the ol' wood supply built up to his standards. On these occasions, I'd find one of his famous literary compositions at the breakfast table. A typical example might read: Willie—cut wood. Do not go to ballfield—Dad. Or when Dad found me sort of loafing around the house on a Saturday and said, "What're ya up to today, Mackerels?"

"Uh...I'm just kind of killing time," I said, somewhat unwisely.

"The only way to kill time, Willie, is to work it to death. So get out there on that woodpile."

Dad wasn't exactly what you'd call, "a wordsmith," but he could sure get his point across. And I could always tell when he was sort of perturbed. On those occasions, he always called me Willie instead of Mackerels.

The days spent away from the ball field found me much busier than I would have liked. Armed with crosscut, maul, wedge, and ax, I fell and converted alders into sixteen-inch stove lengths. When this was done, I then had to stack the wood neatly on our covered porch to dry for the good ol' Lang.

I used Dad's folding carpenter's rule to measure off the sixteen inches and then a machete to mark off the spot. One day, though, I had bad aim with the machete. It was a terrible piece of misfortune—I could barely bring myself to look. But the fact remained: I'd accidentally cut one inch off the wooden rule. *I done a bad thing, George.* The ol' rule became a rather treacherous measuring device from that moment on.

One unseasonably cold day, shortly after the Fourth of July, I was unwittingly responsible for the near death of my old nemesis, the wood stove. Mom, in one of her tidying-up moods, had fed it a crumpled, apparently empty, paper bag she'd found littering my bedroom. However, the bag was not empty. Instead, it contained my left-over fireworks, including: four packages of Ladyfingers, five packages of Zebras, and three or four Cherry Bombs. The Lang reacted as though it'd just devoured the spiciest dinner in all of Mexico. It coughed and belched its lids up and down for danged near ten minutes.

Of course, I blame that all on Mom. It was clearly her fault. She was always picking up stuff that should have been left alone for Pete's sake. Heck, I knew where the firecrackers were all the time; they were right there on top of the pile on the floor in the middle of my bedroom. That's where I'd put them away. Mom had never figured out that I had my bedroom all arranged in chronological order—the last thing put away would be right there on top of the pile.

Don't get me wrong. I love good ol' Mom dearly, but she does have some annoying little habits if you want to know the whole truth. Another of her favorite tricks is to tell me to do some chore or another just as I'm already starting to do it. I can be reaching for a piece of wood to feed the stove, and invariably she'll say, "Willie, will you put some wood on the fire, please." She must think the wood I have in hand is for picking my teeth or some goofy thing.

Mom's continual use of the mysterious group known as "they" can also get on my nerves. "They" seem to be her main reference source. "Willy, they say that drinking too much pop will cause pimples."

"Who's they?"

"Well...uh...I don't know, but that's what they say."

Since Lang was robbing me of much valuable practice time for baseball, I was continually on the lookout for shortcuts to help get the ol' wood supply built up. A lot of our neighbors had begun to use modern power saws to speed up their wood production, but Dad would have none of it. "The ol' crosscut is a lot better for you, Mackerels...it'll build some muscle on you and put a little more zip on your fastball."

So, I continued to struggle along with our primitive equipment. The hard work might've added a tiny bit of muscle, but none of it seemed to gain me any more velocity on the ol' fastball. I had to keep relying on my wits and my Eddie Lopat junk.

For some reason, Coach Edwards, of our Kingston kids' team, didn't seem to appreciate the value of a crafty junkballer like me. I got to pitch once in a while, but the coach seemed to prefer Roger Finley's talents on the mound. Roger, one of our older players, could be a trifle wild on occasion but did possess a pretty fair blazer. He sort of reminded me of Teddy Snodgrass from the good ol' Willie's Wonders days.

There was one more thing that reminded me of those days. It seemed that Kingston had been struggling along most of the summer without much experience at the catcher's position. Unfortunately for my pitching career, it didn't take Coach Edwards long to see that I'd had some experience as a catcher. He promptly moved me behind the plate.

"You look real good wearin' the tools of ignorance, Mackerels," he said when I first donned the catcher's gear. "That mask really does somethin' for ya—hah, hah, hah." Coach Edwards is such a funny guy.

We won a few and lost a few, and the final game of the season found us playing Scandia in a rematch on our home field. They'd beaten the heck out of us at their place earlier in the summer.

Scandia was the biggest town in the northern part of Kitsap County, and having the most kids to draw from, were perennially the summer league champions. But this year, the Suquamish team was stealing their thunder. Scandia needed a win over us to salvage a tie for first place and a play-off game with Suquamish.

Since they were the visitors, we let them complete their infield practice first, and then we took the field. Roger Finley was pitching for us and was over on the sideline warming up with his little brother, Elmer. I was catching for the infield practice. It was a warm, muggy day, so I hadn't yet put on any of the protective gear. I knew I'd be plenty warm and sweaty before the day was over.

To begin the drill, Coach Edwards fungoed a sharp ground ball to the third baseman. Bobby McClellan started us off on a snappy note, as he fielded the ball cleanly and rifled it to first. Warren Williamson was our first baseman. He was a big, tall, left-handed kid, with a rather large head and a mop of black hair that was always hanging down over his eyes. His ball cap was always a little too small for his oversized head, and what with the little breeze that was blowing across the diamond, he had a heck of a time making it stay on.

Warren deftly received Bobby's throw and then, as his cap fell off, he whirled and fired to the plate. His throw came in on a nasty in-between hop which handcuffed me and bounced painfully off my left shin.

"Come on, Williamson...get 'em up," I yelled.

Our shortstop took the next ball from Coach Edwards and gunned it across the diamond to first base. This time, Warren sailed his throw to the plate about ten feet over my head and up against the backstop. From there it bounced back and hit me on top of the head. Meanwhile, his cap was doing a pretty fair imitation of a tumble weed, as it made its way out to right field.

"Come on, Williamson, get 'em down," I hollered.

As we continued the drill, Wild Warren continued to alternately bounce an assortment of misguided throws off my poor unprotected shins and chase his ball cap. Fearing the possibility of permanent bone marrow damage, I decided I'd better put on the catcher's gear after all. Roger Finley was finished with his warmups and was sitting down. This left his younger brother free for the moment, so I decided to make use of him.

"Hey, Elmer...wanna come and catch some infield for a minute while I put on the catcher's gear?" Elmer took over as I retired to the bench along the third base line. As I bent over to pick up a shin guard, Wild Warren finally found the target. WHAAAP! His next throw missed Elmer Finley by twenty feet, found its way to our bench, and hit me right in the ol' schnozzola. You should've seen all the blood. My eyes started watering so danged much that I could hardly see. I was temporarily rendered whores de combat, as they say in France.

Coach Edwards immediately dashed to my aid. And after one look, he decided he'd better get me home so my parents could survey the damage.

"Looks pretty bad, Mackerels...it might even be broken. Your folks'll probably want to run you to the doctor over in Scandia."

It was almost game time, but I only lived about a quarter of a mile from the field. Mr. Edwards had time to drive me home and still get back in time to coach the game. Dad was home working on Lang's woodpile; he'd intended to come to the game a little later. The bleeding had stopped by then, but my already slightly-larger nose had swollen drastically and was as sore as the dickens.

Dad made a preliminary examination. "Well, your snout's going to have a little crook in it from now on, but I don't think it's broken. Heck, we'll just rub a little dirt and a little spit on it, and you'll be as good as new."

"Do ya think I can go back and play?" I asked.

"Aw sure...you're a tough guy aren't you? I just hope you can get the catcher's mask on over that nose. It's puffed up pretty good."

Dad drove me back to the field, and I charged on over to our bench. The rest of the team was glad to see me and relieved that I wasn't hurt all that much. We were behind five to two, mostly because Elmer Finley didn't have a prayer of holding on to his big brother's fastball. After all, he couldn't even reach the high ones.

Roger Finley went on from there to pitch his best game of the summer. I'll have to admit it. He had his blazer under control and even threw a few curves that broke for a change. I dropped hardly a pitch, even though I could barely see past my badly-swollen nose.

By the last inning, we'd crept to within a single run of our opponents. Our chances looked pretty bleak, though, when with two outs and no base runners, I stepped up to the plate. So far, I hadn't been able to get my timing down in the country air and all. I was mired in a summer-long slump.

"Easy out," the Scandia shortstop yelled as I came to the plate.

When I settled into the batter's box, I decided to open my stance a bit. When standing in my usual way, my swollen nose was blocking all vision from my right eye. Opening my stance seemed to give me a much better view of the ball. Just as I figured, that little adjustment brought immediate results. I surprised everyone by slapping the first pitch into left field for a base hit. I guess the wind might have been of some help, as it blew the ball slightly out of reach of the diving shortstop.

My teammates were going nuts over on the sidelines, until they realized who was up next. Smiles turned to frowns, and puffed chests turned to sagging shoulders as Wild Warren stepped to the plate. Although Warren had lots of power, he seldom if ever made any contact with the ol' ball.

And to tell you the truth, this trip to the plate didn't look any more promising. On his first two swings, Warren looked like he was trying to become the next Babe Ruth. But all he did was stir up the air and set his cap to sailing. Our situation looked hopeless, to say the least. But for some unexplainable reason, the Scandia pitcher hit a wild streak. His next three pitches were way off the mark, and the balls and strikes reached the count of three and two.

"Good eye, Warren," Coach Edwards yelled "...good eye...a walk's as good as a hit."

On the deciding pitch, it looked as though Warren had paid attention and had earned his base on balls. The pitch was definitely out of the strike zone, but ol' Warren had other ideas. Apparently he wasn't going to be satisfied to get on base with a measly walk. At the last possible second, he went after the high, outside pitch with a wild, tomahawking swing. And just as Coach Edwards was saying, "Oh no," Warren drilled the pitch past third base, just inside the ol' foul line, and it rocketed on over the left field fence for a homerun. Thanks to Wild Warren, we'd upset those rats from Scandia.

As a capless Warren crossed the plate with the winning run, the rest of us mobbed him, and we all went down in a big heap. Later, we all took turns clapping him on the back and singing his praises. He was the man-of-the-hour—there wasn't any doubt about that.

But Coach Edwards said, "Wow, that was sure a lousy pitch you went after, Warren."

"Well, I didn't want no walk," Warren said. "I wanted to win this one for Mackerels. He showed a lot of guts comin' back to play after I practically killed him with my lousy throwin'."

"Then I guess I'd better call Suquamish...and tell them that they've just won the championship...by a nose."

*****

Our bench erupts, and everyone rushes out to congratulate ol' Teddy Snodgrass, who has just struck out the last Happy Valley batter to kill their rally and win the game. Sadly, Trudy Trammell is among the first to reach him. Her radiant smile against the backdrop of farm-girl freckles tears at the ol' heart. It really does.

As I half-heartedly join the festivities, I glance over to the Happy Valley dugout. As hard as it is to believe, those poor sodbusters look even more dejected than I feel. I can't feel all that sorry for the white-haired kid, though, if you want to know the truth. But imagine playing for a team like that. Maybe I shouldn't be so bummed out by my situation after all. At least, I get to wear a real uniform while I sit on the end of the ol' bench.

Nov. 8—51

Dear Auntie,

A quick note before chow. What's the weather like back there in Washington? Wish I was there. We're not doing much fighting right at the moment. Actually, we're fighting the cold more than we are the reds. The winters here in Korea come right out of Siberia. It's hard to get all patriotic about this war, especially when they refer to it as a "police action." What kind of war is that, anyway? One guy in our platoon always says, "It ain't much—but it's the only war we got." (I wish we didn't have any. My baseball career is wasting away). Enough for now. Say hello to Uncle George and Willie for me.

Your loving nephew,
Harvey

Chapter 7

My heart is up in my throat somewhere, as I'm back on our ten yard line awaiting the opening kickoff. The butterflies in my stomach always act up at the start of a game, but today there must be a whole new hatch coming out. It might just be the ol' imagination, but it seems just as though all of our opponents' eyes are fixed on just one player—me. The Scandia Vikings are literally licking their chops. They look like a herd of slavering beasts as they await the opening kickoff. Wait a minute! You're probably thinking. Doesn't Willie Mackerels play for the Scandia Vikings?

Not any more he doesn't. But then, who *does* he play for? Well, you'd never be able to guess in a million years. Because now as a senior, I am the full-fledged starting tailback for the Happy Valley Sod Bus—oops, Milk Maids. No—I'm not kidding. And you can bet your bottom dollar that the good ol' Vikings can hardly wait to get their meat hooks on Willie Mackerels. They look happier than a bunch of lawyers at a car wreck at this unexpected chance to knock the pudding out of their ex-teammate. Maybe now, I'd better go back a ways and do some explaining. Why is it that I presently have the misfortune to be in the Happy Valley backfield?

*****

It was in the spring of '51 that my folks decided upon yet another migration—this time, even farther from civilization. We moved to the little town of Happy Valley, over on the Olympic Peninsula. We were venturing into business there with the purchase of all things, a tavern.

The town of Happy Valley was first settled back in the mid 1800's by two English sailors, who'd jumped ship in Port Townsend. Things must have been pretty danged bad aboard the ol' ship, if you were to ask me. There were several fairly large dairy farms in the valley, and on any given day, the smells from their manure piles would be strong enough to knock a dog off a gut wagon.

Besides the run-down, old tavern, there wasn't a whole lot to the town of Happy Valley. There was a down-in-the-heels Methodist church, a ramshackle post office, an old-fashioned one-pump Mobil gas station, a mom and pop grocery store, the rinky dink school, and a broken-down old hotel that'd been abandoned for the past twenty years or so.

The whole town was pretty much a mess, so I guess we wouldn't have wanted our new tavern to look too good at that. If it didn't look crappy, it would've seemed totally out of place. It'd been closed for the past couple of years, as a state trooper had caught the previous operator selling beer on a Sunday.

My folks bought the liquor license, the tavern equipment, and the inventory for a measly $4,500, and leased the building for a song. As soon as I saw the run-down place, I thought even the song too high a price to pay. I wondered where we'd ever get any customers; there was hardly anyone living in beautiful downtown Happy Valley.

Business was pretty danged slow at first. But it gradually picked up, as word of mouth let the locals know that their favorite watering hole was open once again. Customers began to come out of the woodwork from such backwoods places as Sunny Cove, Larsonville, Ironlock, Muck Muck Bay, and Muskrat Valley.

Dad is sure a glutton for punishment. He helps out the ol' income by commuting all the way to Seattle, while he continues to work at his old job at the print shop. It must be an awful long day for Dad. He has a long drive plus two ferry rides just to get to the danged job. Then, after an eight-hour shift standing in front of the ol' printing press, he has to do the trip all over again just to get back home. Mom works the tavern during the day, and after a quick supper, Dad relieves her until closing time. If Dad likes work, he must be having a heck of a lot of fun since we bought the goofy tavern.

We live in the upstairs of the rickety old building, in what I'm sure you'd call cramped quarters. And it hasn't taken me long to build up a real hatred for the tavern. In fact, the tavern has to rank right up there with Lang and Teddy Snodgrass on my list of all-time worst enemies. The cigarette smoke that filters up through the floor is enough to give a young person an early case of lung cancer. And the noises from the business activities below make it just about impossible to ever get a good night's sleep.

One of the worst disturbances comes from our most steady female customer, the Wicked Witch of the West. At least that's what I call her. I've never actually seen the old hag, as I'm forbidden by the state liquor board to even step foot into the business area. But I have no trouble visualizing her. Her wild maniacal laughter magically threads its way through the porous flooring of bedroom each night and finds its way to my poor ol' eardrums. "Hee, hee, hee," she cackles night after night. I can just picture her and her broom hiding somewhere along the Yellow Brick Road just waiting to ambush poor ol' Dorothy and her crew.

Another sleep-robber is a contraption called Shuffle-Bowl, a miniature bowling game that's played with a metal puck rather than a real bowling ball. It isn't that noisy of a game, until someone bowls a danged ol' strike. Then the pins all fly up with a giant rattle, and Shuffle-Bowl cries out in a high, piercing shriek, "RRrrriiiinggg!" Unfortunately, the danged customers don't realize the evil in Shuffle-Bowl, and he's become one of their favorites.

And if neither the Wicked Witch of the West or Shuffle-Bowl manages to keep me awake, then the good ol' Wurlitzer will do the job. The Wurlitzer is an old-fashioned, dome-shaped juke box with colorful bubbles dancing gaily around its plastic outer edge. The machine looks harmless enough, but don't think for a moment that it won't gobble up all the nickels, dimes, and quarters it can get a hold of. And if the goofy customers aren't feeding the juke box, Dad is. He's painted a whole bunch of coins with red fingernail polish, so he can tell Tavern's money from that of the patrons.

"If *we* play music," Dad says, "it'll stimulate the customers into putting *their* money in. It's sort of like priming a pump, Mackerels." Then we hear another round of Hank Snow singing one of his latest gravelly-voiced hits. Funny thing is, though, whenever Dad opens Wurlitzer to count the money, I notice very few coins without fingernail polish. I don't know how many times I've almost fallen asleep only to have Wurlitzer suddenly blast good ol' Hank Snow and the Rhumba Boogie right on through my bedroom floor.

And if all those noise-makers aren't enough to keep me on a constant state of alert, there's always Skinny and Clyde. I think they're old navy vets from World War I. They live in a rustic, old squatter's shack over on Sunny Cove and drive their old Model-A Ford to the tavern. They'll be there every single night, come hell or high water. After one-too-many port wines, Skinny likes to holler, "Fire one."

"Fire two," Clyde will chip in at the top of his lungs.

"Fire in the paint locker," they'll both yell in unison.

They can get on your ol' nerves. They really can.

I guess I've made it sound as though I hate Happy Valley, but that's not really the case at all. Tavern can be a real pain in the ol' gluteus maximus sometimes, but Happy Valley High has really turned out to be sort of a pleasant surprise. It might be just the missing link I've needed to help turn around my sagging academic, athletic, and social fortunes.

At Scandia High School, quite a few of the kids live right in the town of Scandia, itself. There's lots of blue-eyed blondes with names like Ole and Ragnar, and Hilda and Olga. They can be a little clannish, if you want to know the truth. If you ask me, they're a little suspicious of Kingston kids in general and tall, dark, and sub-Errol Flynnish ones in particular.

On the other hand, the Happy Valley enrollment seems to be a mixture of kids from Happy Valley itself and all its outlying communities. There aren't any cliques as far as I can tell. In fact, I've pretty much been welcomed with open arms here. The kids here seem to appreciate having any new warm body to turn out for their athletic teams.

So far, the school work seems to be easier here at Happy Valley. I hope that it's not some sort of illusion, as I could sure use some decent grades to tell you the honest truth. In earlier years, my folks had great designs for me as a scholar but have pretty much given up all hope by now. Last spring, at Scandia, when I brought home four D's and a C, Dad said, "Willie, this is just terrible...what the heck's the matter with you, anyway?"

"I guess I probably concentrated too much on the one subject," I said, somewhat lamely.

Boy, that was a tough quarter. All my valuable time that I could have been using to practice my Eddie Lopat deliveries was filled up with Shakespeare, algebraic equations, and good ol' Spanish. Habla—hablas, hablamos, hablah, blah, blah... And all that meaningless junk was sandwiched between long, boring rides on the school bus and tedious sessions of gathering wood for that darned ol' Lang. I wasn't having too much trouble with the Shakespeare and was managing to stay sort of even with the algebra, but Spanish had me completely at its mercy. It was all Greek to me.

"Me no comprende Espanol," was about the only thing I knew. After all, it hadn't been my idea to take a stupid ol' foreign language in the first place. I would've taken an easier elective or maybe another p. e. class, but my folks had other ideas. They'd both taken Spanish in high school and thought it would be valuable for me. Yeah—right—you never know if I might get the opportunity to go into business, some day—down in Venezuela or one of those other big Mexican towns.

Since Teddy Snodgrass never took any classes as tough as Spanish, I felt free to sit close to Trudy Trammell whenever I possibly could. Not only was she the best-looking girl in the whole danged school but she was the smartest too.

One morning, Miss Swanson, our somewhat senile, old, language teacher, announced that we would be having a test the following day. This was bad news for me. I'd already flunked the first two tests and a third washout would no doubt give me a dirty ol' failing notice. And it would not be a heck of a lot of fun explaining that turn of events to Mom and Dad.

"Dang," I whispered to Trudy, "I just don't get this stuff. I never have understood how you're supposed to subjugate these here verbs."

Ol' Trudy raised her eyebrows, made an interesting little laughing sound deep in her throat and said, "You don't subjugate these here verbs, goofy, you conjugate them."

"Whatever."

Well, then she moved her desk right up close to mine so she could see what it was that was giving me so much trouble. As she leaned over my desk, her hair brushed against my cheek—Lord—her honey-colored locks felt as soft as a mouse's ear. And she was so close, I could feel the heat from her body and also a slight pressure from her ample breast against my arm. Wow! Between that and the scent of her lavender perfume, it was kind of tough to concentrate on the upcoming test. At that point, I was pretty well subjugated—I can tell you that much for a fact.

The next day, during first period English, the class was assigned another real exciting chapter of Hamlet. I had trouble concentrating, though, as unpleasant pictures of the impending Spanish crisis kept rattling around in my head. But suddenly, my eyes were drawn to old Miss Swanson—she was writing some stuff on the blackboard. What the heck is she doing? I wondered. Then—I could hardly believe my eyes. She was writing the questions for the upcoming Spanish test in preparation for third period. She must have forgotten that I was in both classes.

I wondered just what ol' Hamlet might have done in this situation. To cheat or not to cheat? That was the question. Considering my current predicament, the answer came surprisingly easy. I got out my notebook and began scribbling the Spanish sentences as fast as good ol' Miss Swanson could put them on the board. I couldn't get over my stroke of good luck. I had a second period study hall and plenty of time to look up all the translations.

Second period came and went. I had no trouble looking up the answers, and I entered my third period class all ready to apply the ol' coupe de ville.

Fortunately, Miss Swanson wasn't all that strict about seating arrangements, so I selected a desk that was sort of away from the main body of the class. Today, I even kept my distance from Trudy Trammell. The last thing I needed was to be accused of copying her paper.

I fell to work quickly, writing down the English translations I'd memorized in study hall. Though I was a complete dunce in Spanish, rote learning was not that tough for me. Keeping track of all the major league ballplayers' batting averages had pretty well strengthened me up in the ol' memory department. So it turned out I'd never taken an easier test in my whole life. What a snap.

Miss Swanson had the test results all ready for us the very next day. She was in the habit of reading them out loud to the class. I usually dreaded hearing the results; in the past, they'd always been real embarrassing. But that day, I'd felt much like the poker player, who having been dealt a pat royal flush, was now only waiting for someone to open the ol' pot.

It must have been a fairly difficult test at that, as the grades seemed pretty low on the average. Even Trudy Trammell only had a B plus. Her pretty lips formed sort of a pout at the announcement of her grade. I don't think B plusses were up to Trudy's standards at all. But to tell you the honest truth, I thought the pout made her all the more attractive.

When my name was finally called, faces turned in my direction. It's said that misery loves company, and good ol' Willie with his usual F would be a welcome companion on this Black Tuesday. But when my A grade was announced, leering grins turned quickly to scowls of disbelief. I just leered back, as I thought to myself, Muchos gracias, Senora Swanson. But as for all you other gringos y gringettes, remember, por favor, that from now on, El Mackerels es numero uno.

*****

The kickoff doesn't reach me back at the safety position. Their kicker appears to squib it on purpose, and we down the ball on our own thirty-yard line. Are they afraid of my awesome broken-field abilities? But as we head for the first huddle of the day, my stomach feels like another new squadron of butterflies is emerging from the ol' cocoon. And for good reason—the Vikings are huge and are leading the league. We, on the other hand, have only Scandia standing between us and a perfect season. We're zero and seven for the year.

On the first play from scrimmage, we line up in our old-fashioned single wing formation, and I try the center of the ol' Viking line. I swear we must be one of the last teams in the United States of America not to have switched to the T. Pop Warner would be proud.

The Vikings seem real glad to see me come plunging into their midst. Eleven blondes practically trip over one-another in their haste to welcome me. Then there's a great gnashing and rendering of bodies, as they greet me with an assortment of earth-shaking collisions. Some of my old buddies are apparently determined to separate me from my head, as they tug and twist upon it. Others seem more content to take vicious bites at my slightly-bigger nose.

At the bottom of the pile, a voice sounds in my right ear. "Mackerels, you dirty sonofabitch, whatever gave you the idea you could play football?"

In my left ear, someone whispers, "You Benedict Arnold piece a shit, if you think you're gettin' outta this game alive, you got another think comin'."

Actually, I'm quite touched by the fact that they've taken the time to renew old acquaintances like this. I never dreamed they'd be so glad to see me and all. But I have to admit that the weight of all the bodies on top of mine is beginning to get on my nerves a bit. And as the referees try to sort out all the players and reduce the size of the pile somewhat, I feel the ol' brain damage begin to seep in, and my mind sort of slips back to another pileup from an earlier time.

>   Welcome to Tom and Esther Michaels, the proud new owners of
> the Happy Valley Tavern. Mr. and Mrs. Michaels and their son, Willie,
> moved here recently from Kingston. Willie will be a senior this year
> at Happy Valley High. Mr. Michaels told this reporter that he is very
> happy to be here on the peninsula. Mr. Michaels has wanted to get
> into the tavern business for some time, and being in a very dilapi-
> dated condition, he was able to buy it quite reasonably.
>   —Dora Dingley
>   The Happy Valley Harbinger, September 1951

Chapter 8

It was during my seventh grade year that I got pretty hot and heavy into football. And it was at that time that I must have suffered the irreversible brain damage. My grades started to go down at that point, and it could all be pretty much blamed on those early football experiences.

The kids from good ol' Fairview Elementary had now moved on to John Marshall Junior High School. We were no longer the big fish in the little pond. Fairview was just one of many elementary schools feeding into the John Marshall melting pot. If you want to know the whole truth, junior high proved to be quite a shock to our fragile nervous systems. Not only was the schoolwork a lot harder and all, but we also had to get used to new classmates, new teachers, and a whole bunch of new rules and regulations. Besides that, good ol' Jessica Bell was just one of the many distractions at John Marshall.

Marshall was also the Seattle School District's designated learning center for the city's handicapped children. Hard-of-hearing students, deaf mutes, and those suffering from cerebral palsy were just some of the special members of Marshall's student body.

I'd always received pretty good grades at Fairview, but when Dad saw my first junior high report card, he was a little miffed. "They don't send all of Seattle's retarded kids to Marshall too, do they, Willie?" All his fears were realized when the next report came out—it was even worse. Mom and Dad blamed my poor grades on laziness, but I was convinced that the real culprit was brain degeneration caused by playing too much football while wearing inadequate headgear. A new leather helmet would probably have solved the situation, but Dad never bought into that explanation.

I first became attracted to the game of football while watching the recaps of college games on Movietone News. Army was my favorite team. Led by Doc Blanchard and Glen Davis, Mr. Inside and Mr. Outside, the Cadets of West Point were the nation's hot-shot team in the mid-forties.

I also rooted for the local heroes, the University of Washington Huskies, but if you want to know the truth, it was sort of a waste of time. At the start of each new season, Royal Brougham, the sports editor of The Seattle Post Intelligencer would write about the awesome potential of that year's Husky squad and would have them projected as a national powerhouse. Dad was usually skeptical, but I always allowed myself to get sucked in by the P. I.'s propaganda and jumped on the Husky bandwagon with both feet. But by mid-season, Dad would be justified, and the Huskies' fortunes would be as dark and gloomy as Seattle's November skies.

The kids in our neighborhood played their sandlot football a few blocks from our house at Mapleleaf Playfield. There were three separate playing fields at Mapleleaf, but only two of them were worth a darn. The two good fields were both monopolized by the big kids, so we were shoved off to the field on the side hill.

The side hill was pretty darned steep, so naturally, almost all of our running plays were designed to go downhill. A ball carrier running *down* the hill could run nearly as fast as Glen Davis, but a runner trying to run *up* the hill, would look a heck of a lot more like Francis the Mule.

Once in awhile, for variety, we might try a play up the middle. We hoped that fat Rollo Bean, our center, could fall on an opponent or two and open up a hole. Much like baseball, where fat kids were always catchers, our football customs required that they play center.

Since I was one of the faster runners, and also sort of a glutton for punishment, I was often called upon to carry the ol' pigskin. A typical play might find me receiving the hike from Rollo and then taking off around end (down the hill, of course) as fast as I could go, while everyone else blocked. Sometimes I made some pretty good yardage, but a lot of my runs were doomed right from the beginning. It didn't take a bunch of rocket scientists to figure I'd be running down the hill, so the opponents were often just lying in wait to pull the ol' head-em'-off-at-the-pass trick. Then I'd be swarmed under and piled upon by their whole danged team.

Not only was our field and our play selection quite primitive, but our protective equipment was not exactly up to code either. Hardly any of us had shoulder pads, and to tell you the truth, our cheap wartime helmets didn't offer a whole lot of protection to the ol' noggin. Being a child of the Great Depression, Dad wasn't going to cough up the price of one of those expensive leather helmets, and the new plastic ones, like Army's, were not yet available to the general public. Most of us had cheap helmets made of a war-time material called reinforced cardboard, although I've never been able to figure out what they were reinforced with—unless maybe it was a second coat of paint.

Quite often, after being swarmed on by the opposition, I'd get up with a good-sized dent in the cardboard helmet. I got so good at repairing dents, that I probably should have grown up to be a body and fender man. But it was those danged dents that probably gave the creeping brain damage its start. I didn't always understand things so well after my Mapleleaf Playfield days. It was no wonder that my junior high grades weren't always up to par.

I remember the last game I played at that play field. It was a Saturday, and we'd challenged the kids from 84th Street to a game at Mapleleaf. We started early, in hopes of getting one of the better fields, but once again, had to settle for the side hill. It was a beautiful autumn day, with scarcely a cloud showing in one of Seattle's rare totally clear skies. But the wild blue yonder darkened a little, when Teddy Snodgrass chose this particular Saturday to make one of his uncommon visits to one of our games. A speedy, powerful runner, Teddy normally was chosen to play with the big kids on one of the better fields. The few times he had ever played with us, he wanted to be quarterback, coach, referee, and the whole danged shooting match all at the same time. And to top it all off, he could be very critical of the football skills of the players relegated to the side hill.

"Uh...sorry, Teddy...er...we already got our sides," I said. This took more than a little courage on my part, if you want to know the truth of it all. You never knew when ol' Teddy might resort to some bullying tactics to get his way. I'd calculated that maybe enough of the other side hillers might back me if it came to such a thing.

"Ah, I don't wanna play with you creeps, anyway," Teddy said, as he turned and sauntered back towards the main playing field.

The game became sort of a marathon event that saw the score seesawing back and forth as the afternoon gradually slipped away. By 3:30, the 84th Street Gang had taken the lead by a score of seventy-three to sixty-eight. At that time, George McCorkle, their captain and fastest runner, made an announcement.

"I gotta be home by four," he said. "Let's play ten more minutes, and whoever's ahead by then wins the game."

Since they had the ball at the time, it looked like a really rotten deal for us. But, we couldn't very well complain, because we were using George's ball. It looked like we were a beaten team, to tell you the honest truth, but good ol' Jerry Robbins gave us a fighting chance by intercepting an ill-advised pass at mid-field.

However, our limited play selection was beginning to wear thin, as was Rollo Bean's physical condition. The 84th Street kids were on to my downhill running, and poor ol' Rollo was having a heck of a time opening anymore holes up the middle. Fat kids often lacked the stamina for games lasting all day.

"Let's quit this stupid game and go to the Triple XXX for some hamburgers," he said suddenly.

"Come on, Rollo," I said, "hang in there—the game's nearly over."

Rollo agreed to stay, but it didn't take a brain surgeon to tell his heart was no longer into the game. Any success up the ol' middle was probably finished for the day.

After two downs, we'd made hardly any yardage at all, and the situation looked pretty danged bleak, to tell you the ugly truth. On third down, I tried yet one more downhill sweep, but had no luck at all. Once again, I was swallowed up by a whole herd of 84th Streeters. Wearily, I got up from beneath the pile, fixed the dent in my cheap helmet, and wobbled back to the huddle.

"This'll be our last play, Mackerels," Jerry Robbins said. "What're we gonna do?"

He certainly had a good question there. To tell you the truth, I had a heck of a time thinking of an answer. Then, it came to me. I suddenly remembered a trick play I'd seen used by Army on Movietone News at the Green Lake Theater.

"We'll try something different," I said. "Rollo'll hike it to me on three. Jerry...you stay back with me, and I'll hand it off to ya. You go straight into the line and..."

"Aw, that'll never work," Jerry said.

"I ain't done yet, Twink. Just as you get to the line, you turn and throw it back to me...I'll have dropped back a little. Meanwhile, Brantley'll be across the goal line for a long pass."

Sure you can get it that far, Mackerels?" Kenny Brantley asked. That's what I liked—supreme confidence in my play-calling abilities by my teammates.

"Hurry up, you guys...you're takin' too long in the huddle," George McCorkle yelled.

The play went as planned up to the time I gathered in Jerry's return pass. But when I looked up the field for Kenny Brantley, I saw that the 84th Streeters weren't fooled at all. They were all over ol' Kenny like flies on a manure pile.

I had to do something in a big hurry. A quick glance to my right told me I could forget about running down the hill again. George McCorkle and several others were already there, just licking their chops. Without much further thought, I took off up the hill, something I'd tried only once or twice before during my entire career at Mapleleaf Playfield.

I'll have to tell you. I was real surprised when the uphill strategy seemed to catch the 84th Streeters off guard. It actually looked as though I had room to go all the way for the winning score. But there was one thing I hadn't thought about: it seemed I wasn't cut out to be an uphill runner. With leaden feet, I struggled onward and upward but made very little progress. I could just as well have been trying to climb Mt. Rainier in my snow shoes.

Unfortunately, the opposition had hardly any difficulty with the side hill. Like a herd of playful mountain goats, they bounded on up the incline to greet me, well-short of the goal line. This time, when I got up from the bottom of the pile, I had two dents in the cardboard helmet.

COMMUNIST CHINA TO ENTER WAR?
    By Carol Cunningham
    The Associated Press
    Tokyo, Japan

    Inside sources report that the People's Republic of China is gearing up to enter the Korean War on the side of North Korea. Understandably, intervention by Communist China has the United States Joint Chiefs of Staff somewhat worried. Efforts are going on within the United Nations Security Council to seek a way to discourage the red Chinese from taking aggressive action.

Chapter 9

It's a miracle. The fourth quarter has just begun, and we're tied with the mighty Scandia Vikings. And if you knew the bitter truth, we ought to be ahead. It'd be the first time to be ahead of anyone all season long. We'd just tried the flea flicker, the old Army play from the Mapleleaf Playfield days. Only this time it would've worked like a charm—if it hadn't been for good ol' Roderick Remblinger. I swear, he'll be the death of me yet. As I received the pitchback, I could hardly believe my eyes. Roderick was all alone there in the end zone. I reared back and put everything I had into the throw. It was a heck of a toss, as it covered nearly thirty yards in the air. And it was right on the money. Roderick must have had his seasons mixed up, though, and thought we were playing basketball. He made a perfect hoop out of his arms, and the ball went right on through and lit on the ground at his feet. But what could you expect? Roderick is just this side of a turnip, anyway.

A few minutes later, though, we did take the lead, when I acted as the decoy on the ol' buck lateral play. I took the snap from center and plunged straight ahead on an apparent buck up the middle. But just as I reached the line of scrimmage, I slipped the ol' ball to Buddy Pringle, our quarterback, before continuing my fake on into the line.

Well, the Vikings went for the ol' fake—hook, line, and sinker. It seemed they were more interested in crippling and maiming their former teammate than they were in stopping the play. As I went down in a heap of arms and legs and assorted other body parts, it must have looked a lot like a feeding frenzy of lions, jackals, and hyenas fighting over a fallen wildebeest. And while the young gentlemen from Scandia were busily punching me, and gouging me, and whispering sweet nothings into my ear, I couldn't help being reminded of my brief football career as a Viking.

*****

As you might expect, I was pretty pumped up on my first day in attendance at Scandia High. As you might also expect, I wasn't thinking so much about academics either. But this would be my first taste of organized football and a chance to play on a real team, with a real coach, and real equipment. No longer would I have to pound dents out of a goofy cardboard helmet. Maybe the creeping brain damage would abate somewhat.

But football at Scandia didn't turn out to be any cup of tea, if you want to know the truth. Each practice session began with a brutal regimen of calisthenics, which included such all-time favorites as, sit-ups, push-ups, jumping jacks, four-count-burpees, six-count-burpees, and even eight-count burpees. The burpees, progressive combinations of squats, leg thrusts, and pushups weren't all that bad, actually. But the real gut-buster was a torture called leg lifts, which found us flat on our backs holding our heels six inches (no more or no less) off the ground until our stomachs felt like they'd soon catch on fire. We were expected to hold on to the pain a little longer each night. The worst of all, though, were the tortuous cut-aways. First, we did a push-up, which we held in the "up" position for about a minute, and then on the command of, "Cut-away," we had to throw our arms to the side and just let ourselves go. KABBAANG. Then the earth would shudder, as approximately forty chests and bellies hit the ground all at once. I doubt if this was any good for the ol' liver, if you want to know the truth. This torture chamber was followed by endless laps around the track and gut-wrenching sets of hundred-yard wind sprints, too numerous to count.

Then we got down to work. We spent the next hour or so on a bunch of boring old blocking and tackling drills, all of which were designed to put me in a great deal of pain. Most of these contests of brute strength ended up in piles of bodies with an assortment of bulky blondes on top and yours truly on the bottom. All that could be seen of me would be one skinny arm or leg sticking out from beneath the rubble. Those Norwegians were tough and strong. I've got to admit it. The creeping brain damage, that had sort of been in remission, broke out once again, this time in real earnest.

What I'm saying is, that I'd been used to a much different format back at good ol' Mapleleaf. There, we never did any calisthenics, laps, or wind sprints. We just chose up sides and started playing. We also had fun. But at Scandia, I'm afraid, football just became a drudgery, mainly I suppose, because I just wasn't up to the rigorous physical demands of football as played by the Vikings.

I'd grown pretty fast the previous year, and my muscles and coordination had failed to keep pace, I'm afraid. The sudden growth had sapped my long-tall, skinny body of most of whatever endurance It'd ever had. By the time we'd finish all the stupid exercises and drills and finally get to playing football, I wouldn't have strength enough left to pull the skin off of a rice pudding. In fact, I guess you could say that strength was my biggest weakness.

Originally, I'd hoped to become the starting tailback for the Scandia Vikings, but those fantasies quickly went down the drainpipe with the unexpected arrival of the great Teddy Snodgrass upon the scene. Although he had no Nordic blood to speak of (none that I'd ever heard about anyway) Teddy's running abilities very quickly established him as the team's star running back. Not only that, but Teddy, not what you'd call a great admirer of me as a person, seemed to get his kicks by goading the brutes of the team into saving their hardest blocks and tackles for me personally. Why did Teddy's dad have to choose Scandia from all the other towns in the whole State of Washington to go and buy a stupid automobile franchise?

It was during those man-killer drills, that I often thought back to the World War II movies at the Green Lake Theater. In my fantasies, a whole squad of big, strapping, fair-haired brutes followed the lead of the young blonde actor (who looked amazingly like Teddy Snodgrass), as he led them along a jungle trail to be ambushed by the Japanese.

For the first time in my illustrious career, I was not considered fast enough to be a ball carrier. I couldn't even make the second string as a tailback. My Mapleleaf, side hill speed seemed to have deserted me on the Vikings' level field, and the coach converted me into a lineman—a tall, skinny, weak, Ichabod Cranish sort of a third-string lineman.

I've got to tell you. There was no glory left for me in the game of football. I managed to finish that one horrible season; I didn't want to be labeled a quitter. But I never again turned out for football at Scandia. I figured there'd be a lot less chance of further brain damage if I just concentrated on my baseball career instead.

*****

I was rudely awakened from my remembrances there at the bottom of the pile when an angry Viking voice shouted into my ear, "There he goes!" The volume nearly blew out my poor ear drum.

Then, I could feel all the massive bodies above me heaving and straining to loosen themselves from the pile. They wanted to give chase, but it was too late. Remember—all the while the Vikings had been busy manhandling their ex-teammate, ol' Buddy Pringle'd secretly had the ball. Then, Gordy Belmont had taken a buck lateral pitchout from Buddy and was scampering around the unprotected left side of North's line for all he was worth. Let me tell you, Gordy Belmont can run pretty darned fast when he's scared (and he is scared a good share of the time). Seconds later, he stood untouched in the end zone after a nifty run of sixty-three yards.

We'd taken the lead by a touchdown. On the extra point, though, a clump of sod appeared out of nowhere and caused me to muff the kick. We were ahead by six points with a chance at our first win of the season, but I wondered if we could possibly go on to hold the lead against the powerful Vikings. They looked awfully stirred up to me. I imagined that there was going to be some rough moments ahead before the Milk Maids could think about coming out with a victory. As we lined up to kick off, my mind wandered a bit back to the early days of the season and my introduction to Happy Valley football.

Sept. 23—51

Dear Auntie,

So Willie is going to play football at his new school? I didn't think he liked the game all that well. I don't know if it is such a hot idea. Football is rough, and football injuries can raise heck with baseball careers. Of course, this damn (excuse the language—ha—ha) war can sure foul up a baseball career for sure. Even though we're just supposed to be in a holding action, there are guys still getting killed or else seriously wounded. Well, good luck to Willie, anyway. I guess the main thing is that he has fun while he can.

As ever,
Harvey

Chapter 10

I'd planned never to play football again, but during the first trip down the hallway of my new school, I noticed a definite lack of manpower. To tell you the honest truth, there weren't many guys that looked big enough to go out for a game as rough as football. Although I did see a couple of girls that looked big enough to play for the Green Bay Packers. Of course, girls didn't turn out for sports. They either made the cheerleader squad or else they sat up in the stands and watched. There didn't seem to be any lack of enthusiasm for the sport, though, and hopes appeared high for the upcoming season and all.

I guess Hapless Valley hadn't always been the runt of the Olympic League, either. Back when there'd been more logging in the area, there'd been some decent seasons. But recent years had pretty much found the Blue and White mired hopelessly in last place.

To open the football season of '51, the poor ol' Milk Maids had no size, no speed , and no experience. I didn't bring a whole lot to that mix, either, and I was still a little leery of physical contact, to tell you the absolute truth. But since it appeared as though I was one of the three or four biggest kids in school and that nearly every boy in school played football, I just about had to turn out. I sure as heck didn't want to start out in my new school being labeled a chicken right off the ol' bat. Besides that, the Milk Maids looked as though they could use all the warm bodies they could find.

To be perfectly honest with you, our prospects looked pretty darned bleak right from the start. For size, there were only two players weighing more than my 160 pounds. For experience, there were only two seniors, including myself, and not counting the Mapleleaf Playfield days, I didn't have a whole lot to brag about. There was just that single, ill-fated season of warming the Scandia bench. There was a handful of juniors, too, but the bulk of the roster was pretty much made up of some real spindly sophomores and freshmen.

Coach Monahan was a beginner, too. Teaching chemistry was what he'd been hired for, but an emergency situation had landed him smack-dab into the position of head coach for football, basketball, and baseball for the mighty Milk Maids. After evaluating the returning athletic material, the previous mentor had wisely skipped town over the summer.

Right off the bat, though, you could see that Coach was a pretty shrewd judge of talent. Before the first practice was half-over, he'd installed me as the starting tailback. It came as sort of a surprise, to tell you the honest to goodness truth. The craziest thing, though, some of the long-lost Mapleleaf speed seemed to have magically returned. But I suppose the crude Milk Maid practice field might have had something to do with that. Composed of dirt, rocks, and boulders, and looking quite a lot like a minefield, it seemed to spur me on to sprinter-like quickness. I didn't plan to be tackled there, if I could possibly help it.

We were a pretty enthusiastic bunch, right up until our first game. In fact, I'd even got fooled into thinking we might not be so bad after all. But that was before we met our first opponents, the Sequim Wolves. During the pre-game warm up, we peeked occasionally to the other end of the field; we sort of wondered what we were up against. I soon wished I hadn't looked. They were huge. Their running backs were bigger than anyone on our whole team, and their linemen were obviously shirt-tail relations of Tyrannosaurus Rex.

Coach Monahan could see that we were completely overawed and about to slip into a state of shock. He decided it was time for a pep talk.

"I see you men looking at the other team," he said in his best imitation of Knute Rockne. "They look big, but if you'll notice...they're soft and flabby. You men are tough and hard."

But to tell the truth, It was puzzling to me how we could have become so "tough and hard" all of a sudden. Our program of calisthenics were nowhere near as tough on the body as the ones I'd suffered through as a Viking. There was not even a burpee to be seen, let alone any cutaways. And to top it off, we'd been cheating something awful. As a beginner, Coach had unwisely chosen to put us in a circular formation to do our exercises, with him leading from the center.

As he could only watch half of the circle at any one time, the other half never failed to clown around behind his back. It was awful. About the only muscles ever exercised by the goof-offs were located in their middle fingers. But it all came back to haunt us, as the "soft and flabby" guys stomped the "tough and hard" ones by a score of thirty-nine to zip. From that point on, Happy Valley football reminded me a lot of the Mapleleaf Playfield days. Only it wasn't the field that went downhill, it was the entire season.

Our play selection also reminded me of the Mapleleaf days. We ran Mackerels left, Mackerels right, and Mackerels up the middle, only we had no Rollo Bean to open up the holes.

"And our defense is pretty offensive, too," I was telling Dad one night after dinner.

"Oxymoron," Dad said. That surprised me, Dad getting insulting about it and all. I tried to overlook it, though; Dad's been working real hard.

"Sometimes I think you have to be about half-nuts to play tailback for a team like this," I went on to say.

"You might be over-qualified," Dad said.

*****

Our defense rises to the occasion, and we hold the Vikings on downs. We're still enjoying the six-point lead. Then the two teams sort of see-saw back and forth until late in the game when the Vikings mount a drive and get down to our ten yard line. Things look real bad for us; there's no doubt about it.

But would you believe it? None other than the great Teddy Snodgrass fumbles on the next play, and Buddy Pringle recovers on our own five. Four plays later, I am standing in my own end zone getting ready to punt. I don't have a lot of room in which to operate, but hopefully, I can get the kick away. I'm going to angle it out of bounds, so the Vikings won't be able to get a long runback or anything like that. Then, if we can hold them for just one play, time'll run out, and we'll have beaten the mighty Vikings. Won't that be a laugh.

But I fail to reckon with good ol' Roderick Remblinger—in punt formation, he is back to help protect the kicker. He gives a little too much ground with the defensive rush and backs right into me just as I go to kick the ball. Well, would you believe it? I kick him right in the ol' buttin-ski, and with time running out, the Vikings fall on the ball in our end zone for the tying score.

And of course, with no clump of sod jumping out of the blue to bother him, Teddy calmly puts the ball right through the uprights to win the game by a point. Sometimes I think Roderick Remblinger would make a danged good poster child for the brain-dead.

Our Happy Valley High School football team suffered a one-point loss Friday night at the hands of the Scandia Vikings. The loss was the eighth straight for our boys, while the Vikings completed an undefeated season and once again claimed the championship of the Olympic League. Being totally out of synch, Coach Monahan blamed the Milk Maids' kicking game for the defeat.
 —Dora Dingley
 The Happy Valley Harbinger, November 1951

Chapter 11

The one-point loss to Scandia definitely has my nervous system all messed up. I have a heck of a time getting to sleep tonight. Although it seems like I toss and turn forever, I guess I must be dozing some off and on at that. I have this dream that I'm back at Mapleleaf Playfield. Rollo Bean has opened this huge hole in the center of the line, and the goal line is right there, just a few yards away. But try as I might, I can't seem to make any progress at all. It's like I'm being held back by giant rubber bands attached to my legs. I continue to struggle for awhile but then slowly drift into a gray, hazy world. But suddenly, I'm aware of voices from somewhere below me.

"Hee, hee, hee," cackles the Wicked Witch of the West.

"RRrrriiiinnggg!" cries Shuffle-Bowl.

"...Then across the water came Cuban Pete...he started the boogie to the rhummm...ba beat..." sings Wurlitzer and Hank Snow, in a beautiful gravelly-voiced duet.

"Fire one!" Skinny hollers.

"Fire Two!" yells Clyde.

"Fire in the paint locker!" they both shout in perfect unison.

CRASH, BANG, RATTLE, SCRAPE!

As I bolt upright in bed and turn on the lamp on my nightstand, I wonder why I'm still mired in the gray, hazy world of my dreams. Then I realize that it's just the accumulation of all the evening's cigarette smoke that has filtered up through the ol' floor.

Dang you Tavern, I think.

"That's it. You two are outta here. Take it on outside...right now!" I hear Dad's angry voice coming from downstairs. What' going on? I wonder...a fight?

I jump out of bed, quickly don an old pair of jeans, and head downstairs to see what's going on. I sneak through the kitchen and peek into the bar. I'm just in time to see Dad ushering a couple of guys out the front entrance. Skinny, Clyde, Mom, and a red-headed lady with a ponytail are close behind. I get my first glimpse of the Wicked Witch of the West seated at the bar. The hag is not following the others; instead, she seems to, be in a semi-stupor and content to sit there admiring the glass of amber-colored liquid that sits before her.

I turn around and scurry out the back door, hoping to get out front before the action is all over. As it turns out, I'm in plenty of time to get a choice ringside seat. The combatants haven't yet started swinging on one another in real earnest. Circling warily, they are obviously still in the feeling-out stage.

I recognize the shorter and stockier of the two as Fran Newfield, a gyppo-logger from Sunny Cove. He's already staggering pretty good, and there haven't even been any punches thrown yet. He's maybe had a few too many cups of tea, I figure. His opponent is a guy called Bernie Something-or-other, one of those wild Finnish names with about four thousand vowels. He's a little taller than Fran but has a much slighter build. Might be a real mismatch, I think, as they continue to keep their distance.

Turns out I'm right, only not the way I had it figured. Either Bernie is too quick or his stronger-looking opponent is too drunk, as the next thing you know, ol' Fran is flat on his back on Tavern's front lawn. With lightning speed, Bernie has closed the distance and unloaded a savage left hook.

"Fire one!" yells Skinny.

As Fran grovels around on the ground in a feeble-looking attempt to regain his feet, I lean over to Mom and ask her what the fight is all about.

"The redhead's Fran's wife, and they say she's been stepping out behind his back with Bernie there." I don't even bother to ask Mom who "they" are, figuring that it doesn't matter all that much anyway. Fran is up, but after another brief session of sparring, he goes down again—this time the victim of a sneaky, overhand right.

"Fire two!" Clyde hollers.

But Fran is tough. Either that, or he's too drunk to feel any pain. Just when it looks like he's about through for the night, Fran connects with a wild bolo punch of his own that sends *Bernie* skittering across the boardwalk on the seat of *his* pants.

"Fire the whole darn crew!" shout Skinny and Clyde in perfect harmony.

From the looks of Bernie, rolling and flopping there on the boardwalk, he evidently can't take a real good punch. He reminds me a lot of a freshly-caught salmon in the bottom of the boat.

"Get up, you dirty bastard!" Fran says, as he stands on unsteady legs over his fallen adversary. Bernie scrambles shakily back to his feet, and the fight is on once again. As it turns out, neither fighter receives much more in the way of punishment. The redhead sees to that, as she bravely jumps between the two weary gladiators.

"Stop it, Fra....," she starts to say, just as Bernie unloads a wild haymaker. She finishes by saying, "...*ah*...an," as the punch falls well-short of the intended target and hits her with a dull thud in the small of the back.

"That's enough, Buh...*er*...nee," she says, as Fran's counter punch catches her right above the kidneys.

She gets whacked pretty good a couple more times before Dad steps in and waves both men to neutral corners. The poor redhead is a little loop-legged by this time.

"That's enough, now," Dad says. "You guys oughtta go home now and sleep it off."

That must seem like a pretty good idea to Bernie, as he immediately staggers off towards his car. Fran just stands there for a moment rubbing his jaw. The redhead looks like she's about to cry any minute.

"Fudge." Fran says, finally. "I'll be fudged if I haven't lost my fudging wristwatch, and that fudger was brand fudging new."

"Watch that language, Fran," Dad says.

Actually, I'm pretty danged impressed with Fran's ability to use a root word like fudge correctly in so many different parts of speech. But even so, I immediately get down on my ol' hands and knees on the grass and start looking for the watch. I'll have to admit, though, that my motives aren't strictly those of the helpful, kind-hearted citizen. There could be a reward involved, especially what with Fran being drunk and all. You never know about stuff like that.

"Why don't you help Mr. Newfield look for his watch, Willie," Mom says (once more after the fact). "Sure, Mom...I'll get right on it...as soon as I'm all through grazing down here," I should've said. As I crawl around looking for the watch, I can't help but think about the toughness both men displayed. Then my mind sort of wanders back to my Seattle days and my own brief pugilistic career.

*****

It wasn't a whole lot of fun getting beat up by Teddy Snodgrass, even if we're just talking about general principle. Besides being downright painful, it was also damaging to my pride. Teddy was already the first chosen for any game we played and had the girls all going ga-ga over him besides. You'd have thought he'd be satisfied with that, but no, he had to get his licks in on ol' Willie Mackerels from time to time, just to sort of rub some salt into the wounds. If you want to know the truth, I don't think he'd ever forgiven me for the lost championship of the Green Lake Recreational League.

It wasn't as though Teddy was all that much bigger than me. In fact, I'd recently passed him in height by an inch or so. But he was built like a brick outhouse and was awfully aggressive. Teddy had my number, and he knew it.

"Oh yeah," he said to me one day. This was before I realized he was still harboring a grudge.

"Yeah," I said. Like I told you before, I've always been known for my snappy comebacks.

At that time, I wasn't too much afraid of Teddy. I sort of thought I'd be able to defend myself pretty well in any kind of skirmish. After all, I put the boxing gloves on with Dad just about every night after dinner. I felt pretty lucky to have a father who'd take the time to show me the basics of self defense. Dad showed me how to keep my hands up and block punches, and he showed me how to throw left jabs and right crosses.

"The ol' one-two gets em every time, Mackerels."

One day, Teddy and I had another of our little conversations, complete with all the usual "yeahs" and "oh, yeahs." But then he suddenly switched tactics on me. I was completely caught off guard, if you want to know the awful truth of it all.

"Wanna make somethin of it?" he said.

Now in the past, I'd always held my own pretty danged well in the "yeah—oh yeah" phase of our previous altercations, but this new "wanna make somethin of it" stage had me temporarily confused. I'll have to admit it.

"Yeah," I finally said, a bit unwisely too I might add. "Certainly not," is what I should have said. Teddy took my answer as a cue to start raining punches from all angles on my poor, unprotected skull.

I tried like heck to remember what I'd learned during the sparring sessions with Dad, but Teddy's non-stop barrage gave me no time to think. Teddy didn't fight by Marquis of Queensberry rules at all. Once, when I tried one of Dad's famous one-twos, I didn't even get half-way through the one, before I received another wind milling knuckle sandwich right in the ol' kisser.

I decided then to abandon conventional style in favor of the lesser-known ostrich defense. I bent over as far as I could and covered my head with both arms. That helped for a short while, but it didn't take Teddy long to find the gaps in this sort of unorthodox style of resistance. Unfortunately, my arms couldn't cover all parts of my head at once, so it wasn't long before Teddy was methodically punching the open spots. He was raising some pretty good-sized lumps on the ol' noggin, if you want to know the whole sad truth.

Then I had a new brainstorm. Maybe if I snuck a glance out from beneath the protective shell from time to time, I might be able to spot the start of the next blow and avoid it somehow. That strategy didn't work either, I'm afraid. At the very instant I tried my first peek, Teddy nailed me right in the eye with yet another lucky punch. I was beginning to just hate that fight, I can tell you that much for sure.

Finally, though, help arrived in the form of a neighbor lady from down the street, Mrs. Katzenberger. "Boys, boys!" she shouted. "Stop it right this minute. Get on home, or I'll call your mothers on you." Mrs. Katzenberger was a saint, I always figured.

I tell you what...I didn't have to be told twice. While ol' Teddy paused for a second to think about what Mrs. Katzenberger was saying, I was out of there and well on my way home. The knots on my head ached like the dickens, and I was pretty sure I could feel the return of the dreaded brain damage.

Fortunately, the one licking seemed to satisfy Teddy, as we never actually came to blows again. He liked to give me a little shot on the shoulder, though, from time to time, just to remind me that I was still on his hit list. It could be real embarrassing when he did that, especially in front of the girls and all.

But one fateful afternoon, spent at the Green Lake Theater, made me think seriously about challenging ol' Teddy to a rematch. What I saw there certainly gave me food for thought.

Jerry Robbins and I, as we often did, had decided to take in a Saturday matinee. And as we stood near the end of quite a long line to the ticket booth, Jerry was beginning to get a little nervous about the main feature. It was a film called Gentleman Jim, and it was starring none other, than my old idol, Errol Flynn. I was still a little put out with Jerry, by the way, for those uncalled for comments about my slightly-bigger nose. For a guy with a neck as long as his, he had a lot of nerve talking about other people's physical deformities.

"Dang!" Jerry said, as we shuffled along with the line. His Adam's apple bobbed up and down along his giraffe-like neck as he spoke. "I dunno. Hope this isn't some weird show about how to be a gentleman or somethin'. I kinda had my heart set on a good ol' scary movie—like Frankenstein or Dracula."

I tried to think on the bright side, but the title made me a little skeptical, too. I'll have to admit it. I would have liked a good ol' Abbott and

Costello movie—or maybe a Roy Rogers. Though I tried to maintain a little faith in the fact that Errol Flynn was the star, I was half-afraid that our feature might turn out to be a musical. I hated musicals. In my opinion, there could be nothing worse than having to spend a perfectly good Saturday afternoon watching Nelson Eddy and Jeanette McDonald singing their lines at one another. I think the theater owners liked to show musicals when they had a surplus of popcorn or candy to get rid of. All the kids would spend way more time running back and forth to the concession stand then they would at watching the movie.

"Well— I've seen Errol Flynn in quite a few movies," I said, "and he's usually pretty good. He's a danged good sword fighter. Maybe it'll be about pirates or somethin'."

Finally, we made it to the ticket taker, paid our eleven cents, and headed eagerly for the concession stand. Visions of scrumptious candy bars were dancing in our heads. But as I'd feared, the pickings were pretty slim. Much like Dad's Lucky Strike Green, most of the decent chocolate bars had gone off to war. There were no Hersheys or Nestles to be seen.

So while Dad was reduced to rolling his own on a Target cigarette machine, us kids were stuck with a wartime candy bar creation called a Buck Private. They were horrible-tasting things that looked like something a real buck private might have to flush down the toilet.

We finally settled for a balanced diet consisting of equal portions of the two main food groups—heavily buttered popcorn and Ludens' cough drops. Unfortunately, the Ludens' seemed like the best candy available. Jerry purchased one Buck Private, though, to save for later. He liked to play crude practical jokes on his little sister.

The movie, as it turned out, was about James J. Corbett, the heavyweight champion of the world and the recognized father of scientific boxing. Of course, that was way back in the olden days. I was pretty danged fascinated by his fancy footwork and all and thought maybe I could use some of the Corbett/Flynn dancing technique to turn the tables on Teddy. Scientific footwork just might be the answer.

I tried some of the Corbett/Flynn moves on Dad one night but didn't get a very favorable response, I'm afraid to say. Once, after a blinding exhibition of dazzling footwork that must've looked somewhat like a sizzling rhumba/cha-cha combination. Dad put a halt to the sparring momentarily and said, "Jesus H. Christ, Willy, what the heck are you doing, anyway? You're dancing around here like a fart in a skillet."

Shortly after that, I sort of forgot about my plan of challenging Teddy to another fight. It seems as though every time I saw Mrs. Katzenberger, it reminded me of how sore I was after the first encounter with Teddy. I decided to let sleeping dogs lie.

*****

Thoughts of Teddy Snodgrass and Corbett/Flynn suddenly fade from memory. From the corner of my eye, I catch the flash of something metallic glistening from beneath the lilac bush on Tavern's lawn. What luck! It's Fran Newfield's brand new gold wristwatch. "Here it is...I found it!" I shout.

As Fran takes the watch from me, he says, "Thanks Kid," and then he grabs the redhead by the arm and off they go towards his old pickup truck. So much for rewards.

"Next time, you can find your own fudging watch," I should have said.

Nov. 12—51

Dear Auntie,

Just a real short note to thank you for the peanut butter cookies. They're my very favorite. They go real good with all the hot coffee I slurp down. Brrrrr!!! This is the coldest place I've ever been. Thanks again.

Your freezing nephew,
Harvey

Chapter 12

The big Tolo comes about on the Saturday following the last football game and is the biggest Happy Valley social event so far this year. I'm invited by a girl I don't know any too well, Rosie Higgenbottom; she's in my fifth period study hall. The main reason I don't know her so well is because she doesn't live right here in beautiful downtown Happy Valley. Instead, she lives way out on the outskirts of the school district at a wide spot in the road called Thorn Point. She's got a real good figure and sort of a pretty face, although she does have quite a few pimples.

When Buddy Pringle and Vernon Windbladd hear about my prospective date, they practically die laughing. They're my two best friends. They just about have to be my two best friends, because they're about the only other kids that live right in the town of Hapless Valley—at least, the only ones who play sports and all.

Buddy is a year behind me, but he's flunked a grade back there somewhere. His academic marks don't really reflect his true intelligence, though; he's got a lot of the ol' street smarts. I have to admit it. Physically, he's somewhat shorter and stockier than I am and is quite mature. In fact, he's so mature, his hair is as white as snow. I don't mean towhead-white, either. It's more like the silvery-white of a real old geezer. If you haven't already guessed, he's the kid who was staring at me and giving me the finger during the North Kitsap-Happy Valley baseball game last year. He likes to think of himself as sort of a man-of-the-world.

Vernon is only a freshman. He's a pretty good kid, although sometimes he goes a little overboard in his efforts to be a Buddy Pringle disciple.

Early on in our relationship, ol' Buddy suggested that it'd probably save us a lot of time and all, if I'd just let him go ahead and make our every-day decisions—without any interference from me. "You can make all the big decisions if you want," he said. It's worked out pretty good I guess, although nothing big has ever come up yet.

"You goin' out with ol' Rosie Rottenbottom?" Buddy asks. Vernon continues to laugh up a regular storm.

"She seems pretty nice to me," I say.

"Ha, ha...she's nice all right. But if you're goin' out with *her*, you'd better be carryin' one of those little things in your wallet, you know what I'm sayin'?" Buddy has that sly, all-knowing look on his face that I just hate.

"Hey, don't worry...I got it covered," I say, as casually as I can. The truth of it is, though, I'm not real sure just what he *does* mean. But I have the two bucks in my wallet that Dad gave me for the dance and all. That seems little enough to me. Dad's not what you'd call a "cash cow."

Although I try not to show it, I'm a little nervous about the whole thing. Girls drive me nuts. They really do. You'd think what with my sub-Errol Flynnish looks and all, there'd be no problem. But I have a heck of a time relaxing around girls and being my normal, suave, witty self.

I get to worrying a little too much about my looks sometimes. *Mirror mirror, on the wall, who's the Flynnest of them all?* I've already explained that my nose might be a trifle too large, but ever since the Wild Warren Williamson fiasco, it has a slight wow in it besides. You don't notice it all that much, unless you're looking right at me. Then it shows up like a sore thumb. It really does. So when I'm around girls, I don't always look right squarely at them. I like to turn my head just a bit to one side or the other, just so they can't get a real good look at the crook in my nose. Of course, I have to be careful not to turn too far; a profile shot makes the ol' snout look all the bigger. It can be a real challenge sometimes, getting my head turned to just the right angle. It's kind of like when a ship quarters its bow into the big waves in a heavy sea.

I'll have to tell you, too, that my teeth are also not quite up to Errol Flynn standards. You'll notice ol' Errol is always smiling—showing these big, white, perfect teeth, even when he's sword fighting or boxing. Our family dentist says that the enamel never really formed that well on my teeth, and that they'll never be what you'd call Errol Flynn-white. In fact, the truth of the matter is, that they can have a slight tinge of green to them at times. Just a teeny bit, mind you, but probably enough to be considered a flaw, just the same. So when I'm around girls, I don't show my teeth that much when I smile. I hope a closed-mouth kind of smile doesn't come out like some sort of grimace, like I have gas on the ol' stomach or something.

I hope I can be more relaxed around ol' Rosie and make a good impression and all. It'd be kind of neat to have a girlfriend here at good ol' Happy Valley High. But one thing's for sure, this tolo can't turn out as badly as the last one I attended, the disaster during my first year at Scandia High.

*****

What I'm saying is, I didn't fare any too well with my social life at dear ol' Scandia. Although I tried real hard to get next to ol' Trudy Trammell, she had no time for life in the slow lane. Her time was pretty well taken up with the great Teddy Snodgrass.

However, another girl did show some interest in me and invited me to the upcoming tolo. Her name was Sigerd Olafson, and while not quite in the same league as Trudy Trammell, she was not a bad-looking girl just the same. I was thrilled. "What's a tolo?" I said.

The Tolo, I found out, was a school dance where the girls invited the boys. It was considered to be *the* social event of the fall season. The girl had to pay for the dance tickets, and her parents were to provide the transportation. I eagerly accepted Sigerd's invitation, but I doubted if her parents would think it was such a hot idea, when they found out just where I lived. The round trip to Kingston was twenty-four miles of twisting roadway, chock-full of bumps and chuck holes.

We probably would've had a great ol' time at the Tolo, if it were not for one minor detail: I didn't know how to dance. I'd sort of neglected to make ol' Sigerd aware of that fact, because I figured once I got there, I could just go ahead and fake it a little. Let me tell you, I quickly dropped that wild notion, when I saw how the other couples were dancing. Some were gliding across the floor just as smoothly as Ginger Rogers and good ol' Fred Astairical.

I tried a couple of slow dances, but my personal rendition of the ol' two-step must have looked pretty weird, if you wanted to know the awful truth of it all. My version was sort of a left-together, followed by another left-together, and then followed by approximately 200 more left-togethers, until ol' Sigerd and I had gone one full lap around the entire dance floor.

"Gosh, that was fun," I said. But I guess that two of these giant counter-clockwise maneuvers were about all Sigerd could stomach. Her usually fair Scandinavian cheeks were so danged red, you'd think she was embarrassed or something.

My goose was *really* cooked when the band started playing jitterbug numbers. Some of the couples had more moves than a basket of pups, especially Trudy Trammell and Teddy Snodgrass. I'd be darned, though, if I was going to get onto the floor with *my* two left feet. I'd be danged lucky if I didn't fall right on my rear end.

Since the stupid band wouldn't stop playing all those fast tunes, Sigerd and I had to spend most of the time over on the sidelines. I quartered my nose to starboard and attempted to salvage the date with some suave small talk. But I didn't have too much success, I'm afraid. Sigerd just didn't seem any too interested in last summer's baseball season, or salmon fishing, or duck hunting, or any number of other exciting topics I was prepared to talk about.

I guess you could say that the rest of the dance was spent pretty much in total silence, as was the 400 mile ride back to Kingston. It was a pretty cozy ride, though, as all the heat radiating from Sigerd's flushed cheeks kept her parents' car nice and cozy.

Afterwards, I was a little disappointed in ol' Sigerd because she made such a big deal out of the whole thing. The first thing you know, the entire school seemed to know about the entire fiasco, and further social obligations on my part were pretty well put on hold. My name was stricken from all remaining dance tickets for the rest of the year.

*****

I'm hoping things turn out a lot better at the Hapless Valley Tolo. I've got high hopes. I really do. For one thing, I now have my own transportation for the dance, my Dad's old '35 Ford pickup. It isn't much to look at, but it sure beats having to be chaperoned by Rosie's parents. The old jalopy has been the recipient of several do-it-yourself paint jobs and is about five different shades of blue all at the same time. Mom calls it "The Old Spotted Hog."

"No back seat, huh," is Rosie's only comment as she gets into the Hog. I'm not sure why she's so worried about a back seat and all, since there's only the two of us anyway.

I don't want to make the same mistake I made at North, so while we're driving, I tell Rosie right off the ol' bat that I'm not the world's greatest dancer. Oh, I've embellished my left-together two-step by now with a couple of little cross-over moves and a tricky spin or two, but I'm still no Gene Kelly, if you know what I mean.

"That's okay," Rosie says, in between some rather furious popping and snapping of her bubble gum. "I don't dance all that much, either." Things appear to be looking more relaxed at this point. As she sort of rolls her eyes and gives me a little wink, she giggles and adds," I sort of look forward to what goes on *after* the dance...don't you?"

I wasn't aware that the school had anything planned for after the dance so I just play kind of dumb, if you can believe that at all. "Yeah, I always look forward to that too," I say. I try not to smile too much when I say it, either, because I noticed earlier that my ol' teeth have picked *this* particular day to be at their very greenest. In fact, I've never seen them so danged green before. You'd think it was St. Patrick's Day, for Pete's sake.

After we got there to the ol' Tolo, we dance a few times, but Rosie is really hard to dance with. You wouldn't believe how tight she can hold a guy. I don't even have room enough to try the new step-through move I've been working on.

I marvel at the size of Rosie's waist. It's downright tiny. Rosie's looking real pretty, though. I have to admit it. And to tell you the honest truth, I won't mind too danged much if this relationship blossoms a little. Since we're both such lousy dancers, it'd seem almost as though we were meant for each other.

I see Buddy and Vernon talking with some other guys over in the stag line. I wonder about this; I'm sort of surprised that no girl asked Buddy to the dance. After all, real live men-of-the-world don't exactly grow on trees, especially here at good ol' Hapless Valley.

Rosie snuggles close enough, when Tony Bennett sings, Because of You, but on the next number, things really get ridiculous. Teresa Brewer is going on about putting another nickel in the nickelodeon, and ol' Rosie's clinging to me like a cheap suit. And then when Teresa sings, "I'd do anything for you—anything you'd want me to—," Rosie goes and puts her tongue in my ear. Dang! That feels really strange, if you want to know the truth of it all. Next, we try a few jitterbug numbers, but we're both pretty bad. It's almost embarrassing.

Finally though, it's intermission. We each get a sandwich and a bottle of pop and sit down at a table over in the corner by ourselves. I notice that Rosie has a nice, big peanut butter cookie, too. I hadn't even noticed those little goodies, I guess.

As we begin to eat, I quarter my nose to port and start to tell Rosie what I think about the upcoming basketball season. She doesn't seem too interested, though, to tell you the truth. She kind of bats her ol' eyes at me and says, "Betcha I know what *you'll* want after this stupid dance is all over."

"Well, that's sure thoughtful of ya," I say. "Thanks...but I think I'd rather have it right now." I reach over and help myself to her peanut butter cookie. Right then and there, I figure ol' Rosie has turned out to be a lot better date than Sigerd Olafson.

But it isn't long after that when ol' Rosie sort of disappears. I don't see her anymore. I don't know how she's going to get home, although some say she's gone with Roderick Remblinger. I can't quite figure that out, if you want to know the truth. It's kind of a mystery to me—sort of an enema, you might say.

Nov. 17—51

Dear Auntie,

Not much going on right now so thought I'd catch up on my letters. We're still sitting here freezing our you-know-whats off. It's getting colder all the time. I hate Korea. There's lots of red-necks in this army and it seems they all like cowboy music. The favorite song is Movin' On by some hillbilly called Hank Snow. It's sort of the unofficial theme song of the war. Seems to me that we could aim a few great big loud speakers at the North Koreans and blast them with good ol' Hank. The war would be over in a week (ha, ha). How does Willie like his new school? I suppose he's got lots of new girl friends by now. Well, that's about it for now.

                      Love,
                      Harvey (your favorite nephew ha, ha)

Chapter 13

Buddy Pringle's Model 97 Winchester is pointed to a spot directly between my eyes. Could this be the end of the line for good ol' Willie Mackerels? Actually, I'm only half-serious. it's the Sunday following the big Tolo and also the last day before the start of basketball practice. Besides that, it is the last day of hunting season, and Buddy Pringle and I have been walking the fields of Happy Valley all day in search of the elusive Chinese pheasant.

It's a real pretty day, even though the autumn colors have faded a bit. The sky is a brilliant blue, and a slight nip in the air suggests that Old Man Winter is just around the corner. It's a chance for a real relaxing outing—a chance to be away from the rigors of the athletic arena.

However, it's pretty danged hard to relax when you're hunting with Buddy Pringle. Buddy is a heck of a shot. There's no getting around that. He's already got six birds for the day. Meanwhile, yours truly has nothing but a bunch of near misses. Buddy is quick, and he is deadly.

Now, I might not be the world's greatest shot, but at least I've been well-schooled in the handling of firearms. Heck. Dad wouldn't even let me have a BB gun until he'd given me a complete course in safety. He was particularly careful to show me the do's and don'ts of hunting with a companion.

"If your partner is behind you," Dad said, "hold your gun out in front of you so the guy won't be in the line of fire. Now, if he's in front of you, you can hold the gun over your shoulder like this." Dad demonstrated the procedure. He rested the gun on his shoulder with the barrel pointing to the rear—kind of like the way soldiers do when they're marching in a parade. "If you have the gun pointed ahead of you and the hammer slips or some damn thing, you're apt to be shooting your partner's ass off."

Evidently, Buddy's father hadn't been quite so concerned about the posteriors of other people. It was obvious that Buddy'd had absolutely no firearms safety training whatsoever. Not only that, but the Model 97 twelve gauge pump was one of the most dangerous shotguns ever invented. It didn't take a heck of a lot to make its ol' hammer slip.

We're walking side by side with Buddy to my left. At present, Buddy's shotgun is pointed back over his shoulder like it's supposed to be—but I am keeping a watchful eye, just the same. You can never tell about ol' Buddy.

Suddenly, there's a whir of wings off to our left. "Hens!" Buddy hollers, as he whirls toward the birds. He doesn't bother to remove the gun from his shoulder, as hens are not legal to shoot. Of course, now the barrel of the tricky 97 is jabbing me just under the chin.

"Hey, watch it!" I shout. My voice is carrying just a hint of annoyance.

"Oops," Buddy says. "Hah, hah, hah—sorry about that—ho, ho, ho."

Just then, a rooster cackles off to our right. In a flash, Buddy is on the bird and torches off a shot over my left shoulder. "Got 'im!" Buddy hollers. I know that's what he said, because I can read lips pretty good. I no longer have any eardrums.

As we go to retrieve Buddy's rooster, he takes the opportunity to bring up the Tolo. "Mackerels," he says, "hee, hee, hee—you're havin' a little trouble getting' your gun off—just like at the Tolo, last night. Har, har, har. Whatever happened with you and ol' Rosie, anyway? I thought she looked hot-to-trot—hah, hah—warm for your form—ho, ho, ho."

"Aw, I dunno," I say. "It was no big deal." I wasn't real sure of what ol' Buddy was talking about, but I continued. "She gets so danged close, a guy can hardly dance, anyway." Buddy looks at me sort of strangely, as he slowly shakes his head from side to side.

We're along a hedge row, now, and suddenly a covey of quail gets up. "Take 'em!" Buddy hollers, as the tiny birds fly in a string directly across our path. Buddy must not be interested in quail, or else he's maybe feeling sorry for me because he'd blown my eardrums out earlier.

Knowing full well the reputation quail have as fast fliers, I swing way out in front of the lead bird and touch off my old double barrel. Down it comes—the straggler at the tail end of the flock. Finally, I have my first bird of the season.

"It's all in how you lead 'em," I tell Buddy.

*****

It's later now, and we're all through hunting. It's been a real hectic day trying to avoid the barrel of Buddy's pump gun. If Buddy's hammer had slipped all the different times the ol' 97 had been pointed at me, I'd be looking like a hunk of Swiss cheese about now.

We're standing there next to the Hog, and our shotguns are pointed to the pavement. It's time to unload. I take both shells out of the double barrel, and Buddy pumps the 97. BLAM! An ugly, jagged hole appears in the blacktop. It's about two inches from my right foot and nearly a foot in diameter. Buddy's hammer has slipped once again.

As I wait for the ol' heart to stop pounding and the knees to quit shaking, a question comes to mind. I wonder what it would have been like to have to abandon my Eddie Lopat techniques in favor of those of Monty Stratton—the one-legged pitcher for the Chicago White Sox.

> The Tolo, the first major social event of the year for the students of Happy Valley High, was held Saturday night in the high school gymnasium. Music was in the form of records brought by the students, while refreshments were provided by the Happy Valley PTA. A good time was had by all, but being a little too dim, some of the boys and girls complained about the gym as a place to hold a dance.
> —Dora Dingley
> The Happy Valley Harbinger, November 1951

Chapter 14

Now that it's time for basketball to start, the ever-hopeful Happy Valley athletes seem to have forgotten all about our rotten football season. We couldn't possibly be that lousy at basketball too, could we?

"You play basketball don't you, Mackerels?" Gordy Belmont whispers during our third period civics class. We're supposed to be studying for an important exam, and his sudden question sort of breaks my concentration.

As much as I hate to, I forget about staring at Rosie Higgenbottom's legs for the moment and turn my attention to Gordy. With most girls, you'd be lucky to see six inches of leg showing between those long ol' skirts and the tops of their bobby sox. Rosie shows a whole lot more leg than that, especially if she thinks you're looking.

I have to be real careful with Gordy, though, and be sure to stay on his good side. He's been real cooperative about letting me copy his papers and all. Gordy's the smartest kid in school, by far, and the odds-on favorite to be the class valedictorian. After my first report card at Happy Valley High, Dad said, "Looks like you got a pretty good chance of being the dumbedictorian at this little school, Mackerels." I could tell that Dad was only kidding, though, because he'd called me Mackerels instead of Willie.

I'm a little surprised by Gordy's question, if you want to know the truth. I guess he doesn't remember last season when I'd gotten in for a brief time for Scandia in the Happy Valley game. I scored two whole points, even if they did happen to go into the Happy Valley side of the score book. You see, I got a little confused and shot at the wrong basket. But it just goes to show that ol' Rattleballs wasn't a whole lot better at coaching basketball than he was at baseball. What decent coach would leave a guy on the bench all that time and then put him in the game stone-cold like that?

"Yeah, I'll be turnin' out," I said.

"Excellent—we need a center...now I think we have an extremely good chance at qualifying for the district tournament." I'll point out here that while Gordy is pretty much a regular kind of guy, he doesn't talk like one. Instead, he always sounds like a college professor. No one ever brings it to his attention, though; about half the school depends on good ol' Gordy for passing grades.

But Gordy's living proof, I think, that scholars aren't always the most practical of people. I could agree with him to a point; we probably need a center, all right—and also a couple of guards, and maybe a forward or two. Other than that, we're likely all set. But after seeing our fantastic athletes in action during the football season, I can't quite share Gordy's enthusiasm for making it to the district playoffs. We might be short, but we're also slow.

Now I probably ought to tell you, that of all the major sports, I'm probably the least-skilled in basketball. It might be hard for you to believe, but I'm probably not what you'd call a natural at the sport. In fact, at one time, I'd just about given up any hope of making much advancement in the game of basketball.

I don't look all that good in a basketball uniform, either, if you want to know the ugly truth. I don't have that really powerful, muscular body that fills out a basketball suit so well. According to what we studied in biology, those kind of guys are called mesomorphs. Ectomorphs, on the other hand, are kind of lean and slightly muscled. I sort of fit more into that category, to be perfectly honest. There's a third group, too. The endomorphs have sort of a prominence of the abdomen and other soft body parts. I sort of fit in there, too. I guess you'd have to say that I'm an ectomorph who's liable to go sort of endomorphic as I get older.

Undoubtedly, I'd have been a better basketball player if I hadn't got such a late start at the game. Basketball was intended as an indoor recreation, but in Seattle's north end, there seemed to be very few indoor facilities in existence for good ol' basketball. The kids in my neighborhood had to play most of their basketball in the streets—and as you well know—it rains in Seattle.

Any basketball hoop we might have would more than likely be mounted on a crude, wooden backboard and fastened to a telephone pole on one of our less-traveled city streets. The rims might or might not be the regulation height of ten feet. If we were lucky, we might get two or three weeks out of the site before the stupid telephone company went and knocked the whole thing down. They weren't real careful how they did it, either. As often as not, the backboards were smashed and splintered beyond salvation, and the hoops were too bent to be of any more use. I guess someone high up in the telephone company must have failed to make his high school team and still carried a grudge against the sport of basketball or some danged thing.

If the telephone poles were watched too closely, we had to put the backboards on someone's garage. That wasn't so good, though, because the garages were usually located on a back alley. Then, we'd just have dirt playing surfaces, which were liable to be pretty danged rough. We usually had enough trouble trying to dribble the ball, without having to put up with rocks and chuckholes as well.

Rubber basketballs were just beginning to appear on the market, and most of us kids had the old-fashioned leather balls designed for playing indoors. After a few voyages across Seattle's world-class mud puddles, the leather balls would be completely waterlogged and would be like trying to pass, shoot, or dribble a medicine ball.

We didn't have any coaching, so to tell you the truth, our games were pretty ragged and disorganized. A couple of the older kids would just choose up sides and sort of act as player-coaches. The big guys passed to us only as a last resort—when absolutely no one else was open. Looking back, I can sort of see why. Passing to one of us little kids was sort of like throwing the ball out of bounds on purpose. About all any of us knew to do was to take off on a mad, head-down dribble, which usually ended up going off our toe and right to the other team.

I've got to admit, though, that basketball was probably the most educational of all the sports we played. It sure taught us plenty about the geography of Seattle's north end. We must have looked a lot like a wandering band of gypsies, as we roamed far and wide to stay ahead of the ol' telephone company. I especially liked the trips to the Roosevelt District. On the way home I could stop at the Triple XXX and replenish my body's lost nutrients. A frosty mug of their root beer and a piece of pie ala mode usually did the trick.

Organized basketball didn't start for me until my junior year at Scandia. I wanted to turn out as a freshman, but Dad didn't think it was such a hot idea. He was still a little concerned about my rapid growth spurt and lack of stamina.

"You remember how pooped you were after football practice? Well, basketball will be ten times worse, Mackerels...you don't get to stand around in the huddle and rest like you do in football."

By my junior year, though, I'd strengthened up quite a bit and was able to go out for the team. I was way behind everyone else in the experience department, but I at least managed to make the junior varsity team. I worked hard and gradually made my way up from the end of the B Squad bench to where I actually got into a varsity game or two.

I was pretty danged nervous when I put on a varsity suit for the first time. I can tell you that much for sure. It was against the Sequim Wolves, a real tough opponent, and to be perfectly honest, I didn't expect a whole lot of playing time. But late in the game, ol' Rattleballs got a little nervous as a lead we'd built up early in the game began to go south on us. All our big guys had fouled out trying to check Sequim's six-six center, and he was starting to go hog-wild on us.

"Mackerels," Rattleball's voice sounded suddenly from the other end of the bench, "get in there and check the big guy." I'll have to admit that I wasn't actually what you'd call cool, calm, and collected, as I started out onto the floor. In fact, I was more nearly in a state of shock.

"No, no, Mackerels," Rattleballs yelled, "you have to report in first!"

I just sort of stood there in a daze. Rattleballs, not wanting me to be called for a technical, jumped from the bench and physically led me to the scorer's table. It was embarrassing. I felt like a penny waiting for change.

Michaels in for Swenson," Rattleballs said to the scorekeeper. Then, he gave me some parting instructions. "Play in front of the big guy and try to keep him from getting the ball."

Well, as it turned out, I followed the instructions pretty much to a tee and did a pretty darned good job of denying the ball to the Sequim big man. I was what you'd probably call a whirling dervish, even if I do say so myself. I really had the kid confused, though, when I continued to guard him down on our end of the court. As my teammates worked the ball around for a shot at the basket, I kept up my tenacious defense. I danced around and around the tall guy, wildly waving my hands across his line of vision. I guess I got sort of carried away with my defensive responsibilities.

"What the heck're ya doin'?" the giant demanded. He had kind of a confused look on his face. "*You* guys got the ball."

"Three-second violation on number twenty-four," the referee said, as he pointed emphatically in my direction. "White's ball out-of-bounds."

Rattleballs jumped to his feet. "Mackerels...only check him when *they* have the ball!"

Well—all that undue attention sort of burned me up, if you want to know the truth of the matter. After all, ol' Rattleballs really never gave me any instructions about what to do at the offensive end of the court. But after that momentary little lapse, we went on to win the game, and Rattleballs started using me more and more as a defensive stopper for the varsity. He was finally starting to show a little sense. Of course, there was that final game with Happy Valley, where I'd had the tough luck with the wrong basket and all.

To tell you the truth, though, the outlook for my senior year in basketball didn't look so awfully hot. I hadn't contributed much at all offensively, and there were some real promising sophomores who looked like they might be ready to move up to the varsity. It'd be real embarrassing to be cut from the squad, what with me being a senior and all. Teddy Snodgrass would get a big kick out of it, though. You could bet your bottom dollar on that bit of information.

But all those fears are behind me now. The move to good ol' Hapless Valley has seen to that. It's easy to see, that the Milk Maids need all the help they can get. Besides, I'm a far better player now than I was at North. I'll bet even Rattleballs would be impressed.

You see, right after my junior season had ended, I discovered a new offensive weapon—the hook shot. It all came about when Dad took me to Hec Edmundson Pavilion, in Seattle, to watch the Huskies play St. Louis University. Bob Houbregs, Washington's All-American center, put on a display of how to shoot the hook shot that you'd have to see to believe. They were high, arching things of beauty, often taken from twenty feet or more.

I'm telling you, Houbregs just flat out destroyed the Billkins that night. The St. Louis guys were running some old-fashioned eastern offense, you know, the kind where they made about thirty passes or so before they ever shot the ball. But then, the Huskies would come down the floor, make one pass to Houbregs, and then watch him hook it up. SWISH! I mean nearly every time.

From that moment on, I read everything I could get my hands on about my new hero. It was said, that in practice he shot one hundred hooks a day with each hand. And what was good enough for my hero was good enough for me. I practiced the ol' hook shot whenever I could, and by the time I moved to Happy Valley, I was ready to revolutionize the entire league.

But playing in the Happy Valley gymnasium can be a pretty interesting experience, if you want to know the truth. It was built only a couple of years ago, but the playing surface is already pretty much ruined. You should see it. The contractor failed to vent the foundation properly, and now the floor is all warped. Giant humps have developed in several places, with the largest being located on the west side of the center-jump circle.

Now, jumping is not exactly my strong suit as a basketball player. I've got to admit it. In fact, just getting both feet off the floor at the same time pretty much constitutes a jump for me. I don't worry too much about it, though. Heck, Bob Houbregs can't jump worth a darn, either. If I have the ol' hump in my favor, I usually get the tip, but if I don't, I'm danged lucky if I can outjump one of the Seven Dwarfs.

You can see some pretty interesting dribbling exhibitions on our court, too. We like to herd the other team's guards toward one of the floor's major mountain ranges. It's great fun to lure the dribbler into the Andes or Himalayas and then watch as the ball caroms off one of the giant humps and goes out of bounds.

But at least the Happy Valley court is regulation size. Many of the others in the league are not, I'm afraid. Lots of the other schools have older gymnasiums that are nothing but tiny cracker boxes. And because of that fact, most of the teams like to use the compact zone for their main line of defense. Some of those zones are so darned tight, it's almost impossible to pass an aspirin tablet through them. Most of your scoring has to come from pretty far out. To tell you the truth, I hadn't thought of that when I first decided to commit whole-heartedly to the Bob Houbreg's School of Hook Shooting.

It's starting to look like maybe I shouldn't have been so quick to put all my eggs in one basket. As we play against one sagging zone after another, I have a heck of a time getting my vaunted hook shot off of the launching pad. Whenever I do manage to get a pass somewhere near the key, I have a heck of a time getting the sweeping hook past the sagging guards and into the air. I guess you could just call me the Hapless Hooker.

I get a little desperate some times. I'll have to admit it. As the season progresses, I go farther and farther outside of the key to get the ball. I wave my hands for the ball, but it's all in vain, I'm afraid. Our inexperienced guards can't seem to figure out what I'm doing so far from the basket. Finally, instead of waiting for them to come to the party, I just run out and grab the ball out of their hands and hook it up. I can tell you, it's raising heck with the ol' shooting percentage.

Needless to say, our basketball season is becoming a carbon copy of our football efforts. Boy, are we ever pathetic. Christmas vacation is here, and we haven't won a single game. And the bad news is, we haven't even played the real tough teams yet. You can't imagine just how discouraged I'm getting. I'd been primed for a really big year, what with my new hook shot and all, but things just aren't working out.

Basketball practices can be pretty danged dangerous, too, if you want to know the awful truth. Roderick Remblinger can't read a lick, but he does like to look at the pictures in the funny papers. His current comic strip hero is Ozark Ike, the guy who has invented the revolutionary peg shot. The peg shot is thrown overhand, much like a baseball, and from almost the full length of the court. Ozark Ike wins a lot of basketball games with the ol' Peg shot. Roderick Remblinger is not nearly as accurate.

Before practice officially starts for the day, we usually just scatter out to the different baskets and work on our own individual shooting skills. Today, Roderick cuts loose with one of his peggers, just as Gordy Belmont is going in for one of his patented double-leg-kick lay ins. Well, Roderick's errant shot slams off the backboard and hits Gordy right in the ol' mush. Of course, Gordy's nose swells up like a poisoned pup, and he has to leave practice and have it checked out by a doctor. I hope it isn't broken.

I told Dad about Gordy's accident and then got to mentioning about what an all-around guy Gordy is. Not only does he play all the sports, but he's also going to be valedictorian and star in the school play. Gordy's also the student body president and captain of the danged debate team.

"He's eclectic," Dad said. Gosh, I wonder where Dad got that bit of information. I've been around Gordy quite a lot and have never known him to have any fits or such as that.

We get our first real break from basketball when a major winter storm hits the area. It's a real doozy, and it comes none too soon for me. If you want to know the honest truth, I'm already a little sick of basketball.

> With their disastrous football season over at long last, the Happy Valley Milk Maids are turning their attention to the upcoming basketball campaign. Coach Monahan hopes that his warriors will have a little more luck at that sport. He reports that the boys are working very hard in an attempt to climb out of the Olympic League cellar—a spot they occupied for the entirety of last season. Although short and not too fast, Coach Monahan hopes the Milk Maids can win some games with superior conditioning and aggressive play.
> —Dora Dingley
> The Happy Valley Harbinger, November 1951

Chapter 15

Ordinarily, western Washington weather can't be counted on for a whole lot of snow. This year, though, we suddenly have a winter wonderland, and school is shut down temporarily. To top things off, the boiler goes haywire, so there isn't any heat in any of the school buildings, including the gym. Coach Monahan just about has to cancel basketball practices.

They'd have been pretty lousy turnouts, anyway, as all us players pretty much have snow on our minds. But as I watch the good ol' white stuff pile up, I can't help but think back to the big storm of '49, back when I lived in Kingston. It was a most memorable time in my life and one that I ought to tell you about.

*****

The drifts in Kingston piled up to an unheard of four feet in some places. Traffic was brought to a standstill, and more importantly, school was shut down. We could hardly believe our eyes, as the snow kept piling up, and the temperature stayed down around the freezing mark day after day. Us kids had a whole lot of fun building snow forts and having snowball fights, and when we got tired of that, we'd head on down to the Dockside Cafe and play rummy and drink endless cups of hot chocolate.

As you might have guessed, though, ol' Lang tried his darndest to spoil all my fun. His bowels were always rumbling, it seemed, as he continued to crave more and more green alder. And since the trail to the neighbors' house was all snowed in, it was taking me three times as long to go and fetch water from their well. But the nights would make up for it all. That's when we did our sledding.

To the north of the Kingston ferry dock, high on a bluff all decked out with red-trunked madronas, was an old strawberry farm. And the hill that led there was about as steep and winding as you'd ever care to see. It was just right for sledding.

Each night, as soon as the ol' dinner dishes were washed and put away, the Kingston kids would gather downtown and make plans for our nightly trek up the long, winding hill. Then up we went, with the sleds trailing behind. Up, up, we'd go, past the big strawberry farm on the right, up, up some more, and the finally to the summit. It was a heck of a long hike and pretty danged time-consuming, too. In fact, that part of it all could be pretty boring, if you want to know the honest truth.

Sometimes, though, I'd get the opportunity to fall in step with Trudy Trammell. That sure helped to take the boredom out of the ol' mountain-climbing expedition. I sort of tried to make a little time with her, while Teddy was stuck over there in Scandia. She didn't show a whole lot of interest, but at least she was friendly enough.

The rides down that long, twisting hill were fun; they'd pretty much take your breath away every time. But it seemed like they were over in practically the blink of an eye, and then you were faced with the long, boring journey back up the steep hill once again.

One night, much to my surprise, Trudy showed up without a sled. I guess hers wasn't working just right. I saw that as my chance to grab opportunity right by the tail and ask Trudy to share a ride with me. To tell you the truth, you could have knocked me over with a feather when she said she would.

We trudged up the hill together, chattering sort of aimlessly about the snow, and sledding, and school, and such as that. In fact, it turned out we had a whole bunch of interests in common. I sort of let ol' Trudy carry the bulk of the conversation. I just loved the sound of her voice and all. In fact, when you come right down to it, I loved just about everything there was about her.

I even liked it when she called me "Curly," although, I just hated it when anyone else called me that. Now, in addition to my slightly-bigger nose and my slightly-greener teeth, I have to admit that I have this one other flaw in the looks department. It would probably be another drawback in case a guy ever was interested in a movie career. Unlike all the movie stars I've ever heard of, I have this wild, crazy, curly hair. I've put grease of all kinds on it and have tried to slick it back, but nothing ever seems to work. It might look okay for a little while, but before you know, it'll pop right back to these goofy curls.

Not a single movie star I know has such curly hair—not Errol Flynn—not Gary Cooper—not John Wayne—heck—not even the young, blonde actor, who always got killed by the Japanese. Harpo Marx is about the only one.

Mom and her friends think it's wonderful, though. One day, our neighbor, Mrs. Abercrombie was going on and on about my stupid hair. "Esther," she said, "Willie is so lucky to have such beautiful, curly hair. My Wilma would give anything to have pretty hair like that. Hers is as straight as a stick." I'm afraid curly hair wouldn't have helped ol' Wilma, though. It's been said that whenever she gets up in the morning, all the clocks in town come to a stop for a full five minutes.

Well, getting back to the trip up the hill, Trudy and I finally reached the top and began to prepare ourselves for the trip back down. I got on the sled first, and Trudy piled on top. Then off we went. The weight of Trudy there on top of me felt pretty darned good, to tell you the truth, and I was sort of looking forward to a long, slow, leisurely ride down the hill. I wasn't going to try and break any speed records, if you know what I mean. Well, as it turned out, I didn't have to worry about that. I guess because of Trudy's added weight, we actually were going a little faster, and about half-way down the hill we overtook little Elmer Finley, who'd taken off just ahead of us.

In an effort to avoid an almost certain collision, I oversteered a bit and turned the sled a little too sharply. Over the edge of the road we went, and from there we tumbled over and over until we finally landed with a plop in the middle of a big ol' snow drift.

Trudy lay pressed against me for the briefest of moments, and my heart was starting to beat a little faster. I could have laid there forever, with her warm face pressed right up against mine. It was a real good feeling. Then unexpectedly, and without a whole lot of fanfare, she leaned over and gave me a quick peck on the lips. Boy! I didn't know what to think of that, to tell you the honest truth of it all. I just laid there for a second or two, I guess, while I tried to figure out what to make of the whole thing. But he who hesitates is lost, as they say. With a giggle, Trudy just bounced on up, scrambled up the bank, and got back onto the road.

My head was kind of in a whirl, as I retrieved the sled back out of the snow bank. Trudy sort of jabbered on about the accident just as though the kiss hadn't even happened, but it was the single most important thing on my mind. You can bet on that.

As the following days went by, I tried with all my might to rekindle that brief spark of romance, but it was too late. The fire had gone out. I followed up with numerous phone calls to Trudy's house but didn't seem to have much luck. She received them politely and with friendliness and all but still continued to go out with Teddy Snodgrass. Finally, the message sunk in: the gold rush was over, and the bum's rush was on. I cut the ol' phone calls back a bit and then finally gave up altogether.

*****

Our snow vacation here in Happy Valley hasn't turned out to be such a big deal, to be perfectly honest about it all. There's hardly any hills here—at least none as big as the one leading to the old strawberry farm back in Kingston. There are no Trudy Trammells here, either, I'm sad to say. I'm actually a little glad now that the storm has cleared and we can get back to playing basketball.

We've fallen right back into our losing ways, though. I'm beginning to wonder if we'll ever win an athletic contest of any kind this whole school year. We almost have a breakthrough over at Bainbridge, but not at basketball, though. We get slaughtered at that once again. But while we are messing around during the B-Squad game, we go into the Bainbridge weight room and get to playing table tennis with some of their varsity kids. In fact, it's not long before we have a little tournament going.

Vernon Windbladd doesn't look all that much like an athlete. He's not very tall and has sort of a plump body with these narrow shoulders and a big butt. But for a freshman, he's a real quick little kid and pretty well-coordinated, too. He's a fair-to-middling shooter, and mostly on the strength of that, he's made our starting team. Now, as we move along in the table tennis tournament, Vernon surprises us all with his skill at that game as well.

Table tennis isn't one of my real strong areas, and besides, I haven't played in a real long while. I lose a skunk game in my very first match. Vernon, though, is something else. He's obviously played before. He stands way, way back from the ol' table and really gets some Chinese mustard into his serves. And he has all these tricky little curves and such. He wades right on through all those Bainbridge rubes, all the way up to the championship match. He's playing a tall, rangy kid, who's their basketball captain. The guy seems pretty good, too. Vernon looks like he's got a real good chance, though, right up to the time when our resident man-of-the-world, ol' Buddy Pringle, has to go and make the bet.

"A dollar the kid takes ya," Buddy says to the Bainbridge guy. Buddy's always betting on stuff, and talking about odds, and giving points, and such as that.

"You're on," the Bainbridge guy says.

Well, Vernon just isn't a money player, I guess. He chokes up tighter than a bull's ass in fly time and loses twenty-one to four. It seems we can't even win a danged ol' game of Ping-Pong.

Well, we cruise right into the final game of the season with a perfect record of zero and nineteen. And of course, the opponents are none other than the Scandia Vikings. As you might expect, they've already got the league championship all sewed up and will be heading off to the district tournament. I'm not looking forward to this game at all, to be perfectly frank about it. The only possible thing in our favor, is that the game is being played at our place. Teams can have a little trouble adjusting to our bumpy floor right at first.

We almost lose a player, though, and right before the big game, too. In the locker room after practice, ol' Roderick bends over to tie his shoe and a package of Luckies (L. S. M. F. T.—Lucky Strikes means fine tobacco.) falls on the floor, right there in front of Coach Monahan. "L. S. M. F. T.," Buddy hollers. "Loose straps mean floppy tits—hah, hah, hah." Coach doesn't kick Roderick off the team, though; he just gives him a big lecture about the evils of smoking. Who knows? Maybe ol' Roderick's Ozark Ike peg shot could be the deciding factor in the big game.

Coach Monahan comes up with a real innovative game plan for Scandia. I have to give him credit. It looks kind of risky, but I guess he figures there's not much to lose.

"Mackerels," he says, "we're going to have to try getting along without your hook shot, tonight. Ah...I don't want you wasting energy running out there to grab the ball out of our guards' hands. You're going to be the key to our defense. You're going to be checking Teddy Snodgrass."

"Uh...but he's a *guard*."

"Yeah, I know...and the highest scorer in the league, too. That's why I want someone right on him at all times."

"Mmm...but what about Swingendorff, their big center? That's who I usually check." I'm a little uncomfortable about checking a guard, if you want to know the truth. I play pretty good position defense on post men, if I do say so myself, but quickness of foot is required for checking all-star guards. And to be perfectly honest, quickness is not one of my strong points.

"We're going to play what's called a box-and-one, Mackerels. You stay right close to Snodgrass, and your teammates'll be backing you up with a four-man zone. We gotta hope they can shut down Swingendorff while they're at it. I've got to tell you, Mackerels...you're the key to this game. If you can stop Snodgrass, we've got a good chance to win our first game of the year."

I don't know if I can handle the pressure of it all, but I grimly accept the challenge. I sort of hate to give up the hook shot, though. But I guess Coach is right; I'll need all my energy and concentration for hounding Teddy Snodgrass from baseline to baseline.

*****

I can't believe the job I've done on Teddy Snodgrass. I've led him through a wide variety of nature hikes over our vast assortment of mountain trails, and he's been dribbling the ball off his foot most of the night. With Teddy not scoring a single point, and with Swingendorff bottled up by our four-man zone, the big game becomes a pretty low-scoring affair. And although they have to do without my vaunted hook, my teammates are scoring surprisingly well. In fact, they're coming through with a variety of shots I never knew they had.

The Vikings are up by ten, though, late in the fourth quarter, and it looks like curtains for us once again. It's sort of embarrassing for me, seeing that it's against my former teammates and all.

Heck—even our cheerleaders are getting shown up. The Viking yell squad is made up of Trudy Trammell and two statuesque blondes, that both look as though they've been poured out of the same Nordic mold. I don't know where we get our cheerleaders. They're all sort of short and dumpy, if you want to know the awful truth. I guess they're not totally butt-ugly, but unless I miss my guess, they're not likely to be attracting the ol' white-slavers, either. Rosie Higgenbottom would have been a pretty good-looking cheerleader, but she's a little too busy with other things according to what some of the guys have been saying.

"He's our peaches. He's our cream. He's the captain of our team. Yayyyy, MACKERELS!" I'd like to die, when our midgets come out with that corny yell.

The Viking beauties come right back with a cheer of their own. "Potato chips, potato chips...munch, munch, munch. Milk Maids, Milk Maids...here's your lunch...EAT IT!"

You won't believe it, but with seven seconds to go, we're ahead thirty-eight to thirty-seven. The good ol' money player, Vernon Windbladd, has just gone hog-wild shooting from the outside. His last long bomb has just given us the one point lead. His fat little cheeks are red as a beet from the effort.

You can hear our cheerleaders in the background. "Lutefisk, lutefisk—raw, raw, raw—Scandia, Scandia—HA, HA, HA."

But it's the Viking's outs under their own basket, and I just know the ball will come into Teddy Snodgrass. And to tell you the truth, I'm just about pooped from chasing ol' Teddy all over the place. I sort of doubt that I have enough energy left to keep Teddy from getting the ball.

Then, I get a glimpse of Coach Monahan, over on the bench. He seems to be making some sort of signal with his hands—it looks sort of like a wave action or something. At first, I don't get it. But that's understandable enough. I'm so danged tired from shagging Teddy Snodgrass, that I'm afraid the ol' brain damage is creeping back in.

Then it comes to me. You'll have to hand it to the coach—he's pretty danged smart, at that. He wants to use the humps on our floor and have me lure Teddy into one of our mountain ranges before he catches the inbounds pass. Since it's nearly impossible to dribble there, he'll have no place to go, and he'll still be too far from the basket to shoot.

Well, it works as slick as a whistle. I shade Teddy a bit but let him go to the pass. He falls right into the trap, or rather, he climbs up to the trap. He's been unknowingly lured into the Himalayas, and by the time he receives the ball, he's teetering right there on the top of Mt. Everest.

I've never seen such panic as there is in his eyes, as he realizes where he is. He knows he isn't going anywhere on the dribble. I've got him now, I figure. Then, danged if he doesn't rear back and start to let fly with a desperation Ozark Ike peg shot. From that distance, though, I figure he's got about as much chance as a one-legged-man in an ass-kicking contest. I don't even try to check him, as I can't risk sending him to the foul line. Lord, oh Lord, we've finally won a game, I think.

Suddenly, a blue and white streak flashes across my line of vision and heads right for Teddy. It's Roderick Remblinger. He's coming to help me out. Either that, or else he just can't stand to watch someone else attempt an Ozark Ike shot. WHAACCCKKKK!

"Foul on zero-zero," the ref shouts.

"Elevator, elevator...we got the shaft!" is the cry of our dumpy, little cheerleaders, but the refs pay no attention. And neither does Teddy Snodgrass. As time runs out on the clock, he steps to the line as cool as a cucumber and sinks two foul shots, Thanks to Roderick, our losing streak's still intact. Roderick's such a duckhead.

Down in the locker room, after the game, Buddy says, "I think Roderick must be a throwback."

"Throwback to what?" I say.

"Those Neanderthal guys we were studyin' about in history the other day. Didja ever notice ol' Roderick's beetle-brows...and that slopin' forehead?"

Gordy Belmont breaks in. "Yes, but he has that protruding mandible, more indigenous to Homo Sapiens. According to anthropological findings, the Neanderthals had virtually no chin at all."

I'll have to stop and tell you right here about the fact that ol' Roderick can swallow half his face. That's the truth. He's got this retractable lower jaw, kind of like a python, and he can put his lower lip half-way up the bridge of his nose. It's really weird.

"And, um..." Gordy continues, "nothing I've ever read suggests that the Neanderthals of the late Pleistocene age ever mixed with the Cro-Magnon, who, of course, were the forerunners to modern man."

"Huh?" says Buddy.

"Uh—he says Neanderthals weren't supposed to have mixed with modern man," I say.

"Well, Buddy says, "maybe they weren't *supposed* to, but there musta been a Neanderthal somewhere in the Remblinger woodpile...there's no doubt about it in my mind. Looks to me like the anthropologists got their theories bass ackwards. You know what I'm sayin'?"

> The Happy Valley Milk Maids lost the final game of the season, 39 to 38, to the perennial league champs, the Scandia Vikings. The game was played on the Milk Maids' home court and concluded another winless season for the hapless Milk Maids.
> In defeat, Coach Monahan praised the shooting of freshman, Vernon Windbladd and the stellar defensive play of Willy Michaels. Being rather warped and lumpy, Coach Monahan had to admit that the Milk Maid gymnasium also played a major role in holding the high-flying Vikings to a mere 39 points.
> —Dora Dingley
> The Happy Valley Harbinger, February 1952

Chapter 16

Tonight, after our disappointing loss to Teddy Snodgrass and the Scandia Vikings, I have a heck of a time getting to sleep. I just can't seem to unwind. I wonder if we're ever going to beat the Vikings at anything. Maybe Vernon Windbladd can beat their Ping-Pong champ or something. So I just toss and turn on the ol' bed for awhile and listen to all the noises coming through the floor. The Wicked Witch is cackling away in fine form, and Shuffle-Bowl is RRrrriiinnnggging up his usual storm. Skinny and Clyde are firing torpedoes, one after the other, and Wurlitzer and Hank Snow seem to be in unusually fine voice.

Then, I start to think about how baseball season is just around the corner and all. Boy! Am I ever glad. I'm anxious now to get on with my real career. To tell you the truth, I've just about given up on winning a football or basketball scholarship with the Huskies. It might have been different if I'd played somewhere other than Hapless Valley High. But I guess I've got to face the facts—the stars from the smaller schools often go unnoticed.

I've got to make some money, though, before the season gets started. I definitely need new baseball shoes, and also, it looks like the ol' fielder's mitt is all worn out. Of course, it's never been much of a mitt in the first place, if you want to know the truth. I won it in a kids' fishing derby back in Port Gamble with a runty, little salmon about twelve inches long. It's one of those rinky-dink three-fingered mitts they came out with there for awhile. Modern pitchers all wear these neat gloves with real long fingers. Mine has three short, squatty fingers. It's a real dumpy mitt. As I lay there listening to Wurlitzer and Hank Snow grind out their rendition of I'm Movin' On, I try to think about how I can earn enough money for the new shoes and glove.

"Fire one," I hear Skinny holler once again. And before Clyde can even fire the second fish, my thoughts sort of drift back to Fran and Bernie and their fight on the boardwalk. I think about how I might have had enough for a mitt, already, if that cheapskate, Fran, had given me the reward I deserved for finding his fudging wristwatch.

Wait a minute—the boardwalk! Why haven't I thought of that before? There has to be scads of money under the ol' boardwalk. After all, it's been there ever since the town was founded. Lord only knows how many sodbusters, with holes in their pockets, have traveled the boardwalk at one time or another.

"RRrrriiinnnggg!" Shuffle-Bowl disrupts my thinking for a moment. I've been wondering what tools Dad might have that I can use to pry up the boards. Shuffle-Bowl quiets back down, and I try to concentrate once again, but flashbacks about Trudy Trammell and the strawberry farm keep interfering. But then, while I try to get my tired mind off non-productive subjects such as that, I drift off to sleep.

*****

It's ten o'clock, bright and early the next morning. It's Saturday and a beautiful cloudless day. I have Dad's old hammer and a small crow bar and am getting ready to attack the boardwalk. There's liable to be a small fortune under there, enough for a new mitt and some shoes, anyway. For some reason, though, I seem to have a little trouble getting started. Every time I put the pry bar under the boards, a chill runs up and down my spine, and I just pull the bar back out. It's almost as though something deep down in my sub-conscience is holding me back. It's kind of eerie, if you want to know the truth. Now, after staring at the walk for another few seconds, the lines between the boards begin to undulate and go into wild, crazy patterns, and I can sense the ol' brain damage taking hold once again. I feel myself slipping back into a different time and a different place.

*****

"EEEAAHHH!" Startled, I jump back as the snake slithers out from its place of hiding. One glance at the forked tongue darting from out of the evil-looking mouth has my heart right up in my throat. Hastily, I tear my gaze away from the malevolent eyes, lest I fall captive to their hypnotic influence. My knees shake uncontrollably, as I retreat and pretend as though I haven't seen the creature. I pray Wilfred hasn't noticed.

It's a beautiful day with hardly a cloud in the sky, a rarity for Seattle in April. Wilfred Jensen and I are in his back yard playing catch with a little rubber ball of his. Tossing the ball gently might be a more accurate description. You can't actually play catch with ol' Wilfred, especially with a real baseball or anything like that. Wilfred's eyes are sort of cocked, and if you aren't careful, the ball is apt to hit him right in the ol' mush. He's thrown the ball wild, once again, and that's why I'm over by the boardwalk in the first place.

Like I said earlier, Wilfred is developmentally disabled. He looks to be about twenty-five or so, but he only had the mind of a small child. Learning to read or write has, so far, been far beyond his capabilities. In fact, if the truth were known, he's still having trouble trying to tie his own shoe laces. We share the back fence with the Jensens, so I play with Wilfred from time to time. Mom has told me to be nice to him and all.

"They say he's not quite right," she once said. He has a mean streak in him, though, and going to Wilfred's house can turn out to be quite an adventure. He can get a little violent at times, just when you least expect it, and he's a whole lot bigger and stronger than I am.

But I'm not nearly as scared of Wilfred as I am of Ingaborg, Wilfred's pet garter snake. Creepy-crawly snakes are definitely not among my all-time list of favorite animals. And just as I'd feared, Wilfred has spotted Ingaborg as she sidles out from under the boardwalk.

With a maniacal gleam in his cocked eyes, Wilfred swoops down on the undulating Ingaborg and grabs her by the tail. The chase is on. AAAHHRRrrggg! Around and around the Jensen backyard we run, with me screaming at the top of my lungs and goofy ol' Wilfred and the dangling Ingaborg in hot pursuit. SHINOLA! I can feel their hot breath on the back of my neck.

*****

BEEP, BEEP. "Why're ya just standin' there with that crow bar, Mackerels? Your eyeballs are all rolled back into your head, and ya look like you're in some kind of trance or somepin." Buddy Pringle has just driven up in his dad's old pickup truck.

"I'm gonna tear up the boardwalk and look for money," I say, as my wandering mind slips back to the present.

"Ha! You might find fifteen cents and a lot of small change, if you look there long enough. Everybody and their brother's had a go at that boardwalk. You know what I'm sayin'?"

Dang! No money there? Even so, I do feel just like a giant load's been taken off my back. For some reason, I'm glad to get away from the boardwalk. There's something evil about that structure, although I can't quite put my finger on it. "I sure want to get some money for a new mitt and some baseball shoes," I say to Buddy.

"Why doncha ask your folks?"

"Nah." Actually, I've thought of my parents, but I'm a little afraid to ask, to be quite frank. Lately, Dad's been cooler to me than the other side of the pillow. He had a little tough luck last weekend, when he went to build some more shelves for all of Tavern's empty beer cases. He had everything all planned out and had the boards cut and ready to nail and all, but that was before he discovered the little accident I'd had with his wooden carpenter's rule.

"Hop in, then," Buddy says, as he looks at his wristwatch. "Time is money—in fact, it's already about twenty dollars after ten—hah, hah, hah. We'll go for a ride, and I'll show ya a little place where we prolly oughtta be able to make some dough." Now, you've got to understand about ol' Buddy Pringle. Even though he's a legitimate man-of-the-world, and all, he just murders the King's English. He'll say "prolly" for probably, "splain" for explain, and "posta" instead of supposed to. He talks weird. Sometimes, if the truth were known, I don't really talk all that good, myself. But you don't want to sound like a sissy to the other kids and all. The only guy who can get away with fancy language is ol' Gordy Belmont. With Buddy, though, it's kind of hard to tell whether he knows any better or not.

Well, we take off in Buddy's truck, and it's not long before we reach the Muskrat Valley Road. Buddy drives almost to the end of it, before he finally pulls off onto the shoulder, right before the East Valley turns on to the road to Larsonville.

"What're we doin' here?" I say

"See that place down there?" He's pointing to a rustic-looking old farmhouse, complete with barn and silo to the rear.

"Yeah...that's the old Baer farm...so what?"

"Well, ya see that wooded area over there about a hunnert yards behind the barn?"

"Yeah."

"Know what's in there?"

"Trees, I guess."

"But, what kind of trees?"

"Danged if I know."

"Cascaras!"

Feb. 6—52

Dear Auntie,

Here it the week before Valentines Day, and I haven't got my valentines out yet. Knowing army mail the way I do, I don't suppose they'll get there in time now. I imagine you've got a hint of spring by the time you get this letter. Here, things are buried by 3 feet of snow, and now there is a cold dry wind coming from the north. We are sad here, today. One of our missing soldiers was found dead this morning. His frozen body was all ripped apart from mortar fragments. Seriously, Auntie, you better get Willie to try and get his grades up. Maybe college can keep him out of this stupid war. That's all for now. Happy Valentines Day.

As ever,
Harvey

Chapter 17

Cascara trees. They could definitely be at least a partial solution to my financial problems. Back in Kingston, I'd made some pretty darned good money peeling the bark from cascara trees. Cascara bark is a major ingredient for the making of laxatives. It had to be both peeled and dried, before you could take it to the Kingston Farm Store to be weighed and sold. Sometimes, you could get as much as thirty cents a pound for it.

Dad got me started on the venture. He'd made spending money that way, when he was a kid. "Don't ever chew any of it, though, Mackerels. You'll be able to thread the eye of a needle from thirty paces, if you know what I mean."

A sack stuffed with freshly-peeled cascara would weigh a ton, but would lose a whole lot of weight during the drying process. Some kids would put rocks in the bottom of their sacks, to make them heavier and all, but the Farm Store employees were hardly ever fooled by such monkey business. They could tell what a sack should weigh, almost to the ounce, just by lifting it. Any suspicious sacks, they'd jab with a pitchfork—just to make sure we weren't trying any funny stuff. Anyone caught cheating, would be told to take their business elsewhere from then on.

Finding the cascara and peeling it was sort of fun, but protecting the harvest from thieves could be a pain in the neck. The trouble was—the bark had to sit out and dry for quite awhile before it'd be ready to sell. That's when it'd be particularly vulnerable to the bark robbers. I had places behind the house where the cascara would get the maximum sunlight for drying and all. Unfortunately, those spots gave the minimum amount of protection from the Rath boys, Tom and Lester.

The Raths were a born-again hillbilly family that lived in an old tarpaper shack way down at the end of the tidal slough that fed into Apple Tree Cove. Many was the time I'd gone out back to check the drying process, only to see one of the Rath boys slithering off into the woods with a sack of my precious bark. Dad always referred to Tom and Lester as, "The Grapes of Rath."

I couldn't just go to their house and demand the return of my bark, either. It wasn't quite as simple as that, if you want to know the awful truth. Just to get to their ol' shack, you had to wend your way through a maze of old, rusted, junked cars and car parts that littered an already ugly landscape.

Also, the Raths had a whole pack of vicious mongrel dogs patrolling their property, just looking for an unsuspecting leg to chew on. It could be real heart-stopping, if a snarling cur with obvious Doberman, Great Dane, and Rottweiler lineage stepped suddenly out from behind a decaying Model-A Ford and cast longing eyes upon your shin bone.

And to top it all off, the Raths sort of liked to shoot at would-be intruders with their .22 rifles—just to see how close they could come without actually hitting them. I've got to tell you, the cascara business could be quite an adventure back in Kingston.

Buddy's done some research and has found that we can sell our bark to Caselli Brothers' Hardware in Port Townsend. Lately, they've been paying twenty-seven cents a pound for dried bark.

"I scouted it out, Mackerels, and I tell ya, these must be the biggest cascara trees in the whole world. But, we gotta be real careful. Old Sam Baer doesn't want anyone peelin' his bark 'cept his own kids. And they say he's a real mean old bugger. He'll prolly call the sheriff, if he catches us stealin' bark. You know what I'm sayin'?"

That sounds sort of scary to me, if you want to know the truth, but I need the money pretty danged bad, and besides—the idea of sneaking into forbidden territory makes it all the more exciting. "When're we gonna do it?" I say.

The next day, we drive Buddy's dad's old Ford pickup to the Muskrat Valley and park on a secluded back road near the Baer farm. I like it when we take that truck instead of the Hog. It has a radio, and we are listening to Vaughn Monroe singing Ghost Riders in the Sky. I like that song, although Buddy has to go and spoil it with his own brand of off-key singing. For ghost riders, he likes to substitute, "ghost turds." Buddy can be a little crude at times.

One day I asked Dad if he'd ever thought about putting a radio in the Hog, and maybe giving it a new paint job, some white walls, some fender skirts, and maybe some dual Smitty mufflers.

"No—I have never given that even the slightest consideration," Dad said. "It'd be a complete waste of money. You have to remember: a vehicle is only transportation, and that's all it is. All that fancy junk won't make it run one bit better." I suppose Dad was right; he usually is. He's also no fun.

Well anyway, we quietly shut our doors and begin looking around for the best spot to enter the thickly-wooded area. Finally, on tiny cat feet, we take off through the lush undergrowth, and as we creep stealthily along, we keep our eyes peeled for the gray bark of the coveted cascara.

It's kind of tough to spot them at first, because they look a whole lot like the more prevalent alders. Usually, though, they don't get nearly as big, and the bark has sort of a different texture. You can also tell the difference in the leaves.

Suddenly, our eyes are drawn to the most telling feature of all—the faded, yellow trunk of a cascara that's already been peeled. Someone's cut one down, recently, and it's lying on the ground right there in front of us. When we look around, we can see several more close by.

"Dang it, Mackerels, look at the *size* of these things," Buddy says, "they're *enormous*."

Ol' Buddy isn't just whistling Dixie, either. These are easily the biggest cascara I've ever seen. They make the ones back in Kingston look like a bunch of puny, little toothpicks. "Looks like we're too late, though," I say. "I'll bet the ol' Baers made themselves a fortune in here."

"Hey...wait a minute...there's one," Buddy says excitedly. "And there's another one right over there."

I look to where he's pointing, and sure enough, he's spotted two great big ol' untouched cascaras. And as we work our way to them through all the thick brush, I can see a few more great big buggers not all that far away. It won't take many trees like this, before we'll have plenty of money for baseball mitts, and shoes, and such as that.

Now, I've got to tell you. When you're harvesting cascara, you really ought to cut the tree down, first. That way, you can peel the entire thing without having to do any climbing. Also, you've got to leave the bark on the stump intact. The stump will send up new shoots, and in a few years, you'll have a multi-trunked tree all ready to harvest again. If you peel the trees and leave them standing, they'll die, and pretty soon you'll be out of the ol' cascara industry.

"Now, Mackerels," Buddy says, "we don't wanna cut any of these trees down." You'll notice that Buddy sort of takes charge on little capers like this, which is no more than right, I guess, what with him being a man-of-the-world and all.

"If we cut any trees," Buddy says, "the noise of our machetes'll have them Baers up here on the dead run. We'll just peel 'em as high as we can reach. And heck, since the trees are just gonna die, anyway, we prolly oughtta take the bark off the trunks, too...right on down to the ground. Boy, that trunk bark is really thick. It'll weigh up fast—you know what I'm sayin'?"

I can understand that, all right—Buddy's making lots of sense. Buddy ends a lot of sentences with, "You know what I'm sayin'?" I guess it's because he's not always sure that I understand. And the sad fact of the matter is: lots of times I don't.

Well anyway, Buddy begins peeling the trees we first spotted, while I work my way on over to the others. The first one I come to is a real beauty—way bigger than I'd ever peeled at Kingston. Visions of long-fingered fielders' mitts begin cavorting around in my head.

I make some slits in the giant trunk with my jackknife; then I slide my hands in between the trunk and the slippery bark and peel off a great big chunk. It must weigh danged near a pound all by itself. It won't take long to fill our sacks with heavy stuff like this. That's good, though, as we sure as heck don't want to be here in Baer country any longer than is necessary.

Now, a tree that's been peeled for some time is sort of a dull, yellowish-tan, but the exposed yellow of a freshly-peeled tree is much brighter. After I've worked the patch over for a half-hour or so, I'm surrounded by a stand of naked trees, whose glaring yellowness would make you think about putting on the ol' sun glasses.

I've got my sack plumb-full and sort of wish I'd brought another, when I hear loud chopping noises not too awfully far away. *What the heck is Buddy doing?* Leaving my bulging sack of bark at the foot of a big ol' fir tree, I take off through the woods in the direction of the chopping sounds.

Suddenly, right there beside me, Buddy bursts out of the brush and likes to scare me half to death. He's breathing real hard and is all humped over from the weight of a full sack of bark. He looks pretty danged agitated, too. Then, with finger to his lips, he signals for silence.

Just then, we hear more chopping noises right there behind us, and my heart jumps all the way up into my throat. It's the *Baers*! And they have to be less than fifty yards away. As Buddy hurries to my side, we can hear the Baers talking.

"Someone's been in my cascara!" says Papa Baer in a great big voice.

"And someone's been in my cascara, too!" says Mama Baer in a middle-sized voice.

"Someone's been in my cascara," says Baby Baer, in a wee, squeaky voice, "and they've peeled all of the bark!"

Buddy and I need to hear no more. As quietly as possible, we scuttle back to where I've left my bark against the tree. When we get there, Buddy's huffing and puffing like the Big, Bad Wolf and sweating like all three of the Little Pigs put together. When I go to lift my sack of bark, I can see why. It must weigh a ton and a half, or more.

As I struggle to get the bulky sack to my shoulders, Buddy searches the woods for the most likely route of escape. It won't be easy; the Baers are between us and the pickup.

Buddy's truck and the Baers are to our east, and deep, dark woods (lions, and tigers, and bears—oh my) are to the west and in the wrong direction to boot. We'd have to circumnavigate the entire globe if we went that way. And danged if the thickest jungle I've ever seen isn't to the north. Even Tarzan would have his troubles if he tried to penetrate that horrible mess. No—the only logical way out appears to be to the south. We won't have to travel too awfully far, before we'll reach a great big pasture.

Buddy agrees. "We can prolly cut across that pasture over there, Mackerels...to that grove of little trees; then we can circle back to the truck from there."

I can understand that, all right. Once again, Buddy is right on top of things. And the Baers will probably never even see us. They'll probably be in the cascara patch a while longer, as they inspect the savage rape of their once-virgin forest.

Slowly and silently, we make our way to the pasture. About three-fourths of the way there, though, I know how Charles Atlas must feel—you know—the guy who carries the world around on his shoulders all the time. My whole body aches like I've just finished one of those horrible football practices back in Scandia, and the salt from my perspiration is stinging my eyes so bad that I can hardly see.

Finally, we reach the fence line and are able to drop the goldarn sacks. If you want to know the bitter truth, my arms and shoulders have never been so sore. As we take a breather, we study the fence for the most likely place to get through.

"Let's try it here," Buddy says, and he climbs the fence to the other side. When he makes it over, I hoist his sack of bark to him over the fence. I lift mine to him, too, and then prepare to tackle the barbed wire myself. I might mention here, that crossing barbed wire fences has never been a particularly strong skill of mine. Climbing over this one looks particularly tricky, so I decide to try going through the fence, instead.

I make it about half-way, when Buddy hollers, "Go back,

Mackerels...and make it snappy!" He sounds more than a little urgent, too.

I scramble back out as fast as I can, and darned if I don't rip the seat of my pants while I'm at it. I jump to my feet to see what the heck Buddy's so excited about, and as I do, I get a full sack of bark right in the ol' mush. "Take this, Mackerels, and here's the other one, too," he says, as he hurriedly shoves the second sack in my direction.

As Buddy struggles back through the barbed wire, I finally have time to glance up and locate the problem. It sure as heck doesn't take long—I can tell you that much for sure. The flared nostrils, the thundering hooves, and the wicked set of horns leave no doubt about it: there's a bull in a Baer market!

"El Bullio!" I cry, adding further proof that the time spent back in Miss Swanson's Spanish class wasn't all in vain.

The beast comes to a screeching halt just inches short of the fence and fixes its evil-looking eyes right on us. And you can tell it's pretty well ticked-off. We walk along our side of the fence for a little ways, just to see what it'll do. Well, the danged thing moves right along with us, step-for-step, except when it stops to paw the ground once in awhile with its big ol' hooves.

"It ain't gonna let us across this pasture, Mackerels...I can tell ya that much right now," Buddy says. "We're gonna hafta go clear around this whole danged field—you know what I'm sayin'?"

I can understand that, all right, even if it is going to take about three times as long to get back to the truck. Anything, to keep from facing Papa Baer. He's big enough to fight real bears with nothing but a very small switch. I sort of doubt, too, that he'll be singing Happy Trails to good ol' Buddy and me.

About a million years later, we wearily load the leaden sacks of cascara into the back of the pickup. You ought to see us; we must be a sorry sight. After fighting our way through endless miles of trees, and branches, and blackberry thickets, our danged clothes are all ripped to shreds and soaked with sweat. And of course, I wasn't smart enough to wear a long-sleeved shirt, so I've got all these scratches on my arms, and they itch like heck from all the sweat. I don't know about Buddy for sure, but I'm tired as all get out and thirsty as the dickens. I'll bet I've lost at least ten pounds on this stupid expedition.

"I wonder how much we'll get for this bark?" Buddy says. He looks pretty darned tired, at that, as he leans wearily against the truck.

"I don't know," I say, "but it sure seems like a hard way to make some easy money." (The weed of crime bears bitter fruit. Crime does not pay. The Shadow knows—heh, heh, heh, heh—.)

Samuel Baer reports that someone trespassed on his Muskrat Valley property last weekend and peeled the bark off most of his cascara trees. Cascara bark is used in the making of laxatives. Mr. Baer had planned to set the money from the bark aside for his son, Teddy's, college education fund.

Standing naked in his cascara grove, Mr. Baer figures that the trees are pretty much ruined forever.
—Dora Dingley
The Happy Valley Harbinger, April 1952

Chapter 18

Well, baseball season is here at last, but evidently, no one's bothered to tell the danged ol' weatherman. Spring has sprung okay, but it's sprung right back into winter. The blustery winds feel like they've taken an express route directly from the North Pole. Coach Monahan keeps our managers busy collecting wood for the bonfire along the third base line. Whenever there's a chance, we dash over to the fire to warm our hands.

"Too bad we don't have some wieners to roast," Vernon Windbladd says.

"Well, there's always Mackerel's arm," says Buddy Wise-Ass Pringle; he's such a funny guy. These sodbusters don't even realize I've been keeping my fastball under wraps until the goofy weather warms up. The last thing I want is a sore arm.

"Did you pitch much over at Scandia?" Vernon asks.

"Uh...now and then." I don't consider that answer to be a lie—exactly—now and then add up to twice, don't they?'

But from what I see here, it looks like I'll get to pitch a whole lot more than that at good ol' Hapless Valley. If you ask me, the Milk Maids seem awfully weak on the pitching mound. Of course, we look pretty weak at a lot of other places, too. Still, I figure we shape up better at this sport than we did at either football or basketball.

Right off the bat, it looks like I might even avoid the Willie's Wonders syndrome for once; Richie Schmutz seems like a pretty decent catcher. Only a sophomore, he's a little rough around the edges but has a heck of a throwing arm. Throwing out base runners was never one of my stronger suits, anyway, if you want to know the truth. I almost envy

Richie, though, as he's probably got the safest spot on the whole team. Our infielders have to deal with all those rocks on the Hapless Valley diamond, while the poor outfielders have to contend with huge boulders. It makes Richie look pretty safe back there behind the plate with all that protective gear he wears.

Buddy Pringle is in left and looks like probably our best hitter. He's not real fast in the field but catches just about everything hit his way. Vernon Windbladd is the shortstop and is really good for being so inexperienced and all. He's got these great reflexes and a fairly decent arm. And though he couldn't hit a bull in the butt with a banjo, Gordy Belmont is a danged good center fielder. The rest of the team seems pretty mediocre, except for right field. That's where Roderick Remblinger plays. Roderick is not just your average ballplayer—he's quite a bit below average.

What worries me the most, though, is the fact we don't have real baseball uniforms. I've finally found out why, now that I'm here at good ol' Hapless Valley. It seems that Roderick's older brother was to blame. At least, that's what's been said by Mom's old friends, they. While in the school's old gym, the older Remblinger supposedly flipped a cigarette butt into a waste basket to avoid being caught while smoking in the men's restroom. Later that night, the whole danged building burned to the ground and most of the athletic equipment as well. So far, the school board hasn't been able to budget any money to replace the baseball uniforms.

Dang, I hate to go out there dressed like a sodbuster," I say to Buddy Pringle and Vernon Windbladd, right after the first baseball practice. "Old football jerseys and blue jeans really make us look bush league."

It's really important to ya, huh, Mackerels?" Buddy says.

"Dang right...you play like you look."

"You probably won't even make the team, then," Vernon says. I reach over and tweak one of Vernon's fat, little cheeks. He just hates that, but it serves him right. Sometimes Vernon can be sort of a smartass, for just being a freshman and all.

"Well then, why don't we just go out and get us some new unies?" Buddy says.

"Yeah...right...and just how're we gonna go about it?" I ask.

"It's simple. We just go around to all the merchants in the whole, danged area and see if they'll each buy one uniform. You know...sorta like a sponsor. You know what I'm sayin'?"

"Hmmm."

"See...we can put their business names right on the back of the unies and all. It'd be real good advertisin' for 'em."

"Hey, that might work," Vernon says.

"Sure it'll work. I thought of it, didn't I?" That's one thing I admire about Buddy: he never lacks for confidence.

"Well, it's sure worth a try," I say, "let's go ask Coach and see what he thinks."

So today after school, Buddy, Vernon, and I are on the road in search of sponsors. We've got Buddy's dad's old pickup. Coach Monahan has excused us from practice to go out and solicit uniforms; he thinks it's a great idea. He checked in an athletic supply catalogue and figured out that each businessman will have to come up with twenty bucks to buy a uniform. He even helped us work out a little sales pitch to try on the merchants. It seems Coach Monahan's dad had been a Fuller Brush man.

Since Happy Valley proper doesn't have all that many business establishments to choose from, we have to range far and wide into neighboring communities to look for help. We've got seven commitments right off the bat, as Buddy proves to be a really good salesman. Caselli Brothers' Hardware, in Port Townsend, is next on our list.

"Now, Mackerels, since you're the one who just had to have these uniforms in the first place, I think you oughtta take a try at the sales pitch, for a change," Buddy says.

"I can ask my dad about sponsoring us. He'll probably want to advertise the tavern."

"Aw...that don't count," Buddy says. "You need to try it with someone different. It'll help give you some self-confidence."

"I don't need any self-confidence."

"Sure ya do. Just look attcha. You're afraid to go talk to a hick storekeeper."

I've got to tell you, it's hard to ever win an argument with a man-of-the-world like Buddy. So, as I head for the entrance to Caselli Brothers', I try to remember the sales pitch Coach Monahan has taught us.

We go right to the counter, but Bonzo Caselli is busy with a customer. We wait there for a few more minutes while they talk, about tees, and elbows, and grease traps, and such as that.

"We better come back another time," I whisper to Buddy. "They're too busy right now."

"That's okay. We're next...besides...we ain't in any hurry."

"Can I do somepin for you kids real quick?" Bonzo has turned his attention to us for the moment. "I'm sorta busy with Mr. Smithers, here, on a big plumbing problem."

"Uh...we...uh...could come back later."

"He wants to talk to ya about baseball uniforms," says the man-of-the-world.

"Yeah, okay...so what's the deal, kid?"

"Uh...well...you see...uh...we need some new baseball uni..."

"How much?"

Oops, I can just tell from the look on his face that Bonzo is not going to want to spring for any uniforms, but I give it the ol' college try anyway.

"Uh...well...uh, if you buy one uniform, you get to have your name on the baa..."

"Yeah, yeah...how much?"

I was right—it was a bad idea to come here in the first place. "Uh, it'd be real good adverti..."

"How *much,* kid?"

"Uh...er...twenty bucks," I say, as I hold my breath.

"We'll take two," says Bonzo.

As we walk back to the truck, I say, "Well, that wasn't so bad. Coach's sales pitch works pretty good, doesn't it?" Before the day is over, we have orders for thirteen suits, and that's all we need. We've suited up the starting team, Coach Monahan, and our three wonderful substitutes. By the way, you can imagine how good they are, if they can't even beat out Roderick Remblinger. We call them, "The Three Stooges."

Well, the new uniforms only take four days to arrive, and if you want to know the truth of it all, they don't turn out to be what you'd call real flashy. They're just plain, white uniforms with no trim. As a matter of fact, they don't even say Milk Maids on the front. The sponsors' names are on the back, though, in very plain, blue lettering. Buddy and Vernon both have CASELLI BROTHERS' on the backs of their uniforms, while naturally, mine says TAVERN. I'm not all that excited about that, if you want to know the truth, but it'd probably hurt my parents' feelings if I wore anything else.

"They're what they call stock uniforms," Coach Monahan explains. "That's all we could get for twenty dollars."

But they sort of look like Brooklyn Dodger uniforms, if you go and use your imagination and all. At least, they're a big improvement on old football jerseys and blue jeans. You've got to admit that.

> Our Happy Valley athletes are busy preparing for the upcoming baseball season, Coach Monahan reports. "I hope the boys can be more successful than they were in the football and basketball seasons," he told this reporter.
>
> It seems too, that the boys have been out soliciting new uniforms for the squad, as well. Although rather plain in appearance, almost to the point of being drab, Coach Monahan says the uniforms will be a big improvement over the jeans and football jerseys the boys had been wearing.
>
> —Dora Dingley
> The Happy Valley Harbinger, April 1952

Chapter 19

"Hi, Butters...tee, hee...how come you lost the game, yesterday? Aren't you guys ever going to win any kind of game this year?" I turn around, and there is Helen Morley and Naomi Panks, two of Rosie Higgenbottom's goofy pals.

Helen is real tall and skinny and wears ugly, horn-rimmed glasses. To make up for her less-than-spectacular looks, Helen wears tons of make-up and drapes cheap jewelry on as many parts of her body as she can find room. You could probably stock the jewelry department of the Bon Marche with all the rings, necklaces, and charm bracelets she wears. But the makeup and accessories haven't done her a whole lot of good, I'm afraid. As Buddy once observed about her, "You can only put so much lipstick on a pig."

Naomi is short and fat, and while she's not into the makeup and jewelry like Helen, she has this one silver tooth that sticks pretty much straight out. A lot of the guys like to call her, "Fang." But since I have this slightly-bigger nose, and these slightly-greener teeth, and this slightly-wilder hair, I've never been too much into name-calling and all.

Ever since I went to the Tolo with Rosie that time, her chums have been calling me "Peanut Butters." Lately, though, they've just shortened it to plain ol' "Butters." I don't even bother to turn around. If I did, though, I wouldn't even bother to quarter my nose. I can tell you that much for sure.

The game they were referring to, was the first one of the season. And wouldn't you know it, but the Willie's Wonders syndrome had to go and rear its ugly head once again. Even after all the babying of my arm during the cold weather, it went and got sore on me, anyway—right in the elbow. I couldn't have thrown a curve, if my life depended on it. I offered to pitch anyway and just stick with fastballs, but Coach Monahan didn't think it'd be such a good idea. I'm not sure why.

He had no one else, so he just about had to pitch Richie Schmutz. Of course, that meant I was stuck behind the plate once again. Catching Richie is no cup of tea, either, if you want to know the awful truth. He can really hum the ol' pill and can throw just about every kind of pitch known to man. Of course, he has absolutely no idea of where any of them are going. What makes it really tough, though, is that his curve doesn't always break. You can't stay down in a catcher's crouch, either, because sometimes he throws behind the batter, and you have to be ready to shift the feet real fast.

Richie threw a no-hitter, but we lost to Central, anyway, twenty-three to one. All the Central guys either walked, struck out, or were hit by one of Richie's non-breaking curves. Said one Central kid, after he'd been hit for the third time," Cripes...don't you sodbusters have anyone else who can pitch? This guy's wilder'n a flea!"

On the brighter side, though, I've started out the year batting .667, with an infield single, a bloop double, and a walk in four trips to the plate. My new glasses seem to be the secret to my new-found success. You see, in addition to my slightly-bigger nose, my slightly-greener teeth, and my slightly-wilder hair, I've also had these slightly-weaker eyes all my life.

I've always sort of resisted the idea of wearing glasses, though, until just the other day. That was right after I thought I saw this sort-of-cute sophomore girl down at the end of the hall. But when I went to strike up a conversation, it wasn't her at all. It was Naomi Panks.

*****

We have a thief on our team—either that—or some outsider snuck into the foyer of the gym during our brief baseball workout. It rained all day, so we couldn't have practice outside. Coach just had us play a little catch in the gym. I didn't actually practice pitching, though, because he made us play in our stocking feet. I'd need more traction than that for my fastball. I don't know why we couldn't have gone ahead and wore our shoes; like I've said, our gym floor is ruined anyway.

We all left our shoes out in the foyer as we warmed up. I usually wear my penny loafers to school; they're easy to get on and off for changing into spikes and such as that. But since Buddy Pringle had been putting quarters in the little slots where the pennies were supposed to go, I thought I would, too. After all, when you've got a real live man-of-the-world showing the way, you really ought to take advantage of it.

Well, as it turned out, someone needed the quarters worse than I did. After practice, when I went to get my shoes, there were notes in the slots where the quarters were supposed to be. THANKS, they said. One thing about it, though, Roderick Remblinger's off the hook. He can't even spell THANKS.

"Well, at least they left ya the shoes," Vernon said.

Then Buddy has to get in his two cents' worth. "Guess they never heard of the old saying: if the shoe fits—steal it—har, har, har."

After our brief workout, Buddy, Vernon, and I go over to the Happy Valley Mercantile. Buddy's kind of a Pepsi addict, (Pepsi Cola hits the spot; be sure that you drink a lot—nickel, nickel, nickel, nickel—) and Vernon and I are thinking about ice cream cones. But because of the danged ol' penny loafer thief, I'm completely broke. I ask Buddy if he might by any chance have the two bucks he borrowed last week.

"Uh—no—uh, I only got enough for a bottle of pop for myself. But don't worry, Mackerels—It's better that I owe ya the money rather than I beat ya out of it."

After Buddy and Vernon exchange sly glances, Vernon says, "Aw, I'll lend ya a quarter, Mackerels—but you gotta pay me back tomorrow without fail, or I'm gonna charge you ten cents interest per day." It's sure a good thing that I have such great friends.

It's times like these that I really miss my days back in Seattle. There were lots of drugstores in Seattle, and most all of them had soda fountains. And they had all sorts of exotic concoctions to choose from. You had chocolate sodas, milkshakes and malteds, and just about any ice cream sundae you could think of. Myself, I always had kind of a hard time choosing between pineapple, marshmallow, and caramel. And lots of times, after I'd been paid for delivering the Green Lake Reporter, I'd splurge and get myself a banana split, even if they did cost fifty cents. You don't have all that variety to choose from at the Happy Valley Mercantile. They have ice cream cones, and that's it. Your choices are: vanilla, chocolate, or strawberry. The biggest decision you're going to make is whether or not you want one scoop or two.

The Mercantile is one of the oldest buildings in beautiful, downtown Happy Valley and is owned and operated by Vernon's folks. Mrs. Windbladd pretty much operates the store, while Vernon's dad works in at the paper mill in Port Townsend.

To tell you the truth, I don't think the Windbladds are cutting any fat hog with the operation of the store. Us kids hang out there quite a lot—buying pop, and ice cream, and candy, and such as that, but I never see a whole lot of other people in there. For one thing, it's as big as a barn and just about as hard to heat. There's an old pot-belly stove way at the back, but you'd never know that when you're standing up front.

"What can I do for you boys, today?" Mrs. Windbladd asks, as we approach the counter. As usual, she is all dressed up in an assortment of woolen sweaters and leggings to combat the arctic cold that leaks in from under the door and around the windows. She blows on her hands while she waits for our order.

"The usual," Buddy says, as he grabs a Pepsi out of the cooler.

Vernon decides on a Whiz bar (Whizzz—best nickel candy bar there izzz), but I've still got a yen for some ice cream. "Uh—I'll take a—uh—er—." Will it be vanilla, chocolate, or strawberry? Since I only have Vernon's quarter to spend, one of the exciting options will have to be left out.

(Decisions, decisions). "One scoop vanilla and one chocolate," I finally say, as with the toe of my now penniless loafer I stir up a couple of the more interesting dust bunnies down there on the old wooden floor. I hold back on the strawberry, in case I might want some variety one day farther down the road.

"Hey, Mackerels," Vernon says, you any good at algebra?"

"Not too bad...at some of it, anyway. What're ya workin' on?"

"Story problems."

Well, lucky for Vernon Windbladd, he's caught me in one of my strong suits, as far as good ol' algebra is concerned. I'll have to admit that I'm not too good at quadratic equations, and polywogials, and such as that. But I'm pretty much a whiz when it comes to story problems, even if I do say so, myself. I don't know why that is, but it's the truth, just the same. I guess they just sort of fascinate me. I especially like the kind where you got a train leaving the station at one speed and another, faster, train leaving an hour later, and you're supposed to figure out when the faster train will catch the slower one. Stuff like that can be pretty practical and all. You never know when you might be caught in a situation like that.

Well, Vernon wants me to come over to his house after dinner to help him with the algebra. He lives in one of Happy Valley's pioneer farm houses, only two doors up the street from Tavern. The Windbladds have their home fixed up pretty nice, for being such an old house, and all. I've got to admit it. Mr. Windbladd was quite an athlete in his day, I guess, and in the rear of the house, he's fixed up this really neat recreation room, kind of like a little gymnasium. You have to go through that room in order to get to the kitchen, where Vernon does his homework.

After the dinner dishes are done, I go on over. Vernon meets me at the back door, but on our way into the kitchen, I can't help but notice the regulation punching bag hanging there in the rec room. Just looking at it sort of stirs up some of the Corbett/Flynn fires that have been lying dormant all these years.

"Hey, a punching bag," I say. "I've always wanted to work out on one of these." I'd never tried it before, but it looked pretty easy in the Gentleman Jim movie. "Okay if I try it?" I figure we have lots of time for the algebra.

Vernon outfits me with some official Everlast punching bag gloves, and I go to work. I think I'll just start in real easy, before I get into anything too tricky. I give it a light tap with my left, but before I can follow up with the right, the danged thing has already come and gone. I just barely graze it, and it proceeds to spin crazily out of control. I try a couple more times, figuring that my natural athletic ability will kick in any second. But I can't seem to get the hang of it, no matter how hard I try.

"You got too danged much air in this thing," I say.

"Hmm...let me try it." Vernon says.

I don't see how any goofy freshman is going to have any luck, if I can't even do it. Like I said before, there's too much air in the danged thing. But then, Vernon takes the gloves and starts in. Ratatattattat atatattattat tattatattat tattatattat. Vernon's hands are flying so fast you can hardly see them, and the bag is nothing but a blur. His chubby cheeks are all aglow with the effort. Then he caps off the dazzling exhibition with a well-timed right hand. VVvvrrooommm the bag goes, and the house even shakes a little bit on its foundation.'

"Now, let's put on the speed bag and give it a try," Vernon says.

"Uh, we better get on that algebra," I say.

Mar. 5—52

Dear Auntie,

Hope this letter finds the Michaels family in good health. I suppose Willie is starting to get ready for the baseball season. Sorry to hear they were so lousy in football and basketball. It sounds like he's awfully serious about his sports. Wish I was there to council him. He wants to try and have as much fun as he can and realize that high school sports are not the end of the world. KOREA is the end of the world. Wouldn't I love to be down in Florida at spring training with the Cardinals, instead of here in this God-forsaken ice box. Yesterday, it was thirty below. By the way, know any good old fashioned home remedies for constipation, Auntie? (ha, ha) Well, it's time to go on patrol now. Write soon.

Love,
Your favorite nephew (ha, ha)

Chapter 20

Tomorrow, we're playing our second game of the season, up at Port Angeles. Lately, the weather has been warmer, and my sore arm is feeling a little better. But I still won't get to make my pitching debut just yet.

At practice today, Coach Monahan says, "We'll rest your arm one more week, Mackerels. I need to try some other kids, anyway. We'll never get through the whole season with just one pitcher." He goes on to explain that since Angeles is so tough, and all, there's no sense in wasting me there if I'm not at my best. And if he's trying a bunch of other kids, he must have given up on the Richie Schmutz experiment already.

"By the way, Mackerels," he says, "you really ought to do something about that complexion problem. You been eating too much candy or drinking too much pop?" What Coach is referring to are these big scabs that have just started to show up on my face. They look really awful, if you want to know the truth. I've been kind of worrying about them. In fact, they make me forget all about my slightly-bigger nose, and my slightly-greener teeth, and my slightly-wilder hair, and my slightly-weaker eyes.

Tonight, after Dad gets home from his commute to Seattle, he says, "Jesus H. Christ, Mackerels, your face looks terrible. You better go on into the doctor in Townsend tomorrow and see what the heck's the matter." So, the next morning I get an appointment and go on in.

"You've got a virus called impetigo," the doctor says. "First of all, you've got to keep the scabs all off...that's where the poison is. Here's some cotton swabs to use with rubbing alcohol. Then, put this salve on the sores. It should all go away in just a few days."

'What causes it?" I ask.
"Have a cat by any chance?"
'Uh...yeah."
"Well, cats quite often are carriers."
"Hmmm."

As I start to leave, the doctor adds, "Oh...and Willie...try not to perspire. Perspiration can cause the disease to spread."

When I get back to Happy Valley, I stop by the tavern before returning to school. Mom will want to know what I found out. But, when I drive up, who do I see sitting there on Tavern's front porch, but the culprit, herself—Tar Baby—our old black cat. She's busily licking her paws, as she enjoys the warmth of the sun. I think back a second to the last contact I had with her—last Saturday, to be exact.

*****

For some strange reason I was in a really nostalgic mood. It was probably due to the World War II movie I'd seen in Townsend, the night before. Those films make me think back to the less stressful times of my youth—the days before Trudy Trammell, and Teddy Snodgrass, and all the losses we've piled up here at Hapless Valley. And once in awhile, I even revert back to my wartime childhood and get out my tin soldiers.

There's a worn spot on Tavern's upstairs living room carpet that Mom tries to hide with a little throw rug. The throw rug not only hides the worn spot but also makes a dandy Wake Island for my tin soldiers to attack.

On that particular Saturday morning, it should have been fairly easy to take the island, for while the real Wake Island had thousands of hostile Japanese to defend its shores, my Wake Island had but one lone adversary—Tar Baby. But that one foe could be pretty darned formidable, to tell you the honest truth. And when she was resting herself on the throw rug, she didn't particularly appreciate any disturbance.

As my tin battleships and aircraft carriers circled the island, I searched carefully for the most advantageous spot from which to launch an attack. I would have to choose carefully—there was no margin for error. Tar Baby's half-closed eyes viewed the armada with apparent unconcern, as she continued to knead the nap of the throw rug with her front paws. Her black tail twitched in spasmodic contentment.

Now, I knew from past experience that any sort of frontal attack by my tin warriors would be nothing short of suicide. Tar Baby's front paws were lightning-quick, if you want to know the truth, and she'd make really short work of any attempted beachheads right there in front of her blazing yellow eyes. I'd mistakenly gone that route several times before.

I've tried attacking from the rear, too, but one swish of Tar Baby's tail can wipe out an entire platoon.

Finally, I decided that a lone soldier would try a solo flanking assault to get to the soft underbelly of the enemy. For this sortie, I selected a tin infantryman that looked an awful lot like the young, blonde actor in all the war movies.

Teddy—er—I mean the young, blonde soldier—crept stealthily up the beach, seemingly unobserved by the foe. Finally, he felt he'd reached a strategic vantage point from which to strike. He moved very quickly, but unfortunately, not quickly enough. After a skirmish of brief duration, there was yet another tin candidate for a posthumous purple heart, and the scratches and fang marks on my hand and wrist would probably require at least two weeks to heal.

*****

"Impetigo, huh? I had that once when I was a kid," Coach Monahan says. "Can't sweat? Well, you won't be able to pitch now, for sure...and I wouldn't imagine it'd be too good an idea to wear the catcher's mask right on top of those sores. Hmmm...well...we'll put you out in center field and let Gordy Belmont start on the mound."

Well, it's Gordy Belmont and a cast of thousands, as the Port Angeles Roughriders proceed to whack the ball all over the lot. Gordy's very first pitch is tattooed to deep left-center, headed for the fence. I take off on an all-out sprint but can't get there in time. Not used to playing the outfield, I misjudge the carom off the wall and am lucky to hold the runner to a mere triple. I'm already sweating like an over-worked mule.

Gordy continues to pitch batting practice for the Angeles guys, and their singles, doubles, and triples keep me on the run for the next several hours, while the Roughriders build up a six-run lead. Meanwhile, I've set a new world's record for gallons of perspiration in a single inning. The impetigo germs must be having great fun, as they gallop back and forth across my weary body.

Coach decides to give Vernon Windbladd a try on the mound for the second inning. "He's got pretty good control," Coach tells me, privately. Coach is right, too. Vernon's control is so good that he proceeds to hit the Port Angeles bats with practically every pitch. I don't think the inning will ever get over. Soon, just about every guy on the team is taking a shot at pitching. All except Roderick Remblinger, of course.

The game comes mercifully to an end after about a year-and-a-half, and we wearily board the bus and head back to Hapless Valley. I've probably lost at least ten pounds, after all the running I've done. On the bright side, though, I'm still batting a hefty .667. The new glasses are definitely the answer to all the problems with hitting I've experienced over the years. The glasses might open up all sorts of new avenues in my baseball career. After all, Babe Ruth was a pitcher, too, when he started out.

April 1—52

Dear Auntie,

No—this is not an April fool's joke. It's actually a letter from your favorite nephew (ha-ha). I only wish that KOREA was an April fool's joke. Seriously, here on the front we've been hearing talks about a truce. Hope THAT'S no joke. The reds are stalling, I hear—something to do with the repatriation of their POWs. Hope this war gets over pretty soon. I doubt that the Cardinals are going to keep a place for me forever (ha-ha). For now, we're just sort of dug in and hoping. There is a terrible rumor going around, though, that Hank Snow is going to replace General Ridgway and march us clear on up into North Korea. April fools! (ha-ha). Tell cousin Willie to get those grades up.

Yours truly,
Harvey

Chapter 21

Today, we're playing at home for the first time. Maybe all the rocks and boulders will give us a little advantage over the South Kitsap Fighting Wolves.

There's a reason why I'm referring to them as Fighting Wolves rather than just plain ol' Wolves like they're supposed to be. The other day, there was an article in the paper about Toutle Lake High School. It's located way down in Southwest Washington, somewhere, and they call themselves the Fighting Ducks. Now, isn't that one of the great nicknames of all time? It brings to mind a couple of fat mallards waddling around the ring with their dukes up and Everlast printed on the waistbands of their boxing trunks. Buddy Pringle is so impressed, he thinks that all mascot names in the whole State of Washington ought to be prefixed by the word, Fighting.

"Of course, I don't know if Fighting Milk Maids sounds all that much better than just plain Milk Maids," he says. "I wonder to myself how Fighting Sodbusters might go over.

Now, after the first inning, the Fighting Wolves are leading the Fighting Milk Maids by a score of six to zip. My arm doesn't feel all that bad, but I guess I've been a little tentative when it comes to breaking off my curve ball. A couple of hits, a couple of walks, and a couple of infield errors have us off to a bad start.

Between innings, the usually mild-mannered Coach Monahan loses his cool and gives us sort of a bawling-out in the dugout. "Too many mental errors," he says. "We're not backing up the bases like we practiced. "And we're just not anticipating the situations. We're throwing to the wrong base. We're not hitting the relay man. We don't even know how many outs there are. He goes on like that for several more minutes, as he continues to point out all our mistakes..

As Coach continues to sputter and fume, Buddy keeps digging me and Vernon Windbladd in the ribs, trying to get us to laugh. Finally, though, he sums up for Coach and helps put it all into perspective. "We gotta get our heads out of our butts," he blurts.

"How's Roderick gonna know which end is which?" I hear Vernon Windbladd whisper.

Well, strangely enough, the Coach's chew-out session seems to have done a lot of good, because the whole team settles down and plays some good ball. The outfielders catch everything hit their way, and the infielders gobble up everything in sight, in spite of all the bad bounces on our rock pile of a field.

Now, a finesse pitcher like myself really relies on his fielders. I've got to admit it. Without a real blazer, I don't strike out all that many, if you want to know the truth. I nibble here, and nibble there, and work the ball up and down the ladder quite a lot. And after Coach Monahan's lecture, I've kind of thrown caution to the wind and am bearing down harder on the curve ball. Even if I do say so myself, I have the Fighting Wolves eating right out of my hand.

Meanwhile, we Fighting Milk Maids have battled back with five runs of our own. I contribute here in the fourth inning with a solo home run, the first of my entire high school career. I manage to work the South Kitsap pitcher to a three-and-two count, and then guess right on the fastball. Hitting curves has so far not been one of my strong points. I wonder how Babe Ruth did with the curve back in his formative years.

Now, we're here in the seventh and final inning, and I mow the Fighting Wolves right down. I even cap things off on their last batter with one of my rare strikeouts. We head to the dugout for our last at bats and a chance to win our first game of the season. Vernon Windbladd catches up to me, as I trudge in from the mound.

"Hey, Mackerels, didja know there's a big league scout up there in the stands?"

'Yeah...right."

"Hey," Vernon says, "I'm not kiddin' ya. Ol' Harry Popolinski's right up there behind home plate. My old man knows him. Supposed to be a scout for the Cardinals. Been up there the whole game."

"The St. Louis Cardinals?" I say.

"What other Cardinals ya know?"

I scan the area behind home plate, and sure enough, there is an older guy up there that I've never seen before. He doesn't look all that impressive, either, if you want to know the honest truth. I can see him pretty good, since I'm wearing my new glasses and all. He isn't dressed like anything special, and it looks like he could use a shave. And from this distance, I'd almost swear he has some kind of nervous tic or something. He keeps flicking his tongue in and out of his mouth like a ticked-off snake of some sort.

Well, the South Kitsap pitcher gets two quick outs on us, before the amazing Roderick Remblinger comes to the plate and draws a base on balls. Why a pitcher would walk a guy like Roderick is sure a sixty-four thousand dollar question. But that brings me to the plate, with a chance to drive in the tying run. Another homer will win it for us.

Their catcher immediately jumps out in front of the plate and motions for his fielders to play back. He remembers my home run back in the fourth. "Back up!" he hollers. "Back up! Tavern's up!" This kid is no dummy. I can tell you that much, right now. But on the other hand, it might not be all that difficult to sense a budding Babe Ruth in the making.

Well danged if I don't work the count to full again and guess right on another fastball. I get everything I have into the swing. KKRRRAACCKK! It's a booming fly ball to left field once again. The Fighting Wolves left fielder goes back, back, back...back...and makes the catch, right at the edge of the fence for the final out of the game. I guess pitching seven innings sapped some of my strength.

We go out and say our "Rah, rah, Fighting Wolves," shake their hands and all, and I head back to the dugout to get my old three-fingered mitt and my warm-up jacket. And surprise of surprises, the old geezer from up in the stands is there to greet me. You know, the scout from the St. Louis Cardinals. He's even got on a Cardinal cap, one of the navy blue ones with the red brim and the big, red St and L monogram. To tell you the honest truth, I've always thought they looked pretty classy.

As he sticks out his hand, he says, "Nice game, there, Mister Michaels. Flick, flick goes the tongue. You made a nice recovery, there, after that bad start, there. *Flick, flick.* That shows a lot of character, there. *Flick.* My name's Harold G. Popolinski, there (I figure the G probably stands for Garter snake), and I do a little scouting here for the St. Louis Cardinals, there. *Flick, flick, flick, flick, flick.* His ol' tongue is just a pink blur, as it slithers in and out of his mouth. All that danged flicking sort of brings back some unpleasant memories of Wilfred Jensen and his pet snake, Ingaborg.

"But...*flick*...you want to keep working on that fastball, there. You can't get by in the majors, there, with just a big, roundhouse curve, there. You have to at least have enough of a fastball, there, to show the hitters, there. You know what I mean, there?" *Flick, flick, flick.*

I understand all right. I'd be glad to show the hitters more of the ol' fastball—if only I had one *there.*

❋❋❋❋❋

No, Wilfred...STOP, STOP! I'm back in Seattle, next door in the Jensen's backyard. Wilfred has me pinned down, right by the boardwalk, and he's dangling ol' Ingaborg right in my face. She's hissing at me something awful and flicking her tongue for all she's worth. She's coming closer—and CLOSER.

❋❋❋❋❋

Then, I sit right straight up in bed; I've been having this terrible nightmare. I finally recognize it as just a dream, when I realize that Ingaborg couldn't possibly be dressed in a St. Louis Cardinal uniform and all.

"Fire in the paint locker," Skinny and Clyde yell in perfect harmony. I must have slept through their first two shots.

"Hee, hee, hee." The Wicked Witch's laughter seems pretty weak and subdued, tonight. In fact, it barely makes it through the bedroom floor. Must be nearly closing time.

"While Madam La Zonga was adoin' the conga in a little cabana in ol' Havana..."

RRrrriiiinnnngggg!

"...they were doin' the Charleston...and ballin' the jaaaack."

But it seems Shuffle-Bowl, Wurlitzer, and the Singing Ranger are prepared to party on.

Now that I'm awake and all, I get to thinking about my old three-fingered mitt. It cost us the two runs, today, that probably lost us the ball game. It was back in that horrible first inning, where the Fighting Wolves had scored all their runs. With two outs and runners on second and third, a line shot came back to the mound that I should have caught for the third out. But wouldn't you know it, the ball kissed right off the top of my lousy short-fingered mitt and skipped on out to center field to drive in both runs.

Lying there in bed, inhaling second-hand cigarette smoke through the floor and listening to good ol' Hank Snow and the Rainbow Ranch Boys, I think about how I just have to have a new mitt. Especially now that the Cardinals are looking at me and all. And maybe the goofy ol' war will get over pretty soon, and I can be reunited with my cousin, Harvey Bodenheimer, somewhere in the ol' Cardinal farm system.

April 17—52

Dear Auntie,

Sorry to hear that the tavern business is not going so well. Tell Uncle George he'd better not work so hard. I'd say, "life is too short," but we don't like to use that term around here (ha—ha). Things don't sound so good with the war. They say that the truce talks are hopelessly deadlocked. We're a little south of Panmunjom, where the truce talks are taking place. We can patrol the roads leading there as long as we move away to either side before shooting anybody. Crazy—huh? Funny thing—you never see any wildlife except on those roads. I guess the deer and foxes, etc., know that's the only place they're safe. Talk to you later—time for patrol.

Your loving nephew,
Harvey

Chapter 22

Buddy and I didn't make all that much money on our cascara venture, if the whole, sad truth were known. We might've done okay if we could've harvested more than just one sack apiece, but the bull and the Baers had pretty well taken care of that idea. When Dad asked how we made out, Buddy made a sour face and said, "Hah...just great. Me and Mackerels are a couple of regular ol' entrepre...uh..new-ers."

Dad put his thumb and forefinger to his nose and said, "Ha! I always thought you two were a couple of new-ers of one kind or another." Buddy got a good laugh out of that. I didn't really understand, but I managed a chuckle, anyway. I sure as heck didn't want to ask Dad what he meant right there in front of the man-of-the-world and all.

I sort of just drag through baseball practice, today. I'm down in the dumps, because I'm still about twenty dollars short of the cost of the glove I want. I've just got to get myself one like the Wilson, Vernon Windbladd just bought. It's a Ted Williams model and has really neat long fingers. Replacing my ragged three-fingered mitt has become an obsession. But when I get home after practice, who should come to the rescue but Mom and her old friends—they.

"They say that Mr. Warfield down at Sunny Cove wants to hire a couple of kids to help him dig a basement." Upon hearing that news, Buddy and I hustle right on over to Sunny Cove to find the Warfield residence. We don't ask Vernon along—Vernon doesn't work. In fact, the few dollars I have to my name right now are from mowing the Windbladd's lawn every week. I asked Mrs. Windbladd one day why good ol' Vernon didn't tend the grass.

"Oh—Vernon's just too tired out after school, what with sports and all," she said. And when I slave away on the Windbladd lawn for my dollar, I often see ol' Vernon through the front window. He's at the dining room table eating peanut butter sandwiches and reading comic books. And whenever I near the window, he checks to see that his mom's not looking, and then he gives me the ol' finger.

Well, getting back to the basement project at Sunny Cove, it turns out that they have given Mom the straight scoop, for a change. "Yup," Mr. Warfield says, "I'm looking for a couple strong young men who aren't afraid of a little hard work." Mr. Warfield looks at us over his wire-rimmed glasses, and if I'm not mistaken, I see a trace of skepticism in his eyes. "I'm digging a basement under my house," he says. "You can help me out after dinner for a few hours and then all day on the weekends, until we get it finished. I pay a dollar an hour."

That sounds fine to us, and we agree to start work the next day. On the drive home, Buddy says, "I wonder how the heck you dig a basement under a house that's already been built? Usually, the basement comes first." As a man-of-the-world, Buddy knows all about stuff like that.

But the next evening, we find that Mr. Warfield has the job well-figured. Even Buddy has to admit it. There's a conveyor belt running out of the prospective basement and up to the bed of an ancient two-ton truck. Mr. Warfield and a helper already have about a fourth of the basement dug.

The helper is a grown man, probably in his mid-forties or so, by the name of Stanley Thorsen. Stanley is sort of a puny-looking little guy who appears to be awfully shy. He never seems to have a heck of a lot to say, and when he speaks at all, it's in a peculiar hissing manner with a slight Scandinavian accent. When we're introduced, Stanley says, "Yaaa, it'sss very nissse to meet you boysss."

Mr. Warfield is also slightly-built and probably in his late-sixties. It's beginning to look like Buddy and I are being counted upon to supply the muscle for the job.

"One of you will have to go below and keep the conveyor belt filled. The other will stay on the truck and guide the dirt off the belt. You have to make sure it gets loaded evenly," Mr. Warfield says. "Stanley uses the pick and keeps the walls straight."

"I'll take the truck," Buddy says, almost before Mr. Warfield has got the words out of his mouth. This surprises me, to tell you the honest truth. I don't remember ever seeing Buddy volunteer for anything before. But I soon find out why he did. Down in the hole, I have to work my rear end off in order to keep the stupid conveyor belt filled with dirt. I'm fairly-well convinced, now, that Buddy's been on to my brain damage for some time. To be honest, it sort of hurts my feelings a little, to think he'd knowingly take advantage of a handicapped friend like that.

It doesn't take long for Conveyor Belt to take his place somewhere near the top of my all-time enemies list, along with such infamous names as Lang and Tavern. As I listen to his never-ending squeaking and growling, I'm almost positive I hear him saying, "More dirt, Mackerels...more dirt." For three solid hours, I shovel nonstop in an effort to keep the ravenous Conveyor Belt filled to Mr. Warfield's rigid specifications.

Up above, I can see occasional glimpses of Buddy's grinning face, as he leisurely guides the dirt off of Conveyor Belt and onto the truck. Behind me, I can hear the slow, gentle scratching of Stanley's pick, as he methodically evens up the walls.

The next morning, as I come awake, the fingers of both hands are all curled up like the talons of an eagle perched on a snag. My penmanship's never been too good at best, so it'll be great fun trying to finish that science report, writing with danged ol' eagle claws.

But two weeks of working after dinner, plus one solid weekend, brings us to D-Day, at last. The digging is finished, and we are ready to pour cement. Mr. Warfield and Stanley have constructed the wooden forms, while Buddy and I are in school.

Mr. Warfield has brought in a big ol' portable concrete mixer, and nearby he has big heaps of sand, and gravel, and an evil-looking pile of cement bags. There's a garden hose close by for our water supply. Wooden planks run here, there, and everywhere, for us to wheel the heavy wheelbarrow to the forms. The whole danged set up looks to me like it could even be more work than Conveyor Belt.

Two of us will mix the cement, while the third takes his turn at the wheelbarrow. Mr. Warfield gives us the recipe for making the concrete: "Use three shovels of gravel, two shovels of sand, and just one cement," he says, "and use enough water to keep the mix a little on the sloppy side. I don't want the concrete to set up too quickly...a large pour like this could develop some cracks if it gets too dry. And by the way...we'll be working long hours. We have to make it all in one pour."

Well, as we settle into the job, it becomes pretty clear that one mixerload of concrete is going to send the wheelbarrow operator on two trips across the wobbly planks. Mixing is a piece of cake, but the wheelbarrowing is a horse of a different color. It's nothing but hard work.

Tipping the heavy wheelbarrow up and getting the concrete to go into the forms without slopping over is the most difficult task. One of my early pours ended up mostly outside the forms. This got me a rather stern lecture from ol' Mr. Warfield.

Buddy and I have each had our two grueling turns at the wheelbarrow, and now it's finally Stanley's turn. After the little man staggers away with his first load, Buddy makes a startling statement.

"Didja know that Warfield is payin' ol' Stanley a dollar-and-a-half an hour...while we're only gettin' a buck?"

"Oh, yaaa, isss dat right?" I say, somewhat pleased with my Stanley imitation. But Buddy is not impressed; he doesn't seem to be in the mood for kidding around and all.

It doesn't seem fair," he says. "Stan the Man just picked, picked, picked away, while you...er...I mean we did all the hard work. In fact, he's been pretty lackadaisy, if you ask me."

I don't bother to point out Buddy's latest mispronunciation. As a man-of-the-world, he doesn't like being corrected all that much about stuff like that. Instead, I say, "Yeah, but there ain't much we can do about it now, though."

"Well...I don't know...hmmm...hey...you any good at fractions, Mackerels?"

"Uh...not too bad, I guess." The fact of the matter is: I've recently taken a refresher math course for some easy credits, and we've just covered fractions. Buddy isn't so much into higher academics such as that.

"Okay then, figure out how much more sand and gravel and cement it'll take to make a quick half-batch, and we'll get 'er all mixed up before Stan the Man gets back from the first load."

"How come?'

"Then, he'll have two more trips instead of just one. He'll be takin' three loads to our two, all night long. That'll give'm a chance to earn the extra half a buck he's makin'. You know what I'm sayin'?"

I can understand that, all right, so I get right to work on the math. Stanley gets back from delivering the cement, and we have a nice, fresh batch all ready for him.

The day drags on and on, but tricking Stanley with all the half-batches keeps us pretty well amused. We wonder if he is ever going to catch on. Finally, after about twelve hours of steady work and getting along towards dusk, Stanley registers his first complaint. He's dripping with sweat and looks a little wobbly on his pins.

"Yaaa, I yussst don't underssstand it, boysss," he says. "Why isss it dat I alwaysss have to wheel tree timesss, and you boysss only have to take two?"

"Gosh, you got me there, Stanley," Buddy says. "I'm not so good at math, myself, so I don't know how that works out."

"Oh...yaaa," Stanley says, as he wipes the sweat from his brow once again.

It seems as though the day will never get over, as we continue to slave away under the strict scrutiny of ol' Mr. Warfield. This job would be too boring for words if it wasn't for getting to watch Stanley's reactions to the half-batches. In fact, as I continue to toil away, my mind goes sort of blank, if you can imagine that at all. I'm on automatic pilot.

I think about how I don't really care that much for work. Then I think about poor ol' Mrs. Windbladd having to freeze to death in that drafty old store day after day and Mr. Windbladd and the boring ol' paper mill. And what about Dad and how he has to work at two jobs to make ends meet?

It doesn't seem as though Dad is having as much fun as he used to. He looks a little tired lately. I sure hope the dang ol' Cardinals will come through with a contract.

Well, it's six hours later, and we've finally finished the project. I'm really pooped, but I sort of wonder how ol' Stanley is holding up. I wish I'd kept track of all the extra trips he's taken.

Buddy and I each get fifty bucks for the job, which isn't a whole lot, considering all the hard work. But at least I'll have enough money for the new mitt and maybe enough left over for one of those neat turtleneck sweatshirts like all the major leaguers wear. Anything to keep Harry Popolinski interested for the Cardinals and all.

I'll probably stay away from the Sunny Cove area for awhile, though. I'd be a little afraid to look at the Warfield's basement, to tell you the honest truth. Some of our half-batches were sort of thrown together in a pretty big hurry. We were always sort of afraid that Stanley and his wheelbarrow might get back a little early and catch us tampering with the cement mix. Besides, I never told ol' Buddy that I wasn't all that confident about passing that danged fractions test.

> Mr. and Mrs. Claude Warfield of Sunny Cove recently added a new basement underneath their house. Mr. Warfield was aided by Mr. Stanley Thorsen, Mr. Buddy Pringle, and Mr. Willie Michaels. Mrs. Warfield is very happy to have the additional space to store all her preserves and canned goods. But Mr. Warfield is somewhat worried about the quality of the cement that went into the job. Being pretty-well cracked, he wonders if the basement will stand up.
> —Dora Dingley
> The Happy Valley Harbinger, May 1952

Chapter 23

Today is a big day in sixth period study hall—Buddy Pringle is going for the school record. He's put nineteen tacks on Miss Burnside's chair. I love sixth period. It not only signals the end of the school day but also gives us lots of opportunities for self-expression. Buddy Pringle likes it, too. He's really into expressing himself and such as that.

The study hall is under the supervision of the infamous Abigail Cecelia Burnside, or A C B, as we like to call her. She arrived at Happy Valley at the start of the school year, supposedly from a job she'd held at the mental institution in Sedro Woolley. We're all convinced, though, that she was an inmate rather than a teacher. That's if the real truth were known.

She has this wrinkled, prune face, topped off by a mass of spit curls piled high on the top of her head. It's hard to say which is crazier, her looks—or her personality. You cannot reason with her on any subject. The kids detest her raving, tyrannical ways, and she's become without a doubt the most unpopular teacher in the whole school.

Lately, we've been having lots of fun in study hall with the well-known thumbtack-on-the-seat trick. Buddy started the whole thing innocently enough with the placement of a single tack upon Abigail's chair. She didn't seem to feel it, but Buddy was up to the challenge. As a bonafide man-of-the-world, he doesn't like anyone to get the better of him. The next day found two tacks upon the teacher's chair. Again, she never even batted an eye, as she settled her more-than-ample bottom on Buddy's crude booby trap. Undaunted, though, Buddy came back the following day with *three* tacks. *Still* no rise.

So it's several days later, and Buddy is going for nineteen. All eyes are on A C B, as she settles on a bed of tacks fit for a Hindu fakir. We're all ready for the coming explosion, and it couldn't happen to a nicer teacher. But, what a disappointment. She wriggles in her seat a tiny bit but never flinches for even a second. She gets up a few moments later to sharpen a pencil, and, "Ping, ping, ping," go the tacks, as they drop harmlessly on the floor.

"Geez," Buddy whispers, "she must be wearin' a girdle four inches thick, for cryin' out loud."

For the moment, anyway, Abigail seems to have won the Great Thumbtack War, but Buddy doesn't give up easily. He has another trick up his sleeve. He's noticed, that unlike most instructors, who take roll with the use of a seating chart, A C B prefers the old-fashioned way. She calls the roll from a long, alphabetized list. I should have seen this coming. Just before Abigail had come into the room, I'd noticed Buddy slinking away from the teacher's desk with sort of a smirk on his face.

In her high, falsetto voice, Abigail begins to sing out the names. I wonder why Buddy seems so attentive, as A C B works her way through the list. Normally, he'd be using this time to be throwing spit wads across the room.

"...uh...Catherine Melheim?"

"Here."

"Joe Miller?"

"Present."

"Pete Moss?"

There is no response, except a few muffled giggles aimed in the direction of Buddy Pringle.

"Uh...Peter Moss? Hmmm...uh, William (I hate it when she calls me William), go to the office, please, and tell them there is no Pete Moss here." Well, after all the laughing and general uproar dies down, and I've left for the office, I guess Buddy scores once again when he tricks A C B into calling for, "Jean Poole."

Abigail teaches art, too, and always initials everything, including report cards, with a big, sprawling A C B. I always sign up for art class. It's an easy credit and all, and besides, I like drawing, and painting, and all that kind of stuff. I guess I've always been sort of artsy-fartsy. But the bad thing is, my folks expect me to bring home good grades in art. They think I'm sort of like the second coming of Picasso or Leonardo Da Vinci, or one of those other French Impressionists. They might turn the other cheek at my geometry or physics grades, but they expect an A in art. One day, Mom was wondering how it was I could do so well in art and so lousy in all the other subjects.

"Maybe he's one of those idiot savants," Dad said. I think he was just kidding, but he might have been about half-right, at that.

Well, this past quarter, I've been goofing off in class a little too much. I've got to admit it. Therefore, I'm afraid the art grade isn't going to be all that hot. The report cards are coming out tomorrow.

It hasn't all been my fault, though, if you were to know the whole truth. You get a lot of guys in art class that don't have any Picasso or Leonardo Da Vinci abilities at all. In fact, they don't have the least bit of art ability whatsoever. I mean, a stick figure would be a real big achievement for these guys. They're just in there, because they think art's an easier grade than most other electives. It didn't help, either, that Buddy Pringle and Vernon Windbladd decided to take art this quarter. I mean, who could work with those two idiots around?

Well anyway, I'm pretty worried about my art grade and all, and the suspense is dang near killing me. I guess Buddy can tell that something is wrong. "Whattsa matter, pal?' he says. Well, I decide to tell him about the art grade and my folks and all.

"No problem, chum." he says. Ask ol' Abby for permission to go to the art room to work on some extra credit. Hah, hah...then ask if I can go, too...um...let's see...uh, to be a model for ya or sompin'. Tell her ya need a quiet place so you can concentrate." When I look a little hesitant about the whole thing, he says, "Come on...*do* it...it's yer only chance."

Well, much to my surprise, Abby gives Buddy and me permission to go to the art room. Immediately, I hear a stage-whisper coming from the back of the room—it might be goofy ol' Vernon Windbladd. Why wouldja wanna draw anybody that ugly, Mackerels? Har, har, har."

As soon as we're safely in the art room, Buddy says, "Stay by the door, Mackerels and keep a sharp lookout...just in case Abby decides to come over here for some stupid reason or another." Then, he goes right to Abby's desk and starts rummaging through the top drawer. What's he doing? I wonder.

"Don't go drawin' me in action, just yet, Mackerels. It could be used as incriminatin' evidence...hah, hah, hah. Aha! Here's what I'm lookin' for, the good ol' report cards." Buddy proudly holds them up for me to see.

"Um...uh...What'd I get?" I ask.

"Hmm...let's see, now...Kellen, uh...Kilmer...Langworthy...aha, here it is, Michaels, William, P. What the heck's the P for, Mackerels...Pin head—or Pussy? Ho, ho, ho. Ah...it says here you got a C-. What the heck...that's passin' ain't it?"

My stomach sort of rises up into my throat, if you want to know the awful truth. I'm sort of panic-stricken. "Dang!" I say, "My folks will kill me over a stupid C- in art."

But now, Buddy holds up another, smaller pile of cards. "Here's the answer, then, amigo."

To tell you the eerie truth, having Buddy call me "pal," "chum," and "amigo," all in the same day is making me a little nervous. I'm more used to "retard," "dimbulb," and "air-head."

"Whattaya got, there?" I ask, as I take a nervous glance in the direction of the study hall.

"Blanks."

"What good'll they be?"

"*Retard,* do I hafta splain everything to ya? We'll just forge a new grade on one of these here blanks and stick it in with the real grades. Crazy Abby'll never know the difference. What grade do ya want?"

"Um...well, uh, I guess a B+'d probably do the trick."

"That's the trouble with you, dimbulb. You're always settin' your sights too low. Go for the gusto, for Pete's sake. We'll give ya an A. With that said, Buddy begins the task of forging the grade. I can tell he's putting forth his very best effort, as sweat forms on his brow, and his tongue is tightly clenched between his teeth. Good ol' Buddy. I leave my post at the door and step over to the desk to check on his progress.

"*Air-head,* get back over there and keep watch. I don't want Abby to come bouncin' in here and catch me red-handed."

Seconds later, Buddy is all through, and he brings the new report card over to the door. "Whattaya think?" he asks, as he holds it up for my inspection. It looks perfect to me. It'd take the head of the F.B.I., ol' Herbert Hoover, himself, to tell the sprawling A C B signature at the bottom was nothing but a fake.

Well, Buddy slips the bogus report card in with the real ones, and it looks like he's saved the day. I guess I owe him a debt of gratitude—it'd be shame to get Mom and Dad all worked up over a silly art grade and all. But if guys like him and goofy Vernon Windbladd would just take typing, or woodshop, or any elective except art, I wouldn't have to go through all this hassle in the first place.

TRUTH TALKS STALL—Boys not coming home soon
P-I News Services
Tokyo, Japan

Truce talks to end the Korean War have become firmly deadlocked once again. According to P.I. sources, voluntary repatriation remains as the main bone of contention. Fighting continues along the battle line.

Chapter 24

We got thumped in our game over at Scandia. I just hate losing to them; they're such an arrogant bunch. Teddy Snodgrass is the worst. He really is.

"Where'd you sodbusters get the chintzy uniforms?" was the first thing he asked, as we got off the bus. When I didn't answer, he said, "Kind of a waste of money, ain't they? Haven't helped ya win any games I know of...hah, hah, hah. Might just as well as saved yer money and stuck with those old crummy football jerseys...ho, ho, ho."

What a twink! I would've liked to have struck him out about four times, but I didn't get to pitch. It'd only been two days since I'd taken the mound in a three to two loss against Port Townsend, and my arm was still a little stiff. We had the Town game in the bag, too—until Roderick Remblinger came to their rescue.

We were ahead two to one going into the last of the seventh. Two outs later, the Fighting Redskins threatened with an infield hit, a walk, and a double-steal. This put runners on second and third. But the next hitter lofted a routine fly to right field for what should have been the final out. Balls hit to our right fielder, however, can become an adventure—that's where Roderick plays.

At least ol' Roderick judged the ball correctly for a change, as he settled under the fly, apparently ready to make the catch. But the ball tore through his outstretched hands as though it'd just visited from outer space. It hit him right between the eyes and ricocheted twenty feet or more towards center field. But by the time Gordy Belmont could get to the ball, the winning run had crossed the plate for Townsend. Coach

Monahan is sitting Roderick out for this game. "I don't think the school is covered by workman's comp, Roderick," I heard him say.

"Least he was tryin' to use his head, Coach," Buddy chips in.

Since Coach was giving me a rest on the mound, that meant we got to see Richie Schmutz and his 200 mile-an-hour fastball again. And of course, that meant yours truly was behind the plate. Richie was a lot better than the last time he pitched, though. I'll have to admit it. He can be pretty danged awesome when he gets the ball over the plate and all. Before the inning starts, I like to have him throw one or two warm up pitches up against the backstop. This gets the hitters' attention and sort of plants the seed that Richie can be a little wild with the ol' hummer. Then, when he comes in with a little chin music, it's sort of fun to watch their knees turn to jelly.

I tried having a little fun with Teddy Snodgrass by giving the target right up alongside his head. But Richie couldn't seem to hit my mitt, or else he just wasn't paying attention. He walked Teddy on four straight pitches—all low and away. Richie cut way down on his walks and hit-batters, though, and we only lost nine to one.

I spotted Trudy Trammell up in the stands, and she's still looking pretty darned good. I can tell you that much right now. Before the game, I'd talked briefly with my old friend, little Elmer Finley, and he mentioned that Trudy and Teddy might have broken up. That was sure good news if it was true. Anyway, I couldn't help but glance up in her direction from time to time. I didn't want to be too obvious, or anything like that, but it was sort of hard to resist an occasional peek.

The weather was sort of mild—not too hot and not too cold—and Trudy was wearing this real tight sweater. She looked to be in awfully good form, too, if you know what I mean. It was a real pretty blue sweater. It was almost enough to make a guy want to go back to good ol' Scandia, even if he would be sitting on the darned ol' bench.

Since I couldn't pitch, I wish I could've socked a homer or two for Trudy's benefit. But instead, I went hitless for about the umpteenth game in a row. After those first three games, I've gone into a slump. I just can't seem to get used to those danged glasses.

Today, a bunch of us jocks are sitting in the school cafeteria eating our lunch, when the new sophomore girl sits at a table across from us. It's the same table where Rosie Higgenbottom and all her crew are sitting. I'm kind of glad to see she isn't actually with them, though. I haven't thought of her as being that kind of a girl, if you know what I mean.

The new girl's name is Brenda, I've found out. She's not as well put together as Trudy Trammell, mind you, but she's got those same wholesome girl-next-door type of looks. Her hair is sort of honey-colored, and she's got a few freckles—not too many—but enough to remind you a little bit of Trudy. Brenda might just possibly be a good prospect for the Senior Ball that's coming up pretty soon. If you want the awful truth, things have been looking a little grim in the ol' social engagement department.

I sort of quarter my nose to starboard a little and give her one of my very best tight-lipped smiles; I'm not too sure as to what degree of greenness my teeth have reached today.

But my hair is sure in better shape than usual. I can tell you that much for a fact. I have it all slicked down with some new kind of hair lotion I found in the Rexall Drugs in Town. It contains this new stuff called lanolin and really seems to be doing the job. In fact, if you want to know the truth of it all, right now my hair is probably the most Errol Flynnish it's ever been.

"Whattaya got for lunch, Mackerels?" Vernon Windbladd rudely breaks into my thoughts about my looks and the new girl and all. Vernon is all the time wanting to trade desserts with me. Of course, that's a danged good deal, as far as I'm concerned. Mrs. Windbladd makes the most delicious cakes and banana breads that you'd ever want to taste. She really does.

All I ever get in *my* lunch is some morsel from the tavern, like a sack of peanuts, or a Hershey bar, or some danged thing. Today is peanut day. Vernon especially likes peanuts, so the trade is made: two five-cent sacks of Planter's Peanuts for the biggest, most scrumptious piece of chocolate cake you'd ever want to see. It's three-layered and even has walnuts scattered on top of the thick, rich frosting.

I steal another glance at the new girl and am sort of surprised that she's already looking my way. She has a real nice smile on her face, too. I give her another of my tight-lipped specials and go back to finishing my tuna fish sandwich.

When I sneak another look, she's still smiling at me. Well actually, it's more of a grin, if you want to know the truth. But good ol' Rosie Higgenbottom is grinning at me too—and so are the other two vestal virgins, Helen Morley and Naomi Panks. In fact, that whole danged table of girls is staring and grinning to beat the band. Some appear right on the verge of laughing out loud, for Pete's sake. As she chortles away, I am particularly fascinated by the ray of light that comes through the cafeteria window and reflects off of Naomi Panks' silver fang.

"Hey, Mackerels, what kinda gunk you got on yer head, anyway?" Buddy Pringle says.

"Aw, I forget the name of it...but it's got some new kind of stuff called lanolin."

"Ha, ha...lanolin?" says the know-it-all man-of-the-world. "That's the stuff they get outta sheep. Hah, hah, hah...no wonder all them flies are buzzin' round yer noggin. They prolly think you're a sheep's butt."

Dang! Buddy's right! I'll bet every fly in the entire cafeteria is swarming around my head. You'd think I was a stupid ol' manure pile or something. By this time, of course, Rottenbottom and her raunchy crew are practically in hysterics. The new girl is laughing too, but not maliciously, like the others, if you know what I mean.

A few days later, I am over my embarrassment about the flies and all and muster up the courage to ask the new girl to the Senior Ball. I haven't heard of anyone else that's asked her.

"I don't dance," she says.

"Well, I've got to admit," I say, "that I'm not the world's greatest dancer, either."

"No," she says, "I mean I don't dance, *period*. It's against my family's religion."

"Oh...well...er...um...maybe we could go to a movie sometime, then," I say hopefully.

"Sorry. Our religion doesn't permit movies, either."

Well, so much for the girl-next-door. I don't suppose her religion will allow some of the other things I had in mind, either. And so much for the Senior Ball, too. I guess I'll be spending the evening up in my room, dancing the Rhumba Boogie with Wurlitzer and good ol' Hank Snow.

May 3—52

Dear Auntie,

It is a sad day for me—some guys from my old platoon were hit while on a daylight patrol. Seems as though their lieutenant got them lost, and they missed their checkpoints. They were like sitting ducks and got hit by incoming Chinese mortar and small arms fire. One of my old buddies got hit in the groin by shrapnel—I think he's going to lose his private parts.

Some of the guys have been coming down with bad cases of nerves lately and are becoming sort of useless—can't really blame them though. That's all for now—hope this letter hasn't been too depressing. Keep me in your prayers.

With love,
Harvey

Chapter 25

Today is Saturday, and Vernon Windbladd and I are playing a little catch out on in the alley that separates Tavern from the old, deserted hotel. There'll be no ballplaying tomorrow. Being Sunday and all, I have to sweep and mop Tavern's floors, get rid of all the empties, and restock the walk-in box. That pretty well shoots the whole day, if you want the sad truth of it all. Dad's been on me pretty good, lately. Working at two jobs seems to be getting the better of good ol' Dad, and he's been a little cross. I told Vernon that if he'd help me a little, we'd have time for some ball during the afternoon. He wasn't interested. I'll just have to get all my throwing in today.

I've only had my new mitt for a week, and it still isn't quite broken in the way I want . It's great to have it, though. A guy looks a lot more like a real ballplayer if he's got a neat-looking mitt. The turtleneck sweatshirt helps out in the looks department, too. I just wish my uniform had something other than TAVERN on the back. It makes me look sort of bush league, to tell you the honest truth. The other day, Roderick Remblinger (who obviously can't read) asked me what my folks did for a living.

Roderick talks real funny, possibly due to his Neanderthal heritage, and Buddy can never understand a word he says. I figure since Buddy doesn't use very good English himself, he probably doesn't have much of a comparison base. But after I interpreted for him, Buddy gave Roderick his answer. "They run a T. A. Vern franchise," he said.

"Huh...dadamn—wha kina sumanabit zazat?" Roderick asked, "sumah nuuu chaing owfih or sumin'?" Roderick's voice has a really strange quality to it. It isn't actually what you'd call nasal. Instead, it's as though it's come from deep within the bowels of a dark, dank cave, one with crude drawings of woolly mammoths upon the walls.

"What'd he say?" Buddy asked.

"God damn—what kind of a sonofabitch is that—some new chain outfit or something?" I interpreted.

"Yeah, T.A. Vern is somepin' like that," Buddy said to Roderick, as he turned away to hide the big ol' smirk he had plastered across his face.

Well, getting back to Vernon and me. I'm just getting warmed up pretty good and getting ready to break off a few curves, and Spud Wilcox comes ambling along. He's headed for the tavern, no doubt—he's the town drunk. It's mid-day, and he isn't staggering or anything yet, but by late-afternoon, he'll be stiffer than a plank. You can bet your farm on that bit of information. Dad has eighty-sixed him out of the tavern several times for mooching drinks but hasn't kicked him out for good, just yet. Dark port is his drink of choice, but Dad says Spud will drink anything loose at one end, if someone else is buying.

For some unknown reason, Spud is looking particularly ratty today. Of course, that's just my humble opinion. He hasn't shaved for several days, and his clothes are a mess. It looks like he's wearing last night's dinner on his old, faded, blue work shirt. There's stains on the crotch of his worn, pinstriped suit pants, too, but it's hard to tell if he's spilled wine there or peed himself instead.

"How's it goin', boys?" Spud says. He's always seems friendly enough, as far as I'm concerned, anyway. I've never seen him belligerent, or anything like that.

"Not too bad, Spud," I say.

"I used to play a little ball," he says. "It was a long time back, though."

"Oh," was about all I could think to say.

Vernon looks like he's about to come up with something smart-assed; he doesn't always have the proper respect for his elders and all. Sometimes, you can't trust Vernon any farther than you could throw him by the tail. You have to watch him like a hawk to keep from being embarrassed and all. I shoot him a real evil look and make little pinching gestures with my thumb and forefinger. At the sight of that, his little fat cheeks light up like a glow worm's, and he dummies up real quick.

"Yep...used to do a little pitching," Spud says. "For the Dodgers."

I find that pretty hard to believe, if you want to know the truth of the matter. Spud is only about five foot two and probably weighs no more than 130, wringing wet. He's wearing a beat-up, old Brooklyn Dodger hat, but I don't imagine he ever got it playing for the Bums. He must've bought it at a rummage sale somewhere. "You pitched for the Brooklyn Dodgers?" I say.

"Nope," Spud says. "The Happy Valley Draft Dodgers—hah, hah, hah."

"Wyncha give'm the ball, Vernon. Let's see what kinda stuff ol' Spud has goin' for him." I suspect Spud'll have more stuff between his toes than he'll have on the ball, but anyway, we'll soon find out. I get down in a catcher's crouch and put up my new mitt for a target.

"My arm's probably not in too good of condition," Spud says.

I can understand that all right. After all, the rest of him's in pretty lousy shape.

"There might not be too many pitches left in the ol' rag, so I'll start right out with my money pitch," he says, "the knuckleball."

Whoa, I think, this oughtta be good. I dang near burst out laughing at the thought of Spud being able to throw a knuckler and all. About the only thing he can throw, I figure, is a fit of some sort. Vernon must be somewhat amused, too, as once again, he's got that big, silly grin plastered across his pie hole.

Well, Spud takes the ball from Vernon and immediately goes into sort of an old-fashioned windup, one with the double-pump of the arms and all. Then after a little hesitation, he lets loose with kind of a stiff-looking sidearm throw. The ball comes in so slowly, I don't think it'll ever arrive. I can probably eat a sandwich in the time it takes to get to the target. But in it comes—swooping, swishing, darting, and dipping. You can count every single stitch on the ol' seams, right up until it takes one, last, savage plunge and digs right into the tender flesh of my inner forearm.

"Shinola!" I holler. I've never before been hit by a pitch that hurt so much. I guess it must be because a knuckler has practically no spin to it. It's a real, heavy, dead pitch. As I spend a second or two rubbing my forearm, Vernon's doubling up and laughing his fool head off.

"Let's see that one again," I holler to Spud."

I figure the pitch has to be a fluke, but Spud comes right back with one that flutters even more, if that's at all possible. This one nails me on the outer part of the forearm and hurts even worse than the first one. Spud throws two or three more of the lively dancers and then hands the ball back to Vernon.

"That's all, boys...I don't want to get a sore elbow." I can understand that, all right. As he heads off for the tavern, I can see that he has more important things planned for his elbow.

"Hey, Spud," I holler, "first show me how you throw that thing...okay?" Well, Spud tells me as how the knuckler isn't actually thrown with the knuckles at all.

"It's a misnomer," he says.

"Oh," I say. I don't understand that—but I guess it doesn't matter all that much. Spud goes on to show me how you grip the ball on the seam with your fingernails and then flick the fingers as you release the pitch.

"It ought to be called a fingernail ball," he says.

As Spud heads off to the tavern, I try throwing a few knucklers to Vernon but don't have too much luck. Very few do what they're supposed to. It might be because my fingernails need filing or something. Anyway, I make up my mind to keep working on the flutter ball—I'll tell you that much for sure. I need a new pitch to give me something to go along with the fastball and the curve. My change-of-pace doesn't seem to be fooling anyone; the batters can't seem to tell the difference from it and my hummer.

BEEP, BEEP. I look up just in time to see Buddy's dad's pickup go flashing by. All the road dust it raises, however, make it tough to tell who is driving. It seems as though if it were Buddy, he would have stopped. But as the dust settles, I can see Buddy's white hair through the back window. But something's wrong.

"Dang!" I say to Vernon. "I must be havin' a sunstroke. I could swear ol' Buddy's got two heads."

"Hah—he's got a girl friend is what he's got. She sits so danged close, it just looks like he's got two heads."

"Who the heck is it?" I ask.

"Goofy ol' Rottenbottom."

May 10—52

Dear Auntie,

Well, the weather here is finally warm enough to play a little catch. Another guy in our platoon was a catcher in the Yankee farm system. It's a good thing—not too many of the other guys can hold my hummer. The ex-Yankee likes my stuff—says the ol' fastball is really hopping. Like me, he can hardly wait for this "police action" to get over so he can resume his career. A ballplayer only has so many years in which to make it. I guess the ol' Cardinals will just have to struggle another year without me (ha—ha). The war is sort of at a standstill, but that doesn't mean there's no fighting. But it's sort of small unit stuff. We fight by night, since the artillery on both sides is too deadly. Well, I think I'll catch a little nap.

Your loving nephew,
Harvey

Chapter 26

Today is Wednesday, and it looks like it's going to be a real nice day. We're up three to two in the top of the seventh and have two outs on the Fighting Roughriders from Port Angeles. It looks like maybe we'll be able to eke out our first win of the season in this rematch here at our rock pile. They have a runner on first, though, because of a bad-hop ground ball that got by Vernon Windbladd out at short. He was a victim of our own rocky infield. Their cleanup hitter has worked me to a full count, but I have him all set up and right where I want him. I've been getting him out with the curve, all day long.

Then, ol' Richie Schmutz has to go and mess me up. Richie, you see, has never learned to hide the signals from the batter. A catcher is supposed to give them up in his crotch and shield them from the batter with his catcher's mitt. But not Richie. Instead, he likes to put his fingers right down there on the ground. Then, everyone in the whole danged ball park can see the signs before I do, what with me and my bad eyes and all.

So, for the most crucial pitch of the whole game, there's Richie's two big fingers down there in the dirt signaling for the curve. And of course, the Angeles batter is standing right there eyeballing the sign for all he's worth. You can bet it takes all the guessing out of it for him. He's sure the ol' yellow hammer is on its way.

Well, I just figure I'll cross the hitter up and sneak a fastball right on by him. It turns out, though, I'd have a better chance of sneaking a sunrise past a rooster. I don't get much zip on the ball, and the batter sneaks it on over the fence, instead. We don't get any runs in our half of the inning, so it's Dear John: that's all she wrote. We lose four to three—thanks to Richie Schmutz and his big ol' fingers.

After the game, I'm just standing over behind the dugout trying to sort my thoughts, and Harry Popolinski comes up to me. I'm sort of glad to see the old fellow, if you want to know the truth. I guess that even though we lost the game, the Cardinals must still have some interest in me.

The game has evidently excited Mr. Popolinski a little, as his tongue is flicking a mile-a-minute.

"That was a tough one to lose, there, Mr. Michaels." *Flick, flick,* the tongue shoots in and out. "You had the curve, there, *flick,* going pretty good, there, *flick, flick.* But keep working, there, on that *flick* fastball, there." *Flick, flick, flick.* With that said, he scurries off in the direction of the Port Angeles bus. I guess he wants to talk to the Fighting Roughriders' cleanup hitter, "there."

Dad finds me next. He left the print shop a little early today, in order to watch me play. He hasn't had a chance to see many of our games.

"Tough one to lose, Mackerels." He pats me on the back. "I thought you pitched pretty well, though...but how come you didn't throw that big kid another curve?"

I explain to him about Richie Schmutz and the fingers in the dirt and all, but Dad just shakes his head. He obviously doesn't agree.

"You shoulda stayed with your best pitch," he says. "I don't think that kid coulda hit a curve ball with an ironing board, even if he did know it was coming. By the way, what was Harry Popolinski talking to you about? You know...the old guy with the tongue problem."

I explain to Dad about how Mr. Popolinski is a scout for St. Louis and all. I figure Dad will be real proud to think that the Cardinals are after his only son.

"A scout for the Cardinals? Hah, hah. I'd be surprised if old Harry was even a Boy Scout. I doubt if he knows a baseball from an over-ripe cantaloupe. I wouldn't get too excited about anything he says, Mackerels."

I guess Dad isn't all that impressed by Mr. Popolinski's credentials and all. But just in case, I'll keep working on the ol' fastball, anyway. It'd sure be nice to sign up with the Cardinals.

CLARK REPLACES RIDGWAY
    By Jillian Botnen
    The Associated Press
    Tokyo, Japan

    General Mark W. Clark has replaced General Matthew B. Ridgway as Commander in Chief of the United Nations Command in

Korea. General Clark, a 1917 graduate of the U.S. Military Academy at West Point, commanded Allied forces (1943-44) during the hard-fought and successful Italian campaign. Also, as commander of the 15th Army Group, Clark received the surrender of stubborn German forces in the north of Italy on May 2, 1945.

Chapter 27

Friday is the first showing of the spring school play. Miss Burnside is in charge. Earlier, she tries to get me to try out, but I pretty much gave up on acting as a career back when I discovered I had this slightly-bigger nose, and these slightly-greener teeth, and this slightly-wilder hair and all. Besides, studying for a part in the play would take too much time away from the development of my knuckle ball.

However, A C B does manage to talk me into being part of the stage crew; she needs my artistic abilities for drawing and painting the back drops. It only takes a little of my time in the evenings, and besides, it gets me out of both study hall and art class. I'm supposed to get some extra credit for my art grade, too, and I figure it might also be a good thing if I got away from troublemakers like Buddy Pringle and Vernon Windbladd for awhile.

But wouldn't you know it? Abigail goes and recruits Buddy, too. She needs his man-of-the-world talents to help build the props and all. Buddy is real handy with tools. I have to admit it. About that time, of course, good ol' Vernon Windbladd has to go and volunteer. He figures both art and study hall will be too boring without me and Buddy. Miss Burnside makes him the head janitor. He's in charge of sweeping and picking up litter and such as that. Seeing ol' Vernon actually doing some work is a real novelty, I might add.

Today is the final rehearsal. The props and backdrops are pretty much all taken care of, but A C B wants me and Buddy to show up, anyway. We don't mind; it'll be more fun than either study hall or art class. She puts us on Vernon's crew to help with the sweeping and the like. Of course, Vernon has to go and clown around and make a big deal out of being our boss and all. Buddy and I go along with it, though, just for laughs.

Another member of Vernon's crew is a huge girl by the name of Patty Maloney. Most guys refer to her as "Fatty Patty"—but not to her face, of course. Patty is about six feet tall, probably weighs in the neighborhood of two-fifty, and has a voice like an unmuffled Jake Brake. She can be pretty danged mean, too, if you want the awful truth. She'd tried out for the female lead in the play, but Miss Burnside managed to convince her that she'd probably be miscast in the role of Sleeping Beauty. Abigail surprised us all with the tact she showed there.

Instead, the lead role is going to be played by Rosie Higgenbottom. I can tell now why it was that Buddy was so eager to be the handyman. And I guess even ol' Abby can see that Rosie's the only girl in the whole danged school that comes anywhere close to resembling a beauty—except, of course, Brenda, the cute sophomore girl. But I don't suppose her religion would allow her to be in any ol' play.

Well anyway, all of us in Vernon's crew are just loitering around behind the scenes, just leaning on our push brooms and trying to stay out of trouble. I've done some pretty danged good set design, too, even if I do say so, myself. You ought to see Sleeping Beauty's castle; it's a real work of art. A C B even says so, and I can just see the extra credit rolling right on in to help beef up the ol' art grade a little. I don't want to undo any of that by joining into any monkey business with Buddy and Vernon. Believe you me, I am going to keep my slightly-bigger nose real clean.

It's about fifteen more minutes before school is out for the day, and Fatty Patty bends over to sweep some stuff into her dust pan. Of course, she would happen to be right in front of me, and her big ol' behind looks to be about as wide as two ax handles and a plug of Star. That old jingle starts going through my mind—you know—the one that goes: I see London, I see France, I see Patty's underpants. And to be absolutely honest, I can't say which of those geographic locations has the greatest area. I can't help but chuckle a little. I look across to Buddy and Vernon and make this little fake gesture like I'm going to whack Patty in the butt with my broom.

Of course, they immediately start grinning and nodding their heads and all, but I shake my head, "No." They must think I'm some sort of fool. But then Buddy puts his hands up under his armpits and starts flapping his wings like a chicken. Of course, Vernon has to go and join right in. Patty doesn't see them, as she is still busy with the dustpan.

Well, I don't know what comes over me, but the next thing you know, I rear back with the broom and give it a swing Babe Ruth'd been proud of. WHAAACCCKKK!!!

"OUUCHHH!!! SONOFABITCH!" Patty turns around and sees me standing there with the broom. I don't like what I see in her eyes, to tell you the awful truth. Hell hath no fury like a fat girl smacked on the butt with a broom. It's time to pull a Hank Snow—and get to Movin' on!

I drop the broom and head for the back door of the stage. And don't think I'm not going as fast as my ol' legs can carry me. Patty's in hot pursuit. I can hear her heavy footsteps pounding along behind me. I try to slam the door in her face, but that ploy doesn't work. Patty dang near tears the thing right off its hinges. Over my shoulder, I can hear Buddy and Vernon lending their support. "Get im, Patty...don't let the dirty fig plucker get away!"

On the dead run, I head for the main building. I figure I'll just go around and around it, until Patty gets tired. It should be no problem at all to outrun a big moose like her. But I guess the flow of all that adrenaline has sapped some of my stamina. Patty is gaining! I go for one more lap around the building, but my legs have turned to lead. And to top things off, my lungs feel like someone's set them on fire.

I can practically feel Patty's hot breath on the back of my neck. Now I know how King Arthur and all those guys must have felt when they were being chased by those fire-breathing dragons.

Then, up ahead, I spot the partially-open window in Mr. Dunlap's science room. It looks like a tight fit, but I have no other choice. Besides, if it's going to be a squeeze for me to get through, then it'll be danged near impossible for Patty.

I launch myself into a perfect dive and sail through the opening as pretty as you please. I hit the science room floor with a beautiful head-first slide right on up to the front of the room where Mr. Dunlap is lecturing. I hear gasps of surprise from the class, but Mr. Dunlap never misses a beat. He crouches right down on one knee like a baseball umpire and thrusts both arms straight out to the side. "Safe! he hollers. You have to hand it to Mr. Dunlap. He has a sense of humor. I'll have to admit it.

I take a glance back over my shoulder, and there is Patty's big, red, ugly face plastered right up against the science room window. The snot from her nose is running down the glass in grotesque rivulets. You should see her. She's a terrible sight. Well, I am up and out the door faster than you can say, "Rhumba Boogie." I kid you not. I head on down the hall and hide in the boiler room, until well after the final bell; I know Patty will have to catch the school bus on out to Mountainview, where she lives.

I make up my mind right here and now to quit hanging around Buddy Pringle and Vernon Windbladd. Those two are always getting me in trouble.

Last week, the Happy Valley High School thespians, under the able direction of Miss Abigail Burnside, put on their version of Sleeping Beauty. Miss Burnside was very pleased with the way that the drama went, even though some foolishness by non-actors prior to the play threatened to ruin the set. Built along sturdy lines, Miss Burnside was relieved when the backdrop was able to survive the horseplay.

—Dora Dingley
The Happy Valley Harbinger, May 1952

Chapter 28

Buddy Pringle drops by after dinner to tell me what Miss Burnside had to say about the rumpus. It seems she blames me for the whole danged thing, so she's decided not to give me the extra credit, after all. I guess the play went pretty well, though, except for one slight goof by Gordy Belmont. He was playing the role of Prince Charming.

In the final scene, when Gordy comes on stage and sees ol' Sleeping Beauty asleep there on the bed, he's supposed to say, "Aha! Methinks I will snatch a kiss." But when ol' Gordy saw Rosie Higgenbottom lying there all seductive-like, he choked up and muffed his lines. "Aha!" he said, "Methinks I will kiss a snatch."

"Ya oughtta heard all the laughin', Mackerels," Buddy said. "Things went pretty good after that, though—but, hey—the kids in the play are gonna have a beach party, Saturday night...to celebrate the end of the play and all. They want all us maintenance guys there, too."

"What're they gonna do there?"

"Aw...you know, have a beach fire...and roast some wieners, and...uh...prolly drink a little beer."

"Drink beer?" I say. I'm not so sure about drinking any beer, what with me being an athlete and all. Besides, I've tried it a few times, and if the truth were known, I'd have to take Pepsi any day. "Weeell...I dunno," I say.

"Aw, come on, Mackerels. It'll be a lot of fun. Besides, there'll be lots of girls there."

"Patty Maloney won't be there, will she?"

"Naw...ha, ha, ha...nobody'd ever invite her. Cripes, if she ever had a bottle of beer, she'd prolly go nuclear on us."

"We hafta bring anything?"

"Naw. They furnish all the stuff...'cept the beer."

"Well, I really don't want no beer, anyway," I say. I know that alcohol is supposed to destroy the ol' brain cells and all, so I've always figured a guy like me ought to be real careful with alcohol and such as that.

"Hey...ya gotta have a couple, or you'll look like a real twink."

"Where we gonna get any beer, anyway?"

"Geez, Mackerels, your folks own a tavern, don't they?"

"Sure...and I'm gonna go ask 'em for some beer. Ha, ha. That's so funny, I'm almost laughing."

"Hey, they're always havin' ya bring beer in from the shed and puttin' the empties away, ain't they? Geez...use your imagination a little. Do I hafta splain everything to ya? While you're workin', just casually put a full case of Rainier out in the bushes behind your shed. No one'll know the difference."

I guess I can understand that, all right. It's amazing, though, how Buddy always has an answer for practically any problem that might come along. I imagine, though, that you'd expect that from a man-of-the-world and all.

Sure enough, later that evening Dad asks me to take some cases of empties out to the shed and then bring in more beer to restock the walk-in box. On each trip, I think about nabbing the case we need for the party, but I'm having trouble working up enough nerve. What if Dad comes out to check on me and catches me in the act? Man-o-man, I'd be busted forever. Besides, there's a full moon tonight. That will make it all the easier to be spotted, I'm afraid. Speaking of that, I learned something the other day about how to use the moon to prognosticate the weather. It was Buddy that told me. "My old man says that if there's a full moon, the weather's either gonna change or stay the same."

I had to think about it for awhile, but finally the wisdom of that old adage sunk in. Buddy must have inherited his man-of-the-worldliness from his father's side.

But moon or no moon, I finally I make the move. As I whisk around the corner of the shed with the case of Rainier, my knees have got a bad case of the shakes. I feel sort of like a crook, if you want to know the whole sad truth. Not only am I stealing, but I'm stealing from my own parents, the people who brought me into the world and all. It's pitch-black outside, but I find a spot for the loot beneath some bushes under an old maple tree, about fifty feet or so behind the shed. Just as I come back around the corner of the shed, Dad steps out of Tavern's back door.

"How's it going, Mackerels?"

"Uh...gulp...just fine, Dad...almost done." My poor heart is going about 500 beats a minute and is stuck right up there in my throat next to my Adam's apple. It hasn't had a workout like that, since the Patty Maloney crisis.

The weather turns kind of warm on Saturday afternoon, and the folks and Tavern are doing what you'd call a landslide business, at least for a place like Hapless Valley. Buddy drops on by to see if I've managed to grab the case of beer.

"How'dja do, Pal?"

"No problemo," I say in my best Spanish.

"Where'dja hide it?"

"Come on...I'll show ya."

I peek into the tavern, first, to make sure the folks are still busy and all. I figure a guy can't be too careful on a caper like this.

"Hee, hee, hee."

"RRrrriiinnnggg."

"Big eight-wheeler movin' dowwwn the track..."

"Fire one."

"Fire two."

Everything seems in order, so I lead Buddy back to the old maple tree. We have to negotiate a few blackberry vines, but finally we make it into the clearing.

"It's right over there," I say, pointing to the base of the old maple.

Buddy reaches the tree first. "Where?" he asks.

That's just like good ol' Buddy—always kidding around. I just laugh.

"*Meathead*, where at *is* it?" Buddy has this real serious look on his face, like maybe he's not kidding after all. I get this sinking feeling in the pit of my stomach. If Buddy is acting, then he ought to have had the lead in the school play, instead of just being a handyman. But when I look, it's just as I'd feared—the beer is *gone*.

"Dang! It was right here!" I say.

"Sure ya got the right tree? It was prolly dark, wasn't it?"

I don't get into the subject of the full moon and all. I look around, but this is the only maple of any size in the area. It has to be the one.

"Who'd go and swipe beer, like that?" I say. "You can't trust anybody these days."

After that, we just sort of wander around the town. Buddy wonders if I'll be able to get any more beer, but I know the chances are slim to none. I doubt if I'll have any more access to the shed in the near future; I pretty well stocked things to the gunnels the night before.

We walk up in the direction of the school but then change our minds and cut across a back alley and head towards the tavern. We are licked, and we know it. Buddy is really bummed-out about the beer and all.

Then we hear the singing. It's coming from an old abandoned garage, two doors from Vernon Windbladd's place. The singing's pretty horrible, if you want to know the honest truth.

"Gimme that old time religion...gimme that oohhhlld time religion..."

Buddy and I sneak up to the garage and peek in. The door on the decrepit old building has been gone for as long as I've been in town.

"Aha! There...za ol' basheball player. Howza knuckle ball doin' that I showed ya? Hah, hah. Betcher shtandin' all 'em those batters right on their earsh...hah, hah, hah."

Well, there's ol' Spud Wilcox sitting on the floor of the garage with his feet straight out and his back up against the rear wall of the old garage. A bottle of beer is in his hand. An opened case of Rainier and a dozen or more empty, brown bottles are on the floor beside him.

"Hic...I don't like beer too much," Spud says, "but since—*sinch*—I was lucky enough to find this case—*cayshe*—o' mountain fresh Rainier, I thought I better drink 'er up...can't look a gift horse—*horsh*—in the mouth—*mouf*...hah, hah, hah. But, I'm not under the alfluence of inkahol, though many thinkle peep I am, ho, ho, ho."

"Dang! That's our beer," I whisper to Buddy.

"*Was* our beer," says Buddy. "What're we gonna do...go and tell your dad that Spud stole our gol dang beer? How could he have found it hidden under a bunch of brush that far off the road in the first place? The old boozehound must be able to *smell* the dang stuff."

Well, I for one, never wanted any ol' beer from the very start. Besides, if the knuckle ball will just come through for me in the North Kitsap game, ol' Spud will have earned his case of beer.

> Over the weekend, members of the Jefferson County Sheriff's Department raided a teenage drinking party, held on the beach at Sunny Cove. The party was evidently held in conjunction with the conclusion of the school play, Sleeping Beauty. Several cast members were present. Being rather tipsy and unable to drive safely, the deputies escorted the teenagers to their homes and remanded them to their parents.
> —Dora Dingley
> The Happy Valley Harbinger, May 1952

Chapter 29

"Hee, hee." Dad is chuckling at the breakfast table, as he reads this week's edition of the Happy Valley Harbinger.

"What's so funny, Dad?" I say, as I wipe the sleep out of my eyes. It's good to hear Dad laugh once again.

"Oh...I get a kick out of this column by Dora Dingley...she's sure a master of the dangling participle."

"Yeah...she's a pretty good writer, all right," I say. The truth is, though, I'm not quite sure just what a dangled participle is. Never having paid that much attention in English class, I haven't even learned how to split my infinitives or mix my metaphors.

"By the way, Mackerels," Dad says, "you won't be driving the Hog anymore."

"Uh...why...is there...um...uh, somethin' wrong with it?"

"It's okay."

I wonder now if I've done something to upset Dad, but he doesn't seem angry or anything. Besides, if he was ticked at me, he'd be calling me Willie, instead of Mackerels.

"Your Uncle Frank is going to give you his old Hudson."

"Wow!" I holler. My Uncle Frank lives in Seattle and works as an automobile mechanic. He always keeps his cars in tip-top shape, and if I'm not mistaken, he completely overhauled the good ol' Hudson not too awfully long ago. He's a real nice uncle, and for some strange reason or another, I think I've always been one of his favorites.

"Yeah," Dad says, "he bought a brand new Pontiac yesterday, and says the trade-in on the old Hudson wasn't going to be enough to put in your eye. Thought he'd just as soon give it to you."

"Hey, that's neat. When am I gonna get it?"

"Today. He's going to bring it down to the shop after work, and I'll drive it home."

It's kind of hard to imagine having my very own car, to tell you the absolute truth. I haven't really driven a whole lot, as Dad isn't all that generous with the Hog. It's the only vehicle we have," he says, "and the way the business is going, it might have to last us for a long while."

I think about the car all day at school, but from baseball practice on, the ol' time really seems to drag. I can hardly wait for Dad to get home from Seattle; it's been quite awhile since I've seen the Hudson. I keep a vigilant watch for Dad and my new car, but dinner comes and goes, and still there's no sign of them. I hope they haven't got in a wreck, or some danged thing.

I told Buddy and Vernon about it at school, and they both come over after dinner to see the new automobile. Being a man-of-the-world and all, Buddy knows quite a lot about cars, and I'm quite anxious for his expert appraisal.

It's pretty nearly dark by the time Dad finally does show up. I guess Uncle Frank was a little late getting to the print shop, so Dad missed the ferry. But finally, here it is, parked along the boardwalk, my very own 1936 Hudson. Uncle Frank has obviously just washed and waxed it, for its shiny, black surface sparkles in what little is left of the late-afternoon sun.

As Buddy, and Vernon, and I inspect the old vehicle, I don't notice a single dent or scratch anywhere. The body is flawless. Upon sudden inspiration, I decide to name my new acquisition, "Pristine," in honor of the way my good ol' uncle has kept her.

"Geez, Mackerels," Buddy says after he's completed the inspection, "this ain't exactly a hot rod is it? Too bad yer uncle could'na given' ya a Ford V-8 or sumpin'." He obviously isn't all that impressed with Pristine. I'll be the first to admit, though, that she isn't the typical kid-type of car. In truth, it's kind of a big, clunky 4-door with sort of a top-heavy, bloated look to her. The designer might have been the same guy that created all those blimps and barrage balloons they had back there during the war.

Buddy might think he's hurt my feelings some, because he quickly adds, "They say those Terraplane engines in 'em are danged good, though."

Sunday comes, and it's a heck of a nice day. The sun is shining, and the wild rhododendrons are in full bloom. I get the crazy urge to take a little trip back to Kingston to show off my car. Maybe I can even find Trudy Trammell and talk her into going for a ride. The sighting of Trudy at the Scandia game and the thought that she might have broken up with Teddy, has kind of stirred up some of the old romantic notions, if you want to know the truth. Lately, I've had a tough time getting her wholesome freckle-faced looks out of my mind. I think about that pretty, blue sweater some, too.

I leave about noon and just sort of take my time. I switch on Pristine's radio, just to check the reception.

"...then across the water came Cuban Pete...he's doin' the boogie to the RHUMMMBA beat..." I quickly switch stations and am fortunate enough to tune in on Fibber McGee and Molly. I laugh as ol' Fibber opens up the closet door and all the junk falls out. Mom won't even listen to the program for that very reason. She says that Fibber's closet scene reminds her too much of my messy bedroom.

What with the ferry across Hood Canal and all, I don't get to the Trammell driveway until about two o'clock. Actually, the Trammells' house isn't right in Kingston proper. They live about six miles out of town, at a wide-spot-in-the-road, known as President Point. By the time I get there, I'm real anxious to see ol' Trudy. I've got to be honest about it.

As I pull into the front yard, I notice both the Trammell vehicles in the carport. The Trammells are fairly well-to-do; Trudy's dad is a commercial fisherman and owns his own purse seiner. But parked in the driveway is another automobile. It's a real eye-catching machine, too. There's no doubt about it. It's a '36 Ford coupe—you know—the one with the spare tire kit mounted on the trunk. It's got fender skirts, and the spotless whitewall tires make a real nice contrast with the sparkling, emerald-green body. I guess you'd have to call it a classic. I wonder if it belongs to Trudy.

I'm about to get out of the car, when suddenly, Trudy steps out onto her porch. I have to tell you—my heart misses a beat or two, when I see her standing there. She's wearing blue jeans, saddle shoes, bobby-sox, and a loose-fitting blouse. The blouse doesn't show her figure like the tight, blue sweater, but she looks really super, just the same.

When she recognizes it's me sitting out there in Pristine, she gives me a little wave and flashes me a great big smile. The sun is reflecting some of the reddish highlights in her hair, and I can see the freckles on her cute, little nose.

But as she starts my way, another figure appears in the doorway, and now the sun is bouncing off a vaguely familiar mane of blonde hair. My heart sort of sinks, if you want to know the awful truth. It's *Teddy Snodgrass*. What in the H. E. Double Hockey Sticks is *he* doing here! I thought Trudy was supposed to be through with the jerk.

"Hey, Senor Curly," Trudy says, "como esta usted?" Ever since that day when I aced her out in Miss Swanson's class, she's liked to talk

Spanish to me. She knows danged well I don't understand a word of it. Then she sort of giggles in that special way of hers and comes over and gives me a big ol' hug that danged near pokes a couple of holes in my chest.

I get a little embarrassed at this show of affection, if you want to know the truth. Our family's never been too much into hugging and such as that. Mom's not much of a hugger. And I can't remember the last hug I ever got from Dad. Come to think of it, none of my aunts, or uncles, or cousins, or any of my relations go in much for that kind of stuff. I guess what I'm saying is: there's been hardly any incest in our family.

"Well...if it ain't the travelin' sodbuster. Where'dja get this clunk? Ya oughtta get yerself a real car—hah, hah, hah." Teddy has the usual big smirk on his face, as he makes a sweeping gesture towards the neat-looking Ford. It takes a little wind out of my sails. I'll have to admit it. I spent nearly all morning Simonizing Pristine's bloated, black body, but now she looks disgustedly plain when compared to Teddy's glistening coupe.

Well, Trudy, and Teddy, and I spend a few minutes renewing acquaintances, so to speak. I haven't really had a chance to talk to Trudy for some time now. And of course, I don't really care if I ever talk to Teddy, or not. All the while, I'm watching them pretty closely, trying not to be too obvious, you understand. I'm trying to decide if there's anything romantic still going on. Teddy, though, seems a lot more interested in making fun of me and Pristine than he is in paying attention to Trudy. On a scale of one to ten, if you could read between the lines, Teddy has Pristine at about a minus three. I don't think he rates me quite that highly.

"Why the heck didja ever want to go over to that dinky school and be a sodbuster, anyway?" Teddy says. "Imagine—you twinks ain't won a single game all year. Hah, hah...and you only got one chance left...Friday, against us. Looks like a perfect season...ho, ho, ho." Teddy gives Pristine's left front tire a good kick for emphasis. Her tires are just black-walls, anyway, so I guess it doesn't matter all that much.

Trudy sort of cuts Teddy off and saves me from any further embarrassment. "Why don't we take a ride on over to Kingston and see what's going on at the B and E?" she says. The B and E is sort of a kids' hang-out where you can play pool or Ping-Pong, or try to win free games on the pin-ball machines. I'm not too good at any of those kid games, but at least it'll be nice to be around Trudy.

"Sure," Teddy says. "We can take both cars, so the sodbuster won't have to bring us all the way back here when we're done."

I can understand that. And since Trudy hasn't seen me for some time, and since I've got a new car and all, I sort of assume she'll ride with me. Besides, this will give her a good excuse to get away from Teddy. As I get behind the wheel, I'm racking my brain for the right kinds of things to say to Trudy. In fact, I'm getting pretty nervous about it all, if you want to know the entire truth. I want desperately to make a good impression; I don't often have a chance to be around the girl of my dreams.

But then Trudy flashes me one of her radiant smiles and climbs into the front seat of Teddy's snazzy Ford. I'm crestfallen. Just looking at her there, seated next to Teddy, brings my blood dangerously near the ol' boiling point.

I slam Pristine's gearshift into first and put the pedal to the metal. I dig out of the Trammell driveway, leaving a cloud of dust and gravel that brings to mind the deadly fallout at Hiroshima.

My damaged brain has trouble handling the disappointment of it all, as I turn from a Dr. Jekyll into a Mr. Hyde. I am no longer an innocent schoolboy smitten with a mild case of puppy love. Instead, I am a snarling, raving maniac behind the wheel of a drag racer.

I rocket on down the twisting, gravel road leading to Kingston and soon have Pristine up to an unfamiliar eighty miles per hour. The old girl is no doubt alarmed at having to travel at a speed such as this; I haven't been driving all that long, and I suppose my driving skills could be a little suspect. But I keep the ol' foot to the floor, anyway, and the Terraplane engine begins to whine and throb. The speedometer needle shakily approaches the ninety mark.

Suddenly, a forgotten bend in the road looms ahead. I really jam on the ol' brakes in order to make the curve, but when I do, Pristine takes matters into her own hands. She goes into a skid that heads us for an embankment to our left. I yank the steering wheel hard to the right and then sort of lose control altogether. Pristine and I part company with the road and go fish-tailing off to the right and in the direction of a 200 feet drop to the beach below.

Fortunately, a ditch and a small grove of alder saplings block the way. Pristine hits the ditch and does a couple of beautiful half-gainers, before miraculously landing right-side-up in the alders, about ten feet short of the drop-off.

I guess I hit my head on the steering wheel and black out temporarily. As I come to, it's as though I'm having an out-of-body experience, as I hear the voice of an angel talking nearby.

"Oh, Teddy, I wonder if Curly's all right. We'd better get some help."

"Hmmph," says an evil-sounding voice, perhaps that of ol' Beelzebub, himself, "I guess sodbusters ain't any good at drivin', either."

Finally, I snap out of my daze and realize that it's Trudy and Teddy on the scene. As I slowly climb out of my new car, it doesn't seem as though I'm hurt anywhere—although I do have a small scratch on my cheek, probably from the necking-knob on the steering wheel. I'm more embarrassed than anything else.

Good ol' Pristine is not nearly as fortunate, I'm afraid. All four fenders are badly dented, and the front door on the driver's side is pretty well mangled. Everything else seems to be okay, except for all the scratches from the alder branches. Teddy goes to a house nearby and calls Trudy's dad to come and pull me back on the road with their truck.

A short time later, Pristine and I limp back to Happy Valley, both a little worse for wear, I'm afraid. My visit with Trudy had been cut short.

The last I saw of her, she was waving good-bye and hollering, "Adios, Senor Curly. Conducir esmeradamente, por favor."

I gave her a nice, big toothy smile, before remembering that I might be displaying greener-than-usual teeth. Then I called out, "Muchos gracias, Senorita." I wasn't sure, though, if that was the right response or not. She might have been wishing me a safe journey, or she might have been calling me an ugly ol' poophead. I couldn't tell which. Teddy didn't even bother to wave. He just stood there, grinning like a skunk eating manure.

*****

Buddy, and Vernon, and I are headed back home from Townsend. Vernon has just picked up his new letterman's sweater from Martin's Sporting Goods. Now that Buddy's going steady with Rosie Higgenbottom, we don't see a heck of a lot of him anymore. But he agrees to come along and give his expert opinion on Pristine's condition after the wreck at Kingston. Dad doesn't know all that much about automobiles.

"You'll just have to drive it the way it is, Mackerels," Dad had said, "unless you come up with the money to fix it."

After a short time on the road, Buddy says, "It seems to steer okay, don't it?"

"I guess so," I say, "but it's always been a little on the loosy-goosy side, anyway."

About that time, on a straight stretch out in the valley, a beat-up old Dodge pulls along side. It's without a doubt the filthiest car I've ever seen. You can't even tell what color it's supposed to be. Its whole body, including the windows, is encrusted with various shades of dirt and mud. It looks like it's just emerged from a primeval swamp.

Through its earthy passenger window, I barely make out the semblance of a person staring at us. And whoever it is, has flashed us an obscene gesture. As the battered Dodge continues to cruise alongside, It looks as though the mysterious occupants want to race. Buddy sees it, too.

"Go for it, Mackerels! The ol' Terraplane'll smoke 'em."

The highway is all clear for as far as I can see, so I punch the gas pedal for all it's worth. We stay even for a moment or two and then slowly begin to forge ahead.

"Hah...we got 'em, Mackerels," Buddy says, as the speedometer needle approaches eighty. Suddenly, though, Pristine's steering wheel goes into a violent spasm, and her entire bloated body begins to shake, rattle, and roll.

"Slow 'er down, Mackerels!" Buddy yells. "She's got the shimmies."

I cut back on the throttle, and almost immediately, Pristine begins to settle down. Meanwhile, our adversary goes zooming on by. Now, the middle finger is positioned in the rear window and remains there until the flying dirtmobile is gone from sight.

"Looks like ya prolly need some front end work after that wreck, Mackerels," Buddy says. Since Buddy is a man-of-the-world and all, I take his advice and sort of baby Pristine for the rest of the way home.

When we finally get back to Happy Valley, Vernon wants me to swing on by the school; he's forgotten his algebra book. But as we pull into the schoolyard, there's the old Dodge, parked right in front of the main entrance. Then, the mud-encrusted door on the passenger side opens up and out steps the owner of the middle finger. It's Roderick Remblinger. He's evidently come from Martin's, too, as he's also sporting a new letterman's sweater. As he opens his door, I can see that it's his older brother behind the wheel.

"Lets knock the crap out of 'em," Buddy says. I talk him out of it, though—we're going to need Roderick for the game with Scandia. As bad as he is, he's still head and shoulders above any of the Three Stooges.

Roderick flashes one of his patented goofy grins, as he raises the hood of his brother's car. He takes out the oil stick, wipes it on the sleeve of his new sweater, and announces, "Dadamn, dah fo qua." With that, he replaces the stick, slams the hood, and jumps back into the car.

"Wha'd he say?" asks Buddy.

"God damn, down four quarts," I say.

Then, with a screech of the tires and a cloud of blue smoke, the Remblinger brothers go careening out of the parking lot and leave us in a hail of flying gravel.

"Remember in psychology where they said we only use ten per cent of our brains?" Buddy says.

"Yeah."

"Well, what's ten per cent of nothin'?" Buddy says, as he watches the Remblingers rocket on out of sight.

The Jefferson County Sheriff's Department reported a near-fatal accident this past week, out on the Muskrat Valley Road. Reginald Remblinger (twenty-six) totaled his 1937 Dodge, when trying to avoid an animal crossing the road. Fortunately, both Reginald and his brother, Roderick, escaped the mishap sporting only minor injuries. The automobile, however, was totaled. Crossing the road very erratically, Remblinger blamed the accident on a chipmunk.
　　　　　—Dora Dingley
　　　　　The Happy Valley Harbinger, May 1952

Chapter 30

Mr. Small gets his dander up today. Wendall Small is Hapless Valley's school superintendent, by the way, and a real doozy. I mean, the guy just doesn't have a clue. Not only that, but he looks like an owl, for Pete's sake. He's got this big, round face, this really sharp nose like a beak, and he wears these giant, horn rimmed glasses. He parts his hair right smack dab in the middle, and in front, the ends actually curl up and look like owl's ears. I'm not kidding. And when he ties his necktie, practically the whole danged thing ends up in the knot. So he's got this great big huge knot and a tie about six inches long. It's clever, though, how the tie ends right where his pot belly starts. Mr. Small and I have one thing in common, though, we were both newcomers to Happy Valley at the beginning of the school year. Previously, he'd been a high school principal somewhere over in eastern Washington.

Last week, Mr. Small gave this edict that banned any further use of the "steel deals on our heels." All us kids were wearing these steel horseshoe cleats to help save the heels of our shoes. Not only did they help cut down the wear and tear on the ol' penny loafers, but they also made this really neat clicking noise when you walked down the hall. Anyway, Mr. Small said we had to take them off. The janitor had been complaining about all the bad scuff marks on the floors. We didn't like it too much, but what could we do? Out came the screwdrivers and off went the cleats.

Later in the day, Buddy Pringle and I were sitting in study hall playing this game with a little football made of folded paper. We were being real cautious and all, so as not to get caught by Abigail. Click, click, click.

Someone was walking noisily down the hallway not too far from the study hall door.

"Geez, who's got the nerve?" Buddy whispered.

I knew it couldn't be Roderick Remblinger. He was sitting two desks in front of me at that very moment.

The study hall door was partially open, so I craned my neck to try and see who it was. Click, click, click. The noisy footsteps sounded closer and closer, until the shoes themselves finally came into view. You could have knocked me over with a feather when I saw who it was. It was Mr. Small, himself. Well needless to say, in no time at all the "steel deals" went right back on the heels. After that, you could hardly hear yourself think from all the clicking that went on in the halls.

Today, Mr. Small is upset about Pristine. I usually walk to school, but this morning I was borderline-late, so I drove instead. Subconsciously, I guess, I wondered why there were so few cars in the school parking lot, but nothing really sank in. I was more interested in getting to first period on time, to tell you the absolute truth. With the Scandia game only a day away, I didn't want to chance a goofy tardy slip getting me in Dutch with the office. Also, as I sprinted toward the main entrance, I was probably vaguely aware that several student cars were parked in the vacant lot across the street. That was a bit puzzling too, but I didn't really give it a whole lot of thought. Anyway, I made it to class on time by the skin of my slightly-greener teeth.

We're about fifteen minutes into the period, and Mr. Small appears in the doorway. As he peers into the room, he blinks his big, round owl eyes for several moments, as though he's trying to get used to the light or something. The next thing you know, he's beckoning for Buddy to come to the door. As Buddy leaves the room, you can see he's lost some of his normal man-of-the-world bearing. In fact, he looks downright alarmed. He shrugs his shoulders as if to say, "What'd I do?"

It puzzles me, too, because even when Buddy does do something wrong, he usually manages to make it look like someone else did it. I sure hope he isn't in too much trouble. We'll need his bat in the game with Scandia. As he leaves for the office, Buddy's complexion is almost as white as his hair. He is definitely upset.

He's gone for quite some time, and I begin to imagine the worst. He must have been in on some shenanigan or other that I haven't heard about. That'll be just wonderful, trying to retire the Viking hitters with Gordy Belmont as our only decent outfielder. He'd be flanked with Roderick Remblinger on one side and one of the Stooges on the other.

A little later, though, Buddy bursts back into the room. He's got this huge grin plastered across his face and a more healthy-looking color has returned to his cheeks. Things couldn't have gone too badly, I reason.

Buddy starts to tell Vernon Windbladd and me about what happened but is overtaken by a sudden laughing attack. But after several false starts, all interrupted by an assortment of giggles, snorts, and hiccups, he finally settles down and tells us the story.

"He was real nice and polite," Buddy says, referring of course to Mr. Small. "He had me take a chair and then said we had a minor problem to discuss. Said it'd ony take a couple minutes or so." Buddy goes on with the story. "Hee, hee, hee...'Willie,' he says...hah, hah, hah. He calls me Willie...ha, ha...he's only been here all year long, and he still gets us mixed up. He thinks I'm you...hah, hah, ho, ho." At that point, Buddy gives me a clap on the back that likes to knock me out of my desk.

As the story turns out, it seems Buddy didn't bother to point out the error in identity to Mr. Small. Instead, he just let the twink ramble on and on, thinking all the while that he was talking to Willie Michaels. Buddy had seen the whole thing as a really good opportunity to spend some time out of a boring history class. Buddy went on to relate the rest of the one-sided conversation.

"Willie," said Mr. Small, "we have a little problem here with your automobile. See...here at Happy Valley, we don't allow students to park their vehicles on the school grounds. Most of the students park in the lot across across the street." Buddy had nodded his head at that point to show that he understood all right.

Mr. Small continued. "Willie, you look like an intelligent boy...and being a senior and all...are very likely a safe and reliable driver. But, Willie, we can't be sure that all the students are that responsible with their vehicles. In fact, Willie, I've seen quite a few of our students do some pretty crazy things out on the highway...hah, hah, hah. So, Willie, we cannot take the risk of letting students park on the school grounds. We wouldn't want some reckless hot-rodder backing up over one of our younger students...would we?"

I guess Buddy had been nodding his head in agreement the whole time—especially when Mr. Small had made the statement about looking intelligent and all.

Then Mr. Small had said to Buddy, "Now, Willie...this might be a bit of an imposition on you, but I think you can see that what's fair for one is fair for all. It won't hurt a big, strong, athletic boy like you to walk a few steps from the parking lot across the street." At this point, I guess Mr. Small had beamed another big ol' smile at Buddy.

"So, Willie, that's how it is here at Happy Valley. Do you understand?"

"Sure," Buddy said, "I understand all right, but I'm not Willie."

"Hah, hah, hah, you guys shoulda seen his face when I said that," Buddy says. "I never seen anything so purple. Then he says, 'Well, whoever you are, you tell the *real* Willie to get his fanny down to this office right this minute!'...ho, ho, ho. So...ha, ha, hee, hee...now it's your turn in the barrel, Mackerels." It's pretty obvious by now that Buddy is pretty danged pleased with himself. After all, he's managed to cut a whole twenty minutes out of the history class.

My visit with Mr. Small doesn't take nearly as long, if you want the whole sad truth. It only takes him about twenty seconds to explain the rules to me.

"Now, I want that car out of the parking lot immediately...and don't ever bring it back again." This time there is no talk about looking like an "intelligent boy" and all. But at least Mr. Small doesn't kick me off the baseball team or anything like that.

*****

RRrrriiinnnggg! I hear a ringing, but for some reason, I can't quite get my act together—my brain seems so fuzzy. I'm racing with this real dirty car and have come to a steep hill. Through the dirt on the other car's window, I see that it's a great big owl doing the driving. It's blinking his great, big eyes and pumping the ol' middle finger for all he's worth. A bird flipping the bird—it's unreal.

I'm losing power on the hill, so I decide to shift down. But when I grab the gearshift, it wiggles and feels all slimy. Then, I hear the horrible hissing noise. AAAaaarrrggghhh—it's Ingaborg!

RRrrriiinnnggg! Shuffle Bowl sounds off again, and I awaken at last. I'm somewhat shaken by my dream. I decide to get up and watch television. Mom and Dad have finally broken down and purchased a fourteen-inch Emerson. I've got to admit: it's quite an invention, even though the screen is snowy at the moment. I adjust the rabbit ears but now the danged thing starts rolling; it must be the horizontal hold. I fiddle with it awhile but finally give up. I'm sort of bored with Test-Pattern, anyway, if you want to know the truth of it all.

RRRrrriiinnnggg! Shuffle-Bowl cries out one more time. As I listen to the noises coming through my bedroom floor, things don't seem quite right to me. It's very puzzling. Although Shuffle-Bowl is in good form, I realize that I haven't heard a thing from Skinny and Clyde. Either they've failed to show up, or else too much fog has set in for any torpedoing. Something else is wrong, too, but I have trouble putting my finger on it. Then it hits me—Hank Snow is missing! In his place, some female singer is going on and on about the cost of some dumb doggy in the window. I wonder if she'd pay a little something for ol' Tar Baby, instead?

"Hee, hee, hee...HEE, HEE, HEE." The Wicked Witch of the West is really in a wing-ding, tonight. I've never heard her quite so wild before.

I wonder what the heck is going on, so I sneak down the stairs and listen from the kitchen. I hear Dad talking to Mom.

"Jesus H. Christ, Esther, did you see that old bag win the Marlin .22 rifle off our new punch board with the very first chance taken on the board. Cost her a quarter is all...and she won the only attraction worth a damn. She's ruined it." Dad is pretty bummed-out. I can tell. "Now, no one'll spend any money trying to win flashlights, and cigarette lighters, and junk like that," he says. "I tell ya, I've about had it with this dump. I'm going to call that guy over in Bremerton, tomorrow."

I wonder what the deal with Bremerton is all about as I go back upstairs. Dad sure seems upset. But as I get tuned in once again to the noises through the floor, I let my thoughts focus on the remainder of the baseball season. There's only three games left, including the all-important one with Scandia. Somehow, we've just got to stop our losing ways. The Fighting Milk Maids just have to win at least one athletic contest this year. I know sports are supposed to teach you a little humility and all, but the amount of humility I've been saturated with this year borders on the ridiculous. It really does.

And as strange as it may seem, in the last game of the ol' season, we have an opportunity to deprive the Vikings of a chance at the league championship. They'll have to beat us in order to gain a playoff with the South Kitsap Fighting Wolves. It's a lot like that summer, back when I was playing for Kingston, and the Suquamish team was challenging Scandia for the summer league championship. But of course, I don't much believe in that "deja vu all over again" stuff.

And I can't forget—it might also be my last opportunity to impress the Fighting Cardinals from St. Louis. It'll be a real important game. There's no doubt about it.

> This reporter recently had a chat with Mr. Wendall Small, Superintendent of Happy Valley School District. He reports that lately there have been several student violations of the school's parking policies.
>
> "We do not allow student-owned automobiles on the school grounds," he stated. "We have primary school children on the campus, as well, and we're just not sure that all of our student drivers are mature enough to handle mixed up students like that."
> —Dora Dingley
> The Happy Valley Harbinger, May 1952

Chapter 31

Well, you'd think it was the beginning of World War III, what with all the bomb shells that have been dropped on me these past couple of weeks. First of all, we've got just one chance left at salvaging any sort of athletic victory for the year. We just got killed by the South Kitsap Fighting Wolves; I'm not even going to mention the score, and we lost a close three to two decision to the Fighting Cougars of Central Kitsap.

I thought we had the Central game in the bag, but once again I failed to reckon with goofy ol' Roderick Remblinger. In the bottom of the seventh, with a one-run lead, and with two outs and a runner on first, I get the Central batter to lift a routine fly to right. I'm standing there on the mound thinking of our first victory and all when the ball kisses off Roderick's glove and is headed for the fence. Well, to his credit, ol' Roderick gets right after it. There'll be no stopping the lead runner, but hopefully we can at least salvage a tie and go to extra innings.

Roderick, though, puts on a clinic on how not to get the ball back to the infield. Not only does he throw behind the runner, but he throws wildly, to boot. The ball ends up in our dugout, while the Fighting Cougar runner crosses the plate with the winning run. Roderick beats anything I've ever seen.

Later, as Buddy and Vernon and I are leaving the locker room, Rosie Higgenbottom drives up in what appears to be a brand new Nash Ambassador. She gives a couple of quick beeps on the ol' horn, leans out the window, and starts beckoning for us to come on over.

"Rottenbottom get a new car?" Vernon asks. Instantly, Buddy has him by the throat. He must be squeezing pretty danged hard, too, as Vernon's normally pink cheeks are now redder than a freshly-washed fire truck. And his eyes look like they're about to pop out of his head.

"That's *Higgen*-bottom to you—you little socktucker. That's my girl you're talkin' about!" Buddy says. Vernon's ol' face is just beginning to change to an interesting mixture of red and blue when Buddy finally lets him go.

There's sort of an awkward silence there for a minute or two, until I finally break the ice. "That Rosie's or her folks'?" I ask.

"Folks'," Buddy says. From that briefest of answers, I can tell that Buddy is still really ticked. Meanwhile, I can tell that Vernon is having a heck of a time to keep from crying. I don't think it's from physical pain or anything like that, but it's easy to see that his ol' feelings are hurt pretty badly. After all, Buddy has pretty much been his hero for quite some time.

"Gosh," I say, "too bad they didn't get a V-8, huh?" I know Buddy's preference for Fords.

"I talked 'em into gettin' the Nash," Buddy says.

This bit of news has me completely dumbfounded, if you want to know the crazy truth of it all. A Nash is a pretty ugly car if you were to ask me. It looks pretty much like an upside-down bathtub.

"Uh—why a Nash?" I ask.

"The back seat makes into a bed," Buddy says.

"Oh," I say, although I can't really figure out why the Higgenbottoms would want a bed in their car. I don't think they ever take many long trips or such as that.

Well as it turns out, of course, ol' Rosie has absolutely no interest in seeing either me or Vernon. Instead she greets Lover Boy Pringle with a lingering soul kiss, and the next thing you know, they're down the road. And through the back window of the Nash, as it speeds away, you can see that the good ol' two-headed driver syndrome has struck once again.

Later, when Dad gets home from his commute from Seattle, he calls me into the kitchen. He wants to have a little talk, he says. I wonder if I've done something wrong.

"Mackerels—," he starts out. Instantly, I feel more at ease. If I were in any kind of trouble, he'd be calling me Willie. "Uh—we've got a good offer for the tavern, and your mother and I have decided to sell. We're not making it here financially, and I just can't keep on with this commuting back and forth to Seattle to work at my trade. It's too tough. We're going to have to move back to the city."

Gulp. I really don't know what to say to Dad, so I pretty much just sit there in shock. If the truth were known, I'm not all that excited about moving away. I've gotten pretty used to life in the country, even though there aren't any ice cream sundaes or banana splits to choose from. I can put up with vanilla, chocolate, and strawberry ice cream cones. Heck— I've even gotten used to Tavern, and Shuffle-Bowl, and Wurlitzer, and all the goofy patrons like Skinny, and Clyde, and the Wicked Witch of the West. I might not be able to sleep so good, anymore, without all the noises coming through the floor. What'll I do without Hank Snow and the Rainbow Ranch Boys? I've sort of gotten used to them. I've made some danged good friends here at Hapless Valley, too, even though I don't see all that much of Buddy anymore, now that he and ol' Rosie are going steady.

"A man from Bremerton wants to buy us out," Dad says, "and we'll actually be making a couple thousand dollars profit out of the deal."

"Uh— how soon we gotta move?" I ask. I'm still finding this whole thing hard to believe.

"Right after graduation, Mackerels. We've already rented an apartment in Seattle—just until we can find another house."

What can I say? If Dad's decided we're going to move, then that's what we're going to do. I've just got to hope, more than ever now, that the good ol' Cardinals come through with a contract. I sure don't want to end up in Seattle working in some ol' boring sweat shop. But then again, if the Cardinals *don't* come through, what am I going to do around here? There's stupid ol' shift work at the mill or working in the woods. What a choice. I guess they make danged good money logging, but you really have to be on your ol' toes. There's lots of accidents in the woods. I'm not so sure it'd be the best place for a slightly brain-damaged individual.

And as far as graduation is concerned, that brings up another bombshell that has thrown me somewhat for a loop. With graduation not all that far away, the list of honor students has already been announced. And you could have knocked me over with a feather when I was named co-salutatorian of the senior class. Of course, I've got to tell you that the class of '52 is the smallest in the history of the school. We only graduate nine. That means that aside from Gordy Belmont, the valedictorian, and Kristina Boobar, my co-salutatorian, I only managed to beat out six other kids. It would have been seven, but Roderick Remblinger is not going to have enough credits to graduate.

I'm pretty danged proud about earning a tie with Kristina Boobar, by the way. I mean, all she ever does is study—if you could go by all the books she carries, that is. And she always carries the whole kit and kaboodle of them snuggled tightly against her chest. The kids all call her, "Kristina Boobless," although I don't know how anyone could tell for sure. The worst part of this whole danged graduation scenario is the fact that I have to come up with a graduation speech. I'm a little worried about that, if you want to know the scary truth of it all. I mean—what am I going to talk about—good ol' Shuffle-Bowl and his effect on world peace?

When Buddy saw the list, it didn't take him long to seek me out. "I gotta ax ya somepin, Mackerels—uh—what kinda grade point ya hafta have for salutatorian, anyway?"

"Three-point-two," I said, somewhat proudly.

"Dang! That's pretty low to be getting' honors, ain't it?

I didn't bother to answer, but I did sort of wonder what kind of average the good ol' man-of-the-world was able to come up with. Later, I found out from Gordy Belmont that Buddy had only managed a four year cumulative score of point 9. The administration is going to graduate him, though. Mr. Small was heard to say that one man-of-the-world every twenty years or so was probably enough.

But then I get to thinking about what Buddy'd said about my G.P.A. being a little low for honors and all. I hate to admit it, but I know he was right. I sort of wish now that I hadn't goofed off so much with regard to my studies. I bet I could have done a whole lot better if I'd only tended to business. The way it stands now, 3.2 is going to look awfully shabby at the ol' graduation ceremony when it's compared to Gordy Belmont's perfect 4.0.

Heck, the alcoholic content of the beer most kids drink is higher than 3.2. And who have I been fooling all this time with all that talk about the dents in the football helmet and the resulting brain damage? Only me.

May 23—52

Dear Auntie,

Thanks so much for the get well card nice letter. It was very thoughtful of you. Please don't be worried about me—I'll pull through OK. With no right arm, I guess the baseball career is over, but I might never have made the grade anyway. I get fitted for my prosthetic device early next week. They say that they've come a long way with those things. Sorry to hear that you're going to have to give up the tavern. I know that you and Uncle George tried your hardest to make it work. Great news about Willie being salutatorian. I bet you're real proud. Maybe now he can get into college and stay out of this damned war. Thanks again, Auntie, for writing so often while I was over in the hell hole. It meant a lot to me.

Much love,
Harvey

Chapter 32

Well, the big day is here at last. It'll soon be time for the recital. First period, I pay even less attention than usual in my boring old history class. All I can think about is this afternoon's showdown with Teddy Snodgrass, and ol' Rattleballs, and the rest of the Scandia twinks. And as for the history class, I've got to admit it's been my worst subject. Last quarter, I only got a D and got into a big hoop-dee-doo about it with my folks.

"You sure missed a lot of simple questions about Asia," Dad said. He was looking at my last test when he said it. It was one of the ones I'd failed.

"Well, there's an awful lot to know about Asia," I said in my own defense. "Asia's a danged big country."

"I don't know why you do so poorly in history, Willy," Mom said. "it was my favorite subject."

"Yeah," I said, "but there wasn't nearly as much history to learn, back when you were in school. A whole lot has happened since then, Mom. Just remember—history gets one day longer—every single day." There was no arguing that point, I guess, as the folks just looked at one another and went off mumbling to themselves.

Buddy flirts with trouble during our humanities class. Miss McQuarry is not amused when Buddy answers that the Fifth Symphony was composed by Ludwig Von Boathaven nor when he says that The Three Musketeers was written by Alexander Dumb-ass. But luckily, he doesn't get sent to the office or anything.

Third period science perks me up a little. Good ol' Mr. Dunlap is in rare form, today, as he sort of branches out into the field of psychology, and hypnosis, and such as that. He tries hypnotizing Roderick Remblinger but can't seem to bring it off.

"Ya can't hypnotize someone who's already unconscious," whispers the man-of-the-world.

Next, Mr. Dunlap tries Rosie Higgenbottom, and it looks like he's succeeded, all right. He's just stuck some pins into her hand, and she doesn't flinch one iota.

"There, class," Mr. Dunlap says, "you can see that Rosie's completely under—she hasn't even felt the pricks."

That causes a few giggles here and there, but one glare from Mr. Dunlap over the top of his spectacles quiets us in a real big hurry. The day of the big game is no time to risk getting into trouble with the office. What with my art training, though, I notice that Buddy's face has turned to sort of a Grumbacher red with just a tiny dab of alizarin crimson added in. I decide against calling his attention to that fact, however.

We've finally made it to lunch, and ol' Vernon Windbladd has traded me a big chunk of homemade Boston cream pie for two Hershey bars. I glance over to the table where all the girls sit, and I see that Rosie Higgenbottom seems completely recovered from her trance. She's gabbing a mile-a-minute to her cronies, Helen Morley and Naomi Panks. Brenda, the cute sophomore girl, is smiling at me once again, but I don't even bother with a tight-lipped special. It'd be a complete waste of time, what with her religious shackles and all.

During art class, ol' Abigail leaves the room for a minute, and Buddy takes the opportunity to draw a cartoon of her on the blackboard. It's real crude, though, if you want the truth of it all. Buddy can't draw worth a darn. You wouldn't even know who it's supposed to be for sure, except he's labeled it: CRAZY ABBY. But while he's up there showing off, I draw a sketch of him and his art work. It's pretty danged good, too, even if I do say so, myself. I got a real fine likeness of ol' Buddy, with his white hair and all, and the perspective is great. I'll shade it later and work on the darks and lights and such as that. It might come in real handy in case I ever need to blackmail ol' Buddy for any reason.

Sixth period study hall comes and goes without a whole lot of excitement. It's pretty boring, actually. Buddy tries to fool Abby with the ol' fake-name-on-the-role trick, once again, but she doesn't fall for "Rose Bush." I think someone down in the office has gone and wised her up.

Then, Buddy turns his attention to me. "What's that you got on your upper lip there, Mackerels?" he asks.

He's looking at the pencil-thin mustache I've been trying to grow for the past three months. I thought perhaps it might make me look a bit more Flynnish. Unfortunately, even though I'm danged near eighteen years old, it seems as though I haven't yet developed much of a beard.

The mustache does look a little scraggly—I have to admit it.

"Ya better put a little cream on it and let that cat of yours lick it off—har, har, har." Smart-ass Buddy always has such great advice.

It's almost game time. I'm lobbing a few with ol' Vernon Windbladd, as the bus from Scandia arrives. As the mighty Vikings are getting off, some of them immediately start tossing barbs in my direction.

"Peee-yyewww! It smells here," says Nathan Risberg, as he makes an elaborate show of putting his fingers to his nose. There's a slight breeze blowing out of the south, and the stench from the honey-wagon in Cy Morgan's dairy farm is a little overpowering. You can't deny that.

"Aw—that's just Mackerel's breath you're smellin'," says my old friend, Theodore Snodgrass. "Hah, hah, hah—hope you're pitchin' today, Mackerels. I could use a few more points on my battin' average—hee, hee, hee." Just one look at Teddy Snodgrass and you'll never need another dose of cascara. I can tell you that much for sure.

>May 24, 1952
>P.O. Box 97
>Hapless Valley, Wash
>Dear Cousin Harvey,
>   I'm not two much of a letter writer but I want too let you know how sorry I am about your arm. I bet you would a been a star pitcher for the Cardinals if it wasn't for that danged shrapnel. I guess the ol' Cardinals are looking at me right now, but I doubt if I'll ever be as good as you. Dad says you had a fastball like Bob Feller. Today is our last chance to win a game, and I'm going to dedicate it to you. Then I know we will HALF to win!!! Well that is about all for now. Hope you are better soon.
>Sincerely Yours,
>Your cousin Willie (alias Mackerels—ha-ha)

Chapter 33

As visitors, the Vikings take infield practice first and look pretty snappy, as they whip the ol' ball around the diamond. Rattleballs has his charges well-drilled. You can't deny it. Even with all the rocks and boulders on our field, I don't see them make a single mistake.

When it's our turn to take infield, I go over behind the bleachers and warm up with one of the Stooges. Even from there, I hear all the Viking hoots and hollers. My teammates must be putting on their usual version of the age-old Chinese fire drill. I try to put that out of my mind, though, as I start working on the ol' curve.

About that time, Mr. Popolinski shows up. To tell you the honest truth, he's dressed a little better than normal. Not only is he wearing the usual St. Louis Cardinal cap, but he's sporting a faded Cardinal warm-up jacket, as well. Underneath, there's a semi-white shirt and tie. He must see this as a real important game. In fact, he even seems a trifle nervous. His ol' tongue is working overtime, as it flicks in and out of his mouth at a furious pace.

"Got a little tip there *flick* for you there *flick*, Mr. Michaels, there. *Flick, flick, flick.* I was behind the other team's dugout, there, *flick, flick,* and overheard their coach's instructions, there. *Flick, flick, flick.* He's telling them to lay for your slow curve, there. *Flick.* Instead, keep the fastball high and tight, there, *flick, flick, flick,* and just show them the curve, there—once in awhile there *flick* to keep them guessing, there. *Flick, flick, flick.*"

With that said, Mr. Popolinski goes scurrying off to the stands behind home plate, *there,* for a better view of my pitches, *there.* I appreciate his advice and all but wonder if my ol' fastball is actually as good as he seems to think. Could it be that I've added velocity without even realizing it?

Well, the Viking jeers seemed to have stopped now, so I figure we're done with the ol' pre-game warm-up. I throw the Stooge one last curve, which he misses, and then head on over to the dugout to see if Coach Monahan has any last minute words of instruction.

"Has anyone seen Roderick?" he asks. It seems ol' Roderick hasn't shown up. And as bad as he is, it'd be a real disaster if we had to play one of the goofy Stooges in his place. I'll grant you, Roderick doesn't catch many balls out there, but after he finally does pick them up, he eventually gets them back somewhere near the infield. The Stooges, on the other hand, are just as apt to throw the danged thing farther out into the field.

"Here he comes," says Richie Schmutz, as he points toward center field. We look, and sure enough, it's ol' Roderick, and he's pedaling his bicycle on in towards the dugout.

"Clack, clack, clickety, clickety, clack," his bike is making a heck of a racket, as he pulls up. He's got a bunch of playing cards clothes-pinned to his rear spokes. What a twink! Sometimes you'd swear Roderick ought to be back in the fourth grade. Buddy gets to looking at the cards.

"Dang! Roderick—these are *baseball* cards. They mighta been worth somepin'. Didn't ya have an old pinochle deck or somepin' else ya coulda used for your bike?"

Roderick swallows his face for a second or two, and then says, "Ekka tekka."

"Wha'd he say?" says Buddy.

"Danged if I know," I say. Sometimes ol' Roderick slips so far back into Neanderthalese that even I can't translate. But regardless, I think to myself, I can't picture a goofy Neanderthal family sitting around the ol' cave playing pinochle or such as that.

"Geez—here's a Ty Cobb," Buddy says, "and a Lou Gehrig—and cripes, you even got a Honus Wagner! Man—I bet you coulda got twenty bucks or so for these here—'til ya went and got 'em all crumpled up."

"Ekkata tekkata" Roderick says, after swallowing his face once again.

"How come you're so late, anyway, Roderick?" Coach Monahan asks. The ol' coach sounds a little ticked, too, if you want to know the truth of it all.

Through my interpretation, Roderick explains as how he'd been looking for his lost baseball socks. Roderick's solved the ol' problem, though—he's put on a pair of red and green argyles. They make a handsome compliment to the rest of a strange ensemble highlighted by a filthy denim F.F.A. jacket. Being in a rural community, Happy Valley High has a chapter of the Future Farmers of America. In place of Farmers, however, Buddy likes to substitute another familiar word beginning with the letter F.

Well, we finally take the field to start the game. And as I trudge on out to the mound, I'm pretty danged confused. To tell you the awful truth, I still don't have a clearly-defined game plan in mind. I'd originally planned to go with my Eddie Lopat junk, but Mr. Popolinski's advice has me all mixed up. Do I dare throw mostly fastballs and hope to get away with it? It seems doubtful to me, but I finally decide to try his scheme on one batter and see how it works.

So as the Viking leadoff hitter digs in at the plate, I shake off Richie Schmutz's opening sign down there in the dirt. With his big ol' fingers, he's signaled for the usual curve. Instead, I'm going to follow the advice of the Cardinal scout and come in high and tight. I feel really pumped, and the ol' fastball might be awesome. But I try a little too hard on the first delivery and overthrow the ball a tiny bit. The result is a pitch a trifle high to call a strike.

"Steee—rike one," the umpire shouts. The batter steps back and shoots the umpire a look of disbelief.

"Get 'em down, Ump," Rattleballs yells from over in the third base coaching box.

"Play ball," says the umpire.

Hmmm, I think, and then I come right back with another hard one about six inches higher than the first.

"Steee—rike two," says the umpire, as the batter takes the pitch with the bat on his shoulder.

"*Dang* it, Ump. Get 'em *down,*" a red-faced Rattleballs calls once again.

Wow! I think. I wonder? Then I fire another fastball nearly a foot too high to be called a strike. The batter, by this time thinking "strike" is the only word in the umpire's vocabulary, takes a wild cut at the highball and misses it for strike three. I set the next two hitters down in much the same fashion, as I continue to take advantage of the umpire's high strike zone.

I lead off our half of the inning but weakly ground out to the shortstop. As I watch Vernon Windbladd step to the plate, it suddenly dawns on me that I've never seen this umpire previously. He isn't one of the regulars we normally see. When I get back to the dugout, I say, "Who's the ump, Coach? I don't think I've ever seen him before."

"Oh—he's an old friend of mine from my navy days. None of the regular umps were available, so he agreed to help us out."

He's helping us out, all right, I think to myself. I continue to work the Vikings up and down the ol' ladder with high cheese, while occasionally sneaking in the ol' curve on the low, outside corner. So far, the Vikings are at my mercy. There's no doubt about it.

As I strut off the diamond, I casually let my eyes wander up to the rather sparse gathering of fans sitting behind home plate. I'm sort of looking for Mr. Popolinski. But as I continue to scan the crowd, my heart does a sudden flip-flop. Of course, it isn't the elderly Cardinal scout who's responsible for that sudden swell of emotion. Instead, it's the unexpected sight of Trudy Trammell.

A vision of loveliness, in a lavender spring dress, she's sitting in amongst a whole bunch of other kids from Scandia. She appears to be involved in quite a lively discussion with two other girls. I try to catch her eye but finally give up and go into our dugout. She's probably just over here to watch her beloved Teddy, anyway. Snodgrass is pitching a darned nice game, too. I have to admit it.

I'm still sort of obsessed with making eye contact with her, though, so I go back out to the head of our dugout steps and fake getting a drink of water. However, she's still busy talking to her friends. So instead, I look up to see what ol' Mr. Popolinski is doing.

He isn't all that hard to spot, dressed like he is in all the Cardinal paraphernalia. I don't know if the ol' tongue is still working overtime or not, because he has his head down. He appears to be writing something in a little book of some sort. I figure he's probably making note of how I'm no longer solely-reliant on the ol' roundhouse curve.

*****

As hard as it may be to believe, it's already the sixth inning of this scoreless pitchers' duel between me and ol' Teddy Snodgrass. KKRRAAACCKKK! Teddy's first pitch of the inning rockets into the catcher's mitt, as Vernon Windbladd takes it for a strike. If the truth were known, I doubt seriously if ol' Vernon even saw the pitch. Teddy's already struck out fourteen, mostly with the ol' hummer.

From the cozy confines of our dugout, Roderick Remblinger hollers out to the Viking fireballer, "Dadamn. Tuh ah, Eeny om—yuu chittensit!"

"Wha'd he say?" Buddy asks.

"God damn. Come on, Wienie arm—you chickenshit." Instantly, Buddy Pringle has a strangle hold on Roderick and explains to him as how he probably doesn't want to get ol' Teddy any more fired up than he already is.

"Ow—dadamn yuuu, BahEEEE. Gnaw aw I tih sih ow yoUUU."

"Wha'd he say?" asks Buddy.

"Ow—goddamn you, Buddy. Knock it off or I'll kick the shit out of you."

"Oh, you *will*, huh—hah, hah, hah?" Buddy says, as he applies one more Dutch rub to Roderick's ol' noggin. But the damage is already done, and Vernon strikes out two pitches later for out number one.

But then, Teddy gets a little wild with the ol' fastball, and Richie Schmutz draws a walk. Then he takes second, as Teddy throws wildly in an attempt to pick Richie off first. That's kind of dumb of Teddy, if you were to ask me. After all, Richie is probably the slowest runner on our team and certainly no threat to steal second. But then, no one's ever accused ol' Teddy of being any smarter than the law allows.

Buddy Pringle is up next. He's probably our best hitter, but so far, Teddy's fastballs haven't been much to his liking. He's already struck out twice.

Roderick hollers, "Dadamn," and something else that I interpret as, "Don't try to kill it, Buddy, just hit it as hard as you possibly can." Sometimes, I don't think Roderick knows if Christ was crucified or chased to death by the Indians.

After a quick glare in Roderick's direction, Buddy takes a peculiar squared-around stance instead of his normal one. He just sort of chops at Teddy's first delivery and sends a poorly-hit ground ball that skips weakly out towards Nathan Risberg at short. The Viking shortstop swoops effortlessly into the grounder and straightens for the routine throw to first. It appears like a cinch second out, and with weak-hitting Gordy Belmont due up next, our chances of scoring look pretty danged bleak.

However, the Vikings don't seem to realize they're dealing with a legitimate man-of-the-world. As usual, ol' Buddy has more up his sleeve than just his arm. He's only traveled about two-thirds of the distance to first, when he suddenly makes a ninety degree turn and heads for second. A startled Nathan Risberg freezes momentarily and holds up his throw. Head down, Buddy keeps right on a course for the bag at second.

But as you probably already know, Buddy is actually out the minute he leaves the baseline. But a confused Nathan begins to advance on Buddy and play on him anyway. Buddy immediately brakes and heads back towards first. Well the next thing you know, they have ol' Buddy in a pickle between first and second. By this time, Richie Schmutz is rounding third and headed for the plate.

To keep Nathan's attention, Buddy stops suddenly, sticks out his tongue, puts his thumbs to his ears, and starts wagging his fingers at the already bewildered Viking shortstop. Well, this makes Nathan all the more furious. I can tell you that much for a fact. With a most horrible scowl fixed upon his face, he starts chasing Buddy for all he's worth. Seven throws later, they finally tag an exhausted Buddy, just as ol' Richie Schmutz chugs across the plate with the go-ahead run.

Three pitches later, Gordy Belmont goes down swinging for the third out. But, now we're headed for the top of the seventh with a one-run lead. Now, it's all up to me. All I have to do is pitch three more outs, and we have our very first victory of the year. I'll also have some very sweet revenge on ol' Rattleballs and Teddy Snodgrass and all the rest of the Scandia twinks.

It is with much sadness that this humble reporter announces that Tom and Esther Michaels and their son Willie will be leaving our Happy Valley community. It seems that they have sold their tavern to a party from Bremerton and will be moving back to Seattle at the conclusion of the school year. We are sorry to see them go but wish them the best of luck in the big city. Not exactly non-existent, but skimpy at best, Mr. Michaels blames the lack of business for their departure.
—Dora Dingley
The Happy Valley Harbinger, May 1952

Chapter 34

As I walk to the mound for what I hope will be the last inning, Roderick Remblinger jogs past me on his way out to right field. I sort of have to laugh; with his ol' hat on sideways and his goofy argyle socks at half-mast, Roderick is sure comical to look at. I'm sure that you'd agree.

I've thought about becoming a cartoonist during the off-seasons of my big league baseball career, and if I ever do, I might use ol' Roderick for a prototype cartoon character. A cartoon featuring a personality that can swallow half his face ought to be an immediate success.

"Hey, Mackerels," Vernon Windbladd says, as he trots on by to his shortstop position, "get these next three guys out and ya got yourself a no-hitter."

Buddy's on his way out to left and overhears Vernon's remark. "Way to go, Dimbulb," says the man-of-the-world. There's a certain amount of malice in his voice. "Go ahead and put a hex on the pitcher, why don'tcha?" It would appear as though Buddy has yet to forgive ol' Vernon for his unfortunate slip of the tongue with reference to Rosie's last name.

"Oh. I would not let superstition enter into your thinking," says Gordy Belmont, as he jogs to his position. "Modern science puts absolutely no credence in beliefs, practices, or rites resulting from ignorance in the laws of nature or from faith in magic or chance. One must never give into a fearful or abject state of mind resulting from such ignorance or irrationality."

Buddy looks at Gordy in a real puzzled way but doesn't ask me to translate. I guess he thinks I have enough to worry about. And I suppose good ol' Vernon shouldn't have been talking about a prospective no-hitter and all, but I was aware of it the whole time, anyway. Wouldn't I just love to give a no-hitter to ol' Rattleballs and tell him to stick it in his — uh—pipe and smoke it.

As I'm taking my pre-inning warmups, I sort of glance up to the stands to see how ol' Trudy Trammell is handling all this drama. She seems to be bearing up pretty well; she's still gabbing away with her girlfriends. I suppose that helps her take her mind off me and the no-hitter and all.

I also take a quick look to see what Mr. Popolinski's reaction might be. I can't tell by his tongue, though, as it seems to be flicking in and out at no more than the normal rate of speed. Finally, though, he catches me looking at him and gives me a quick signal in reply. He's drawing his right hand across his chest, just about arm pit-high. He wants me to go with the high heat.

Well, I start right out on the leadoff hitter by taking him up the ol' ladder with fastballs. I have two high strikes on him, when he lifts a high foul ball to right field. Roderick should have it easily, but going to his left is not one of his strong points. It lights harmlessly, though, just outside the foul line, and the batter still has two strikes on him.

I come in with a big side-arm curve, and the batter smacks it to Roderick again, only this time in the gap towards center. There goes the no-hitter, I think to myself. Roderick is not famous for going to his right, either. But out of the ol' blue comes Gordy Belmont, and the fleet-footed center fielder makes a spectacular grab for out number one.

I try to take the next hitter up the ladder, too, but don't get the ball up quite high enough. He bloops it out to right field. It looks like an easy out, but that's before I remember that Roderick's out there. Coming in on the ball is also not one of Roderick's major strengths. At first, he approaches the ball a bit tentatively but then puts on a big burst of speed. For a second, there, I think he might get to the ball. But instead, he gets there just in time to be too late; he has to play the ball on the hop. The no-hitter is dead; long live the no-hitter. The pressure remains, however. We still need two more big outs to win the ol' game.

After setting up the next batter with high stuff, I throw him a slow curve just a little too wide for a strike. Danged, though, if the runner on first doesn't go and steal second on the pitch. A ground-out advances him to third, but I'm feeling a little safer now, what with two outs and all.

I can't seem to stand prosperity, though, as I proceed to walk the next batter. Now, with runners on first and third, the Vikings elect to steal second. They know ol' Richie Schmutz will be reluctant to throw with a man perched there on third.

Now, I'm in real deep doo-doo. We have two outs, but the Vikings have the winning run out there on second with their number three hitter due up next. He's already hit the ball hard a couple of times, but right at someone on both occasions. Coach Monahan and I have a brief conference on the mound.

"Let's put this kid on, Mackerels," he says. Then, when he sees my look of concern, he goes on to explain his thinking. "He isn't going to hurt us over there at first—the runners on second and third are who we have to worry about. We put this guy on and it sets up a force at any base."

I understand that, all right. As usual, the ol' coach is right on top of things with his strategy and all. The only problem is, though: the next batter is Teddy Snodgrass.

I put the guy on, all right, but then I have to come up with a plan for pitching to Teddy. And the fact he's a left-handed hitter doesn't help matters any. Before I begin concentrating too deeply, though, I take another quick peek into the stands to check on Trudy Trammell. I imagine she's right on the edge of her seat by now, but once again I've caught her just as she's busy talking to her girlfriends. The Cardinal scout is still writing in his notebook at a furious pace.

I think about starting Teddy out with the ol' curve, but its break has been getting slower and slower as the game progresses. Maybe the curve wouldn't be such a good idea against a tough left-hander like Teddy. But on the other hand, the adrenaline that's been giving my fastball that extra zip is about all used up. What am I to do?

While I'm pondering the decision, Coach Monahan makes a move that sort of catches me off guard, if you want to know the truth of it all. It's a brilliant idea, though. I have to hand it to him.

"Time!" he calls, as he bounces up to the top of the dugout steps. "Pringle—switch places with Remblinger," he shouts.

I can understand that, too, after I think about it for a moment. Ol' Teddy's very apt to be pulling the ball to right field, and Coach is obviously sick and tired of watching Roderick fumble around out there. He probably feels a lot more secure with a certified man-of-the-world in that suddenly key position. I do too.

With all the maneuvering finally taken care of, I make a final decision. I'm going home from the dance with the one who brought me— that good ol' fastball up the ladder. Although I don't feel any too strong at the present moment, I'll go with it anyway. One more time, I'll put my trust in Coach Monahan's good ol' navy buddy. With that decision out of the way, I rock back and fire one high and tight—about six inches out of the ol' strike zone.

"Steee—rike one!" shouts the navy buddy.

"What!" hollers Teddy.

"Hey—wait just a danged minute!" Rattleballs bellers. His face is about as red as a baboon's backside, as he stands with hands on hips in the third base coaching box. As he stomps out in the direction of the man in blue, you can tell he's madder than a wet hen.

With his chin jutting out like that of an angry pit bull, ol' Rattleballs stands toe-to-toe with the umpire for several minutes. I can only hear a little of the conversation, but it sounds as though they are mostly discussing the umpire's ancestry and all. Rattleballs even makes reference to some sort of peculiar relationship between the umpire and the umpire's mother. When I hear this, my ol' face turns sort of red, if you need to know the truth. I hadn't known that funny stuff such as that even existed.

Well, when the conversation finally breaks up, I've lost a certain amount of confidence in the ol' navy buddy's ability to help me out with Teddy. After the chewing-out by ol' Rattleballs, the ump looks a little subdued, if you want to know the whole sad truth.

When play is finally resumed, it doesn't take long to confirm the worst of my fears. My next pitch is another fastball, only an inch or so above the ol' strike zone.

"Ball one," the umpire shouts. Apparently, avoiding another confrontation with ol' Rattleballs has replaced allegiances to former navy buddies on the umpire's list of priorities. It seems as though the up-the-ladder strategy could be all through for the day. I'm going to have to rely on Eddie Lopat and all his junk, once again.

So, with the count now one-and-one, I come in with a slow curve via the underground route. That can be a real nasty pitch, especially for left-handed batters. But the submarine delivery is a little too slow, and gravity rears its ugly head. The pitch only travels a distance of fifty-five feet or so, instead of the required sixty feet-six inches. I'm danged lucky that good ol' Richie Schmutz is able to block it and keep the runners from advancing. Now, the count has gone to two and one.

The pressure is getting to me, now. I'll have to admit it. I glance back to the stands to see how ol' Trudy is taking it all. I think she's just too excited to watch, as she's turned back to her girlfriends, once again. The Cardinal scout is paying close attention, though. He's stopped writing, for the time being, at least, but it's easy to tell he's all caught up by the excitement of the moment. His tongue is nothing but a blur, as it flicks in and out of his ol' mouth. And from where I stand, it looks as though he's shaking his head about something or other. Maybe he's disappointed because it looks as though I've given up on the ol' fastball.

But I can't be concerned with what Mr. Popolinski's thinking, or Trudy either, for that matter. I have to concentrate on what to throw Teddy Snodgrass. I decide upon the overhand curve—the one that's consistently been my most reliable out pitch. I throw it pretty danged well, too, if I do say so myself. It goes in about waist high and then drops straight down, just as though it's fallen off the ol' table. Teddy fouls it off and sends it straight back to the screen behind home plate. Now the surprise element is gone from my best pitch. The count's two and two.

Hmmm. I try another Eddie Lopat ploy and come in with a crossfire delivery. I step across the ol' body and throw the curve right at Teddy's hip. When he steps back to get out of the way, it'll sweep right on in over the outside corner for a called strike three, and we will have won the game. But it doesn't break. I'm danged lucky I don't hit Teddy and force in the tying run. He jumps out of the way just in the nick of time.

Now we have a full count. What am I going to do? I can go with the curve once again, but something tells me Teddy is more than ready for that strategy. Or, I can take a chance that the umpire's only weakened temporarily and try the extra-high fastball once again.

When I take a glance at the stands, I see that the old Cardinal scout agrees with that strategy; he's drawing his hand across the armpits, once again. He's signaling for more high heat. Unfortunately, I'm afraid the pilot light has gone out. And what if I'm guessing wrong about the good ol' navy buddy? It'll be ball four, and the tying run will score. The ol' flood gates will be open then. You can bet your bottom dollar on that. I'm out of gas. I've got to admit it. I have barely enough strength left for one more pitch, and with the ever-dangerous Teddy at the plate, it's going to have to be a good one.

Maybe if I just stall for awhile, I can find some inner power that will allow me to throw one last quality fastball or snap off one more decent curve. If only I had cousin Harvey Bodenheimer's fastball. And with that thought in mind, I take a brief stroll off the mound. I have my new Wilson mitt under my arm and am making a great show of rubbing up the ol' ball.

"Time," I call. Then I lob the ball into the umpire and signal for a new one. I get back the rather beat-up one I lobbed in a few pitches ago.

Now, I turn my attention to doing a little landscaping on the mound. I kick dirt here and there with my cleats and even get down on all fours to do some shaping of the surface with my bare hands. As I work, I'm thinking that if only Tar Baby and my tin soldiers were here, I could dig some fox holes and re-fight the Battle of the Bulge.

"Come on—let's play ball," goofy ol' Rattleballs calls from the third base coaching box.

I rather hurriedly finish the earth-moving project and return to a pitching position. I guess I'm going to have to pitch the ball. But then I remember the rosin bag lying there to the side of the mound. Slowly, I bend over and scoop it up. I toss it into the air and then proceed to bounce it off both sides of my forearm a few times. I put on a rather professional demonstration of how a major league pitcher would go about making use of the ol' sack. Then I roll it up one arm, across my back, and down the other arm, from where I neatly drop kick it off the back of my heel and up to my mitt. It's been such a great performance, I think I'll do it all again. In fact, I wonder if Mr. Popolinski's ever seen anything to equal it in the ol' Cardinal farm chain.

"Come on, Mackerels," Teddy Snodgrass shouts from the batter's box. "You in love with that rosin bag, for cripe's sake? You got so much rosin on ya, ya look like the Pillsbury Dough Boy. Come on—pitch the ball."

"Play ball!" shouts the ex-navy buddy.

Sadly, it looks as though all my attempts at stalling have come to an end. And they've all been in vain, I'm afraid, as my ol' arm still feels like a left-over piece of spaghetti. Now that everyone's so danged impatient and all, I've got to make a real quick decision about what to come up with for this game-deciding pitch. I just don't know what to throw, especially now that I've been deserted by both the U. S. Navy *and* Eddie Lopat.

Maybe a spit ball would work. But what with the mountain of built-up tension and all, I can't muster up enough saliva for a ball the size of a pea. I've read where some of the old-time pitchers chewed the bark of the slippery elm for that purpose, but I don't even have any cascara.

Still thinking along those lines, I remove my ball cap briefly and feel of my hair. But there'll be no help there, either, I'm afraid. My hair's dryer than a popcorn fart; I should have used some of that lanolin gunk (Brylcream—a little dab'll do ya). With my hat on and all, the flies probably wouldn't have bothered me all that much, anyway.

Then it hits me: who needs either the U. S. Navy *or* Eddie Lopat? I have another ally I can fall back on—ol' Spud Wilcox. It doesn't take a strong arm to throw the knuckler. In fact, the weaker the better, if you could go by Spud Wilcox at all. I'd tried a few knucklers during the pre-game warm up and had managed to make a few of them flutter a little. If the ol' knuckle ball will just work for me this one time, I'll buy Spud a whole truckload of beer. I'll swear to that much on a stack of bibles.

I take to the rubber, now, with renewed confidence and look into Richie Schmutz for the sign. And as usual, he has his two big ol' fingers down there in the dirt signaling for the curve. Teddy Snodgrass has his peepers fixed right on them, too, but it doesn't matter. I shake off Richie's sign. Immediately, he switches the sign to *one* big ol' finger in the dirt. I can see ol' Teddy smiling, as he thinks about getting a chance to hit one of my fastballs.

Once again I shake my head. Richie hesitates just a bit but then shoves *three* big ol' fingers into the dirt. It's the sign for my seldom-used change-of-pace. Teddy is now grinning from ear-to-ear. Again I shake my head. This prompts a visit to the mound by Richie.

After our brief conference, Richie returns to the catcher's box but doesn't bother to give any more signs. He knows what's coming. But seeing no tell-tale fingers in the dirt, Teddy steps away from the plate. He looks confused as all get out, if you want the truth of it all.

"Play ball!" I holler in from the mound. This gives me an awful lot of satisfaction. I'll have to admit it.

A ferocious scowl takes over Teddy's face, as he gets back into the batter's box. He waggles the bat for all he's worth, and he's gripping the ol' Louisville Slugger so tightly you can practically see the sawdust oozing out the end of the handle. By now, I think he figures that no matter what I throw, it won't be all that much to worry about.

Just to break the tension for a moment, I take a quick scan of the bleachers, hoping to spot Trudy Trammell. But I can't spot her. However, I do see ol' Rosie Higgenbottom wandering over to the concession stand. But is it my imagination, or has Rosie gained quite a lot of weight around the ol' middle since I saw her last? Maybe she's made one too many trips to the hot dog stand.

I get my mind back on the game and just to get the correct feel of the knuckler and all, I go into a Spud Wilcox double-pump windup before I make the final delivery. I have three fingernails digging into the ball's seams, and just as I let go, I give the three fingers a final flick and begin to say my prayers.

I imagine in my mind the sight of the Spud Special dancing and darting its way up to the ol' plate. Won't Teddy be surprised? He'll probably drop a load in his pants. The count is full, so as soon as the ball leaves my hand, the base runners are off and running like a bunch of striped-assed apes.

I had high hopes for the ol' knuckler, but right away I can tell it's no good. The danged ball isn't knuckling at *all*. It goes up to the plate slower than molasses in January and has only a very slight roll. To Teddy, the ball must look fatter than a pair of Patty Maloney's bloomers. At this point, I almost drop a load in *my* pants.

I expect Teddy to waste no time before jumping all over the non-knuckling tidbit, but surprisingly, he holds up his swing. He just stands there with the bat on his ol' shoulder. Will he *ever* swing? I'm beginning to get my hopes up. Maybe the slowness of the ball has him mesmerized or some danged thing.

At the very last moment, though, he takes a vicious swing that could send a ball about half the distance to Norway. KRRAAACCKK! He hits the ball late and off it goes—sailing out to left field. He doesn't get it all, though, thank goodness. It's at least a mile high and looks like an easy can-of-corn for ol' Buddy Pringle. We've *done* it. Against all odds, we've finally won a game. But wait a minute. BUDDY PRINGLE! Coach Monahan switched him to right. RODERICK REMBLINGER is in left field. DADAMN!!!

I drop my eyes from the flight of Teddy's fly ball and try to pick up ol' Roderick. And there he is—coming in on the ball for all he's worth. He's misjudged it. I might have known. Going back on fly balls is the thing Roderick does worst in all this world. That's it. There goes the ol' ball game.

> Oh, somewhere in this favored land the sun is shining bright;
> The band is playing somewhere, and somewhere hearts are light,
> And somewhere men are laughing, and somewhere children shout;
> But there is no joy in Happy Valley—cuz Roderick's such a lout.

Chapter 35

But suddenly, Roderick realizes his mistake. He comes to a screeching halt and then starts backpedaling for all he's worth. It's too late, though. I can tell you that much for sure. We had our chance to win, but once again that danged ol' Roderick has messed things up. There goes our only victory of the year, and in all probability, there goes the ol' St. Louis Cardinals, too. Oh well, they say that to err is human. I just wonder what Roderick's excuse will be.

Roderick's still trying, though; you have to give him credit for that. He's backpedaling as fast as he can. But as you probably know, a good outfielder doesn't go back on a fly ball that way. Instead, you're supposed to turn and run to the spot you think the ball will land and then turn around and wait for it to arrive. But not Roderick. He just keeps backpedaling. Back, back, back he goes, and then back some more. I have to hand it to him, he's probably the most determined backpedaler the game of baseball has ever known.

Can Roderick possibly get there in time? It's almost like trying to figure out one of those train problems in algebra. Myself, I'm betting he won't make it. But then I catch a whiff of a most sickening smell coming in from left field. I know Roderick stinks, but no one person could be responsible for such a horrible odor—not even Roderick.

Then I realize that an ill wind is blowing in from the direction of Cy Morgan's honey-wagon; the breeze from the south has freshened quite a little bit. In fact, it has picked up to nearly gale force. Dang! It's blowing so hard it's gotten its clutches on Teddy's fly ball and is holding it up.

I'm stupefied. I can barely believe what I've just seen with my own eyes. The ball and Roderick have reached the same spot at the same instant. And would you believe it? The ol' horsehide plops right into the webbing of Roderick's outstretched mitt—just as he falls on his ol' kiester.

I sort of stand there in a daze, before I finally realize that Roderick has actually made the catch and that the ball game is over. The Hapless Valley Milk Maids have finally won an athletic contest, and I have a measure of sweet revenge on Teddy Snodgrass, ol' Rattleballs, and the entire Viking clan in general. Oh—the wonder of it all.

I look around for someone to share my happiness but can't seem to find a soul. Vernon Windbladd goes sprinting out to right field where he meets up with Buddy Pringle. Gordy Belmont runs over to join them, and right away, they're doing some sort of Irish jig out there in right field. The rest of the infielders dash out to ol' Roderick Remblinger like he's some sort of hero or something. And Richie Schmutz has joined Coach Monahan and the Stooges over at our dugout. They've all joined hands and are busily engaged in some sort of Ring-Around-the-Rosy escapade.

From behind the protection of our dugout, Coach Monahan's Benedict Arnold navy pal has his eyes trained on the Scandia bench. He's nervously puffing on a cigarette and obviously waiting for ol' Rattleballs to leave the field.

The only person looking as lonely as I feel is poor ol' Rosie Higgenbottom. She's standing in front of our dugout staring out into right field where Buddy, Vernon, and Gordy are still doing their dance. You'd think she'd be elated, since we won our game and all, but instead, she looks as though she's lost her last friend. I've got sort of a sideways view of her, and danged if her ol' belly doesn't look even bigger than I first thought. I wonder if Buddy didn't forget to use one of those little things in the wallet that he warned me about right before the Tolo.

I turn my attention to the stands up behind home plate, but ol' Trudy and all her girlfriends seem to have left already. That really makes me sad. I'll have to admit it. But now I've seen it all. I really have. Up in the top row of the bleachers, behind home plate, a fat lady bursts into song. She must be a Scandia fan, because she's wearing this weird-looking Viking costume. She's got on a big ol' metal helmet complete with horns and is also wearing a big metal bra on the outside of her blouse. I can't believe it. But after seeing Roderick's goofy catch out in left field, nothing seems too crazy anymore.

I listen to her sing for a minute or two but can't understand a word of it. It's got to be a foreign language, but I don't think it's Spanish. She's a pretty good singer, though—I'll have to admit it. One time, I swear she gets right up there to high P. She must be what they call a schizo-soprano.

Then I locate Mr. Popolinski. The Cardinal scout has already reached the field and is heading for the mound. He's walking rather briskly, and as usual, the ol' tongue is keeping pace. I hope that the loss of the no-hitter and all hasn't dampened his enthusiasm for my chances in the majors. Surely he realizes that Roderick Remblinger was the cause of that. As he nears the mound, I can see he has a piece of paper of some sort in his hand. This sort of puzzles me, if you want to know the truth. I hadn't really expected to sign a contract quite this soon.

I reach to him for the congratulatory handshake, but the Cardinal scout doesn't even acknowledge me. Instead, he hurries right on by. Where's he going? Well, you can knock me over with a feather as I finally realize he's headed out to see ol' Roderick Remblinger. I guess Dad was right about ol' Harry Popolinski all along. The old coot ought to be out tending his cantaloupes.

But what's going to happen to me, now that the Cardinals are no longer interested? It might be pretty danged tough to attract the attention of any of the other major league clubs at this late date. I was sort of relying on Mr. Popolinski and the ol' Cardinals, to tell you the honest truth. Could it possibly be, that after all my dedication and hard work over the years I'll never get to be a big league ballplayer?

But sadly, a sort of realization finds its way into my slightly-damaged brain cells. It's a thought that's been festering back there in the recesses of the ol' gray matter, for some time now I guess. I hate to admit it, but I had an awful lot of trouble getting one tiny pitching victory during my entire high school career. Not only did I struggle with the likes of good ol' Teddy Snodgrass—who will probably never play a single game of professional baseball in his entire life—but also, I had a heck of a time with players from such out-of-the-way places as Port Angeles, Bainbridge, and Sequim. So, how in the world do I expect to be able to deal with a Joe DiMaggio, or a Tommy Heinrich, or *any* of the ol' Fighting Yankees, for that matter? And come to think of it, there won't be any old navy buddies to help me out up there in the big leagues. I should be elated about today's big win, but suddenly, I'm feeling lower than ol' Ingaborg's belly.

Head down, I trudge on over to retrieve my warm-up jacket. But on the way, I take a peek over my shoulder at the Viking dugout. It's not a pretty sight. Guys are shouting and pointing fingers at one another, and ol' Rattleball's face is so red, it looks like an over-ripe tomato about to explode. Then, from out of all the hullabaloo, a lone figure emerges and comes to greet me. It's my old friend and battery mate, little Elmer Finley.

"Nice game," Mackerels," he says as he sticks out his hand. Lowering his voice, he adds, "I'm glad you finally got the chance to show ol' Rattleballs a thing or two." Elmer starts on back to the N K dugout but then turns and says, "Oh—uh—by the way—Trudy Trammell wants to see you. She's parked in the vacant lot across the street."

If you want to know the truth, what with my disappointment in the Cardinals and all, I'd sort of forgotten about ol' Trudy. I guess there's times in a guy's life when romance doesn't seem all that important. Besides, it seems sort of surprising that Trudy would want to see me. What would she care about ol' Willie Mackerels? After all, she paid practically zero attention to the most masterful pitching performance of my entire career.

Just the same, I look for her in the vacant lot. I look and look but can't seem to find her. I know both of the Trammell family vehicles, but neither is to be seen. Somewhat disappointed, I head for the locker room and a nice, hot shower. I'm a little disappointed, too, that none of my so-called friends thought to congratulate me today on my eighteenth birthday. Heck of a birthday—now I've got to register for the draft.

Suddenly, I forget about the satisfying win over the Scandia twinks. Instead, thoughts of having to move back to Seattle find their way to my slightly-damaged brain cells. I'm just going to hate leaving my friends, even if they have sort of shut me out of their post-game celebrations and ignored my birthday and all. I worry about ol' Buddy, though. Somehow, I think he's soon going to find out what it's like to have a shotgun pointed in *his* direction. I just hope for his sake it's not a Model 97.

I'm startled out of my thoughts when a musical horn blares at me from less than twenty feet away; it gives me quite a start. I can't quite make out the tune, but it sounds an awful lot like The Rhumba Boogie. Of course, that might just be the ol' imagination working overtime, after a pressure-packed game and all.

In the nick of time, I step back to keep from being run over by Reginald Remblinger. He's here to pick up his goofy ol' brother—the big baseball hero. After Reginald wrecked his Dodge, he got himself a '47 Studebaker. Dang! They're crazy looking. They sort of come to a point both in front and in back, and you can't tell whether they're coming or going. Of course, I doubt very much if the driver knows whether he's coming or going, either, for that matter.

"Dadamn," Reginald hollers. "Wah ow, Mahruls, yuu futtin sittenchit sumanabit—I tit yo ah." Another in a long line of Neanderthals heard from.

"Ekka tekka!" I yell back, as I put a finger up for Reginald—to show he's still number one in my book.

BEEP-A-DOO-BOP-BEEP-boop-boop! Another horn sounds and I soon locate the source. It's coming from a brand new Merc convertible. It's candy-apple red, and the reflection off the glistening chrome work dang near puts out my eyes. If you want to know the truth, it's got to be the neatest car I've ever seen. I'm not kidding. I'll bet it'd even make good ol' Teddy Snodgrass a tad jealous.

"Senor Curly—over here, por favor." Trudy is leaning out over the driver's side and beckoning to me. In the background, I can hear the strains of country music coming from her radio. The blend of steel guitars and castanets sure sounds familiar, and I recognize everyone's favorites, Hank Snow and the Rainbow Ranch Boys. They're singing a new song—something to do with a Spanish fireball. You know—I've never cared all that much for Hank Snow up to now, but under certain conditions he can really grow on a guy.

As I get closer, the familiar scent of lavender wafts its way out of the cherry Merc and sort of overwhelms me. Ol' Trudy has chosen her favorite perfume to match her knockout summer dress. From way out there on the pitcher's mound, what with my slightly-weaker eyes and all, I hadn't noticed the dress's neckline. It's cut real low. I can even see a little of what I've heard referred to as "cleavage." It's definitely a real pretty dress.

If you want to know the honest truth, it's at that point in time that my natural post-game depression and all sort of disappears. I even put my disappointment with Mr. Popolinski and the Cardinals out of my mind. I quarter my slightly-bigger nose to starboard and greet ol' Trudy with one of my very best tight-lipped specials. I have absolutely no idea to what degree of greenness my teeth might have reached after the stress of such a hard-fought game and all. But I take no chances. At least, my slightly-wilder hair is covered up by my Fighting Milk Maids ball cap.

"Curly—don't turn away like that. I love to see that cute, little crook in your nose. And—is that the best smile you can give an old girlfriend?"

Well—I have to think Trudy's being pretty, danged liberal with the term, "old girlfriend," if you want the honest truth. I mean, I've never even been out on a real date with her.

By the way, is that a mustache you're trying to grow there, Curly?" Trudy asks. "Uh—how's ol' Teddy these days?" I change the subject real fast. I'm also trying my darndest not to stare at the cleavage and all.

"He's boring," she says. And when she says it, she has this cute little pout I've always liked so well. "All he thinks about is that hot rod of his. Besides—now, since I got this Mercury for graduation, he's been real jealous. Gosh, I think, if Teddy had to drive either Pristine or the Hog, he'd know what jealous was, for Pete's sake.

"Well, I've got to admit it—you've got a real nice cleav—er—car, there," I manage to say. "Uh—how'dja like the game, by the way?"

"It was great!" she says. "Real exciting. I thought you were really good out there, Curly, even though you didn't make any touchdowns or anything."

Somehow, I sense it's probably a complete waste of time to talk about one-hitters and such as that, so I go ahead and change the ol' subject. "What're ya gonna do this summer?" I ask.

"Oh—probably work at the Dockside Cafè and save up money for school."

"*School?*" I say. I find it hard to believe anyone's thinking about school, when we've worked for twelve years to get out of the danged place. Not only that, but I don't know where I'd get any money for school. I think the folks are just about tapped out from the ol' Tavern fiasco. The $2,000 profit they made has to go toward securing a new place back in Seattle. And it might be tough for me to find a decent job in the city right away—especially since I don't have much in the way of job skills. I doubt if they have any cascara over in the metropolitan area. And I'm not going to be looking for any cement-pouring jobs. I can tell you that much for a fact.

"Yeah," Trudy says, "I got a little scholarship to Walla Walla Junior College—I want to be a language teacher. You ought to go there, too, Curly. It'll be a lot of fun."

Hmmm—Walla Walla—that's way over on the other side of the mountains and is the home of the state penitentiary. The only time I'd ever thought much about that town was when ol' Buddy Pringle and I almost got caught by Sam Baer in his precious cascara patch.

"Well—I'm sort of waiting for the Cardinals and all, and besides that, I don't know where I'd get the money," I say.

"They got birds over there, too, Curly, and besides—junior colleges aren't all that expensive," she says. "I know where you can make some really good money, this summer. Dad needs a skiff man for his purse seiner. Heck—he'll put you on if I ask him, and with a full share, you'll easily make a thousand or so. And anyway—you're really good at art. I remember your cartoons. I'll bet you could easily get some kind of scholarship. And guess what—If you finish in the top two-thirds of your class, you'll be exempt from the draft."

Gosh, I think, a co-salutatorian ought to be able to finish that high, even if he did have only a 3.2 grade point average.

"Why don'cha come on over to my place for dinner tonight," says Trudy, "and we'll take a look through the college catalogue."

"Gosh, I dunno—we'd be pretty late, wouldn't we? I'm not sure what time the last ferry is."

"You could stay over, Curly. Tomorrow's Saturday—no school—and we got an extra bedroom."

Hmmmm. As I listen to ol' Trudy and take in the sight of her sitting there in her pretty summer dress, another hint of the lavender finds its way to my slightly-bigger nose. And if you want to know the absolute truth, the news about the spare bedroom seems rather intriguing. Suddenly, I decide that maybe another year or two of school wouldn't be such a bad idea after all. Forgetting all about my slightly-greener teeth for the moment, I break out into a grin and vigorously nod my head in agreement.

"All right!" Trudy exclaims. "See ya tonight, then, Curly. Let's seal it with a kiss," she says, as she reaches for me out of the cherry Merc. This action catches me somewhat off guard, if you want to know the whole wonderful truth of it all. Always one to do what I'm told, though, I automatically lean forward to deliver a peck on the cheek. And as I do, I catch another whiff of the eau-de-lavender and another glimpse of the ol' cleavage. It's even more impressive than I first imagined.

Trudy really seems serious about me coming over to her place and all. The peck on the cheek turns out to be a full-fledged smack on the mouth, as she grabs me by the back of the neck and pulls my head into the convertible. I guess she is really serious about being a language teacher and all, because there's even a trace of French in the kiss. If Skinny and Clyde were here, I bet they'd holler, "Fire in the paint locker!"

My knees are all wobbly-like, as Trudy finally drives off in her shiny new car. I must look like Bernie Whatsizname, after he'd just been tagged by one of Fran Newfield's roundhouse rights. But though my legs are shaky, my priorities are finally straight. I'm through worrying about Teddy Snodgrass, the St. Louis Cardinals, and Roderick Remblinger.

And I doubt if I'll even try out for the Walla Walla Fighting Sodbusters' baseball team. Instead, I'll be concentrating on my college career, staying out of the draft, and my girl, good ol' Trudy Trammell.